ANNIE KILBURN

a Novel

W. D. HOWELLS

1ˢᵗ WORLD
LIBRARY
Literary Society

Annie Kilburn

W. D. Howells

© 1st World Library, 2006
PO Box 2211
Fairfield, IA 52556
www.1stworldlibrary.com
First Edition

LCCN: 2007920700

Softcover ISBN: 978-1-4218-4015-4
Hardcover ISBN: 978-1-4218-3915-8
eBook ISBN: 978-1-4218-4115-1

Purchase *"Annie Kilburn"*
as a traditional bound book at:
www.1stWorldLibrary.com/purchase.asp?ISBN=978-1-4218-4015-4

1st World Library is a literary, educational organization
dedicated to:

- Creating a free internet library of downloadable ebooks

- Hosting writing competitions and offering book
  publishing scholarships.

Interested in more 1st World Library books?
contact: literacy@1stworldlibrary.com
Check us out at: www.1stworldlibrary.com

1ˢᵗ World Library Literary Society

Giving Back to the World

"If you want to work on the core problem, it's early school literacy."

- James Barksdale, former CEO of Netscape

"No skill is more crucial to the future of a child, or to a democratic and prosperous society, than literacy."

- Los Angeles Times

Literacy... means far more than learning how to read and write... The aim is to transmit... knowledge and promote social participation."

- UNESCO

"Literacy is not a luxury, it is a right and a responsibility. If our world is to meet the challenges of the twenty-first century we must harness the energy and creativity of all our citizens."

- President Bill Clinton

"Parents should be encouraged to read to their children, and teachers should be equipped with all available techniques for teaching literacy, so the varying needs and capacities of individual kids can be taken into account."

- Hugh Mackay

I

After the death of Judge Kilburn his daughter came back to America. They had been eleven winters in Rome, always meaning to return, but staying on from year to year, as people do who have nothing definite to call them home. Toward the last Miss Kilburn tacitly gave up the expectation of getting her father away, though they both continued to say that they were going to take passage as soon as the weather was settled in the spring. At the date they had talked of for sailing he was lying in the Protestant cemetery, and she was trying to gather herself together, and adjust her life to his loss. This would have been easier with a younger person, for she had been her father's pet so long, and then had taken care of his helplessness with a devotion which was finally so motherly, that it was like losing at once a parent and a child when he died, and she remained with the habit of giving herself when there was no longer any one to receive the sacrifice. He had married late, and in her thirty-first year he was seventy-eight; but the disparity of their ages, increasing toward the end through his infirmities, had not loosened for her the ties of custom and affection that bound them; she had seen him grow more and more fitfully cognisant of what they had been to each other since her mother's death, while she grew the more tender and fond with him. People who came to condole with her seemed not to understand this, or else they thought it would help her to bear up if they treated her bereavement as a relief from hopeless anxiety. They were all surprised when she told them she still meant to go home.

"Why, my dear," said one old lady, who had been away from America twenty years, "*this* is home! You've lived in this apartment longer now than the oldest inhabitant has lived in most American towns. What are you talking about? Do you mean that you are going back to Washington?"

'Oh no. We were merely staying on in Washington from force of habit, after father gave up practice. I think we shall go back to the old homestead, where we used to spend our summers, ever since I can remember."

"And where is that?" the old lady asked, with the sharpness which people believe must somehow be good for a broken spirit.

"It's in the interior of Massachusetts—you wouldn't know it: a place called Hatboro'."

"No, I certainly shouldn't," said the old lady, with superiority. "Why Hatboro', of all the ridiculous reasons?"

"It was one of the first places where they began to make straw hats; it was a nickname at first, and then they adopted it. The old name was Dorchester Farms. Father fought the change, but it was of no use; the people wouldn't have it Farms after the place began to grow; and by that time they had got used to Hatboro'. Besides, I don't see how it's any worse than Hatfield, in England."

"It's very American."

"Oh, it's American. We have Boxboro' too, you know, in Massachusetts."

"And you are going from Rome to Hatboro', Mass.," said the old lady, trying to present the idea in the strongest light by abbreviating the name of the State.

"Yes," said Miss Kilburn. "It will be a change, but not so much

W. D. Howells

of a change as you would think. It was father's wish to go back."

"Ah, my *dear*!" cried the old lady. "You're letting that weigh with you, I see. Don't do it! If it wasn't wise, don't you suppose that the last thing he could wish you to do would be to sacrifice yourself to a sick whim of his?"

The kindness expressed in the words touched Annie Kilburn. She had a certain beauty of feature; she was near-sighted; but her eyes were brown and soft, her lips red and full; her dark hair grew low, and played in little wisps and rings on her temples, where her complexion was clearest; the bold contour of her face, with its decided chin and the rather large salient nose, was like her father's; it was this, probably, that gave an impression of strength, with a wistful qualification. She was at that time rather thin, and it could have been seen that she would be handsomer when her frame had rounded out in fulfilment of its generous design. She opened her lips to speak, but shut them again in an effort at self-control before she said—

"But I really wish to do it. At this moment I would rather be in Hatboro' than in Rome."

"Oh, very well," said the old lady, gathering herself up as one does from throwing away one's sympathy upon an unworthy object; "if you really *wish* it—"

"I know that it must seem preposterous and—and almost ungrateful that I should think of going back, when I might just as well stay. Why, I've a great many more friends here than I have there; I suppose I shall be almost a stranger when I get there, and there's no comparison in congeniality; and yet I feel that I must go back. I can't tell you why. But I have a longing; I feel that I must try to be of some use in the world—try to do some good—and in Hatboro' I think I shall know how." She put on her glasses, and looked at the old lady as if she might attempt an explanation, but, as if a clearer vision of the veteran worldling discouraged her, she did not make the effort.

"*Oh*!" said the old lady. "If you want to be of use, and do good—" She stopped, as if then there were no more to be said by a sensible person. "And shall you be going soon?" she asked. The idea seemed to suggest her own departure, and she rose after speaking.

'Just as soon as possible," answered Miss Kilburn. Words take on a colour of something more than their explicit meaning from the mood in which they are spoken: Miss Kilburn had a sense of hurrying her visitor away, and the old lady had a sense of being turned out-of-doors, that the preparations for the homeward voyage might begin instantly.

W. D. Howells

II

Many times after the preparations began, and many times after they were ended, Miss Kilburn faltered in doubt of her decision; and if there had been any will stronger than her own to oppose it, she might have reversed it, and stayed in Rome. All the way home there was a strain of misgiving in her satisfaction at doing what she believed to be for the best, and the first sight of her native land gave her a shock of emotion which was not unmixed joy. She felt forlorn among people who were coming home with all sorts of high expectations, while she only had high intentions.

These dated back a good many years; in fact, they dated back to the time when the first flush of her unthinking girlhood was over, and she began to question herself as to the life she was living. It was a very pleasant life, ostensibly. Her father had been elected from the bench to Congress, and had kept his title and his repute as a lawyer through several terms in the House before he settled down to the practice of his profession in the courts at Washington, where he made a good deal of money. They passed from boarding to house-keeping, in the easy Washington way, after their impermanent Congressional years, and divided their time between a comfortable little place in Nevada Circle and the old homestead in Hatboro'. He was fond of Washington, and robustly content with the world as he found it there and elsewhere. If his daughter's compunctions came to her through him, it must have been from some remoter ancestry; he was not apparently characterised by their transmission, and probably she derived them from her mother.

who died when she was a little girl, and of whom she had no recollection. Till he began to break, after they went abroad, he had his own way in everything; but as men grow old or infirm they fall into subjection to their womenkind; their rude wills yield in the suppler insistence of the feminine purpose; they take the colour of the feminine moods and emotions; the cycle of life completes itself where it began, in helpless dependence upon the sex; and Rufus Kilburn did not escape the common lot. He was often complaining and unlovely, as aged and ailing men must be; perhaps he was usually so; but he had moments when he recognised the beauty of his daughter's aspiration with a spiritual sympathy, which showed that he must always have had an intellectual perception of it. He expressed with rhetorical largeness and looseness the longing which was not very definite in her own heart, and mingled with it a strain of homesickness poignantly simple and direct for the places, the scenes, the persons, the things, of his early days. As he failed more and more, his homesickness was for natural aspects which had wholly ceased to exist through modern changes and improvements, and for people long since dead, whom he could find only in an illusion of that environment in some other world. In the pathos of this situation it was easy for his daughter to keep him ignorant of the passionate rebellion against her own ideals in which she sometimes surprised herself. When he died, all counter-currents were lost in the tidal revulsion of feeling which swept her to the fulfilment of what she hoped was deepest and strongest in her nature, with shame for what she hoped was shallowest, till that moment of repulsion in which she saw the thickly roofed and many towered hills of Boston grow up out of the western waves.

She had always regarded her soul as the battlefield of two opposite principles, the good and the bad, the high and the low. God made her, she thought, and He alone; He made everything that she was; but she would not have said that He made the evil in her. Yet her belief did not admit the existence of Creative Evil; and so she said to herself that she herself was that evil, and she must struggle against herself; she must question whatever she strongly wished because she strongly

　　　　　W. D. Howells

wished it. It was not logical; she did not push her postulates to their obvious conclusions; and there was apt to be the same kind of break between her conclusions and her actions as between her reasons and her conclusions. She acted impulsively, and from a force which she could not analyse. She indulged reveries so vivid that they seemed to weaken and exhaust her for the grapple with realities; the recollection of them abashed her in the presence of facts.

With all this, it must not be supposed that she was morbidly introspective. Her life had been apparently a life of cheerful acquiescence in worldly conditions; it had been, in some measure, a life of fashion, or at least of society. It had not been without the interests of other girls' lives, by any means; she had sometimes had fancies, flirtations, but she did not think she had been really in love, and she had refused some offers of marriage for that reason.

III

The industry of making straw hats began at Hatboro', as many other industries have begun in New England, with no great local advantages, but simply because its founder happened to live there, and to believe that it would pay. There was a railroad, and labour of the sort he wanted was cheap and abundant in the village and the outlying farms. In time the work came to be done more and more by machinery, and to be gathered into large shops. The buildings increased in size and number; the single line of the railroad was multiplied into four, and in the region of the tracks several large, ugly, windowy wooden bulks grew up for shoe shops; a stocking factory followed; yet this business activity did not warp the old village from its picturesqueness or quiet. The railroad tracks crossed its main street; but the shops were all on one side of them, with the work-people's cottages and boarding-houses, and on the other were the simple, square, roomy old mansions, with their white paint and their green blinds, varied by the modern colour and carpentry of French-roofed villas. The old houses stood quite close to the street, with a strip of narrow door-yard before them; the new ones affected a certain depth of lawn, over which their owners personally pushed a clucking hand-mower in the summer evenings after tea. The fences had been taken away from the new houses, in the taste of some of the Boston suburbs; they generally remained before the old ones, whose inmates resented the ragged effect that their absence gave the street. The irregularity had hitherto been of an orderly and harmonious kind, such as naturally follows the growth of a country road into a village thoroughfare. The

W. D. Howells

dwellings were placed nearer or further from the sidewalk as their builders fancied, and the elms that met in a low arch above the street had an illusive symmetry in the perspective; they were really set at uneven intervals, and in a line that wavered capriciously in and out. The street itself lounged and curved along, widening and contracting like a river, and then suddenly lost itself over the brow of an upland which formed a natural boundary of the village. Beyond this was South Hatboro', a group of cottages built by city people who had lately come in—idlers and invalids, the former for the cool summer, and the latter for the dry winter. At chance intervals in the old village new side streets branched from the thoroughfare to the right and the left, and here and there a Queen Anne cottage showed its chimneys and gables on them. The roadway under the elms that kept it dark and cool with their hovering shade, and swept the wagon-tops with their pendulous boughs at places, was unpaved; but the sidewalks were asphalted to the last dwelling in every direction, and they were promptly broken out in winter by the public snow-plough.

Miss Kilburn saw them in the spring, when their usefulness was least apparent, and she did not know whether to praise the spirit of progress which showed itself in them as well as in other things at Hatboro'. She had come prepared to have misgivings, but she had promised herself to be just; she thought she could bear the old ugliness, if not the new. Some of the new things, however, were not so ugly; the young station-master was handsome in his railroad uniform, and pleasanter to the eye than the veteran baggage-master, incongruous in his stiff silk cap and his shirt sleeves and spectacles. The station itself, one of Richardson's, massive and low, with red-tiled, spreading veranda roofs, impressed her with its fitness, and strengthened her for her encounter with the business architecture of Hatboro', which was of the florid, ambitious New York type, prevalent with every American town in the early stages of its prosperity. The buildings were of pink brick, faced with granite, and supported in the first story by columns of painted iron; flat-roofed blocks looked down over the low-wooden structures of earlier Hatboro', and a large hotel had pushed back the old-time tavern, and planted itself flush upon the sidewalk. But the stores seemed very good, as she glanced at them from her carriage, and their show-windows were tastefully arranged; the apothecary's had an interior of glittering neatness unsurpassed by an Italian apothecary's; and the provision-man's, besides its symmetrical array of pendent sides and quarters indoors, had banks of fruit and vegetables without, and a large aquarium with a spraying fountain in its window.

Bolton, the farmer who had always taken care of the Kilburn place, came to meet her at the station and drive her home. Miss Kilburn had bidden him drive slowly, so that she could see all the changes, and she noticed the new town-hall, with which she could find no fault; the Baptist and Methodist churches were the same as of old; the Unitarian church seemed to have shrunk as if the architecture had sympathised with its dwindling body of worshippers; just beyond it was the village green, with the soldiers' monument, and the tall white-painted flag-pole, and the four small brass cannon threatening the points of the compass at its base.

"Stop a moment, Mr. Bolton," said Miss Kilburn; and she put her head quite out of the carriage, and stared at the figure on the monument.

It was strange that the first misgiving she could really make sure of concerning Hatboro' should relate to this figure, which she herself was mainly responsible for placing there. When the money was subscribed and voted for the statue, the committee wrote out to her at Rome as one who would naturally feel an interest in getting something fit and economical for them. She accepted the trust with zeal and pleasure; but she overruled their simple notion of an American volunteer at rest, with his hands folded on the muzzle of his gun, as intolerably hackneyed and commonplace. Her conscience, she said, would not let her add another recruit to the regiment of stone soldiers standing about in that posture on the tops of pedestals all over the country; and so, instead of going to an Italian statuary with her fellow-townsmen's letter, and getting him to make the figure they wanted, she doubled the money and gave the commission to a young girl from Kansas, who had come out to develop at Rome the genius recognised at Topeka. They decided together that it would be best to have something ideal, and the sculptor promptly imagined and rapidly executed a design for a winged Victory, poising on the summit of a white marble shaft, and clasping its hands under its chin, in expression of the grief that mingled with the popular exultation. Miss Kilburn had her doubts while the work went on, but she silenced them with the theory that when the figure was in position it would be all right.

Now that she saw it in position she wished to ask Mr. Bolton what was thought of it, but she could not nerve herself to the question. He remained silent, and she felt that he was sorry for her. "Oh, may I be very humble; may I be helped to be very humble!" she prayed under her breath. It seemed as if she could not take her eyes from the figure; it was such a modern, such an American shape, so youthfully inadequate, so simple, so sophisticated, so like a young lady in society indecorously exposed for a *tableau vivant*. She wondered if the people in Hatboro' felt all this about it; if they realised how its involuntary frivolity insulted the solemn memory of the slain.

"Drive on, please," she said gently.

Bolton pulled the reins, and as the horses started he pointed with his whip to a church at the other side of the green. "That's the new Orthodox church," he explained.

"Oh, is it?" asked Miss Kilburn. "It's very handsome, I'm sure." She was not sensible of admiring the large Romanesque pile very much, though it was certainly not bad, but she remembered that Bolton was a member of the Orthodox church, and she was grateful to him for not saying anything about the soldiers' monument.

"We sold the old buildin' to the Catholics, and they moved it down ont' the side street."

Miss Kilburn caught the glimmer of a cross where he beckoned, through the flutter of the foliage.

"They had to razee the steeple some to git their cross on," he added; and then he showed her the high-school building as they passed, and the Episcopal chapel, of blameless church-warden's Gothic, half hidden by its Japanese ivy, under a branching elm, on another side street.

"Yes," she said, "that was built before we went abroad."

"I disremember," he said absently. He let the horses walk on the soft, darkly shaded road, where the wheels made a pleasant grinding sound, and set himself sidewise on his front seat, so as to talk to Miss Kilburn more at his ease.

"I d'know," he began, after clearing his throat, with a conscious air, "as you know we'd got a new minister to our church."

"No, I hadn't heard of it," said Miss Kilburn, with her mind full of the monument still. "But I might have heard and forgotten it," she added. "I was very much taken up toward the last before I left Rome."

"Well, come to think," said Bolton; "I don't know's you'd had time to heard. He hain't been here a great while."

"Is he—satisfactory?" asked Miss Kilburn, feeling how far from satisfactory the Victory was, and formulating an explanatory apology to the committee in her mind.

"Oh yes, he's satisfactory enough, as far forth as that goes. He's talented, and he's right up with the times. Yes, he's progressive. I guess they got pretty tired of Mr. Rogers, even before he died; and they kept the supply a-goin' till—all was blue, before

W. D. Howells

they could settle on anybody. In fact they couldn't seem to agree on anybody till Mr. Peck come."

Miss Kilburn had got as far, in her tacit interview with the committee, as to have offered to replace at her own expense the Victory with a Volunteer, and she seemed to be listening to Bolton with rapt attention.

"Well, it's like this," continued the farmer. "He's progressive in his idees, 'n' at the same time he's spiritual-minded; and so I guess he suits pretty well all round. Of course you can't suit everybody. There's always got to be a dog in the manger, it don't matter where you go. But if anybody was to ask me, I should say Mr. Peck suited. Yes, I don't know but what I should."

Miss Kilburn instantaneously closed her transaction with the committee, removed the Victory, and had the Volunteer unveiled with appropriate ceremonies, opened with prayer by the Rev. Mr. Peck.

"Peck?" she said. "Did you tell me his name was Peck?"

"Yes, ma'am; Rev. Julius W. Peck. He's from down Penob- scotport way, in Maine. I guess he's all right."

Miss Kilburn did not reply. Her mind had been taken off the monument for the moment by her dislike for the name of the new minister, and the Victory had seized the opportunity to get back.

Bolton sighed deeply, and continued in a strain whose diffusiveness at last became perceptible to Miss Kilburn through her own humiliation. "There's some in every commu- nity that's bound to complain, I don't care what you do to accommodate 'em; and what I done, I done as much to stop their clack as anything, and give him the right sort of a start off, an' I guess I did. But Mis' Bolton she didn't know but what you'd look at it in the light of a libbutty, and I didn't know but what you *would* think I no business to done it."

He seemed to be addressing a question to her, but she only replied with a dazed frown, and Bolton was obliged to go on.

"I didn't let him room in your part of the house; that is to say, not sleep there; but I thought, as you was comin' home, and I better be airin' it up some, anyway, I might as well let him set in the old Judge's room. If you think it was more than I had a right to do, I'm willin' to pay for it. Git up!" Bolton turned fully round toward his horses, to hide the workings of emotion in his face, and shook the reins like a desperate man.

"What *are* you talking about, Mr. Bolton?" cried Miss Kilburn. "*Whom* are you talking about?"

Bolton answered, with a kind of violence, "Mr. Peck; I took him to board, first off."

"You took him to board?"

"Yes. I know it wa'n't just accordin' to the letter o' the law, and the old Judge was always pootty p'tic'lah. But I've took care of the place goin' on twenty years now, and I hain't never had a chick nor a child in it before. The child," he continued, partly turning his face round again, and beginning to look Miss Kilburn in the eye, "wa'n't one to touch anything, anyway, and we kep' her in our part all the while; Mis' Bolton she couldn't seem to let her out of her sight, she got so fond of her, and she used to follow me round among the hosses like a kitten. I declare, I *miss* her."

Bolton's face, the colour of one of the lean ploughed fields of Hatboro', and deeply furrowed, lighted up with real feeling, which he tried to make go as far in the work of reconciling Miss Kilburn as if it had been factitious.

"But I don't understand," she said. "What child are you talking about?"

"Mr. Peck's."

"Was he married?" she asked, with displeasure, she did not know why.

"Well, yes, he *had* been," answered Bolton. "But she'd be'n in the asylum ever since the child was born."

"Oh," said Miss Kilburn, with relief; and she fell back upon the seat from which she had started forward.

Bolton might easily have taken her tone for that of disgust. He faced round upon her once more. "It was kind of queer, his havin' the child with him, an' takin' most the care of her himself; and so, as I *say*, Mis' Bolton and me we took him in, as much to stop folks' mouths as anything, till they got kinder used to it. But we didn't take him into your part, as I *say*; and as *I* say, I'm willin' to pay you whatever you say for the use of the old Judge's study. I presume that part of it *was* a libbutty."

"It was all perfectly right, Mr. Bolton," said Miss Kilburn.

"His wife died anyway, more than a year ago," said Bolton, as if the fact completed his atonement to Miss Kilburn, "*Git* ep! I told him from the start that it had got to be a temporary thing, an' 't I only took him till he could git settled somehow. I guess he means to go to house-keepin', if he can git the right kind of a house-keeper; he wants an old one. If it was a young one, I guess he wouldn't have any great trouble, if he went about it the right way." Bolton's sarcasm was merely a race sarcasm. He was a very mild man, and his thick-growing eyelashes softened and shadowed his grey eyes, and gave his lean face pathos.

"You could have let him stay till he had found a suitable place," said Miss Kilburn.

"Oh, I wa'n't goin' to do *that*," said Bolton. "But I'm 'bliged to you just the same."

They came up in sight of the old square house, standing back a good distance from the road, with a broad sweep of grass sloping down before it into a little valley, and rising again to the wall fencing the grounds from the street. The wall was overhung there by a company of magnificent elms, which turned and formed one side of the avenue leading to the house. Their tops met and mixed somewhat incongruously with those of the stiff dark maples which more densely shaded the other side of the lane.

Bolton drove into their gloom, and then out into the wide sunny space at the side of the house where Miss Kilburn had alighted so often with her father. Bolton's dog, grown now so very old as to be weak-minded, barked crazily at his master, and then, recognising him, broke into an imbecile whimper, and went back and coiled his rheumatism up in the sun on a warm stone before the door. Mrs. Bolton had to step over him as she came out, formally supporting her right elbow with her left hand as she offered the other in greeting to Miss Kilburn, with a look of question at her husband.

Miss Kilburn intercepted the look, and began to laugh.

All was unchanged, and all so strange; it seemed as if her father must both get down with her from the carriage and come to meet her from the house. Her glance involuntarily took in the familiar masses and details; the patches of short tough grass mixed with decaying chips and small weeds underfoot, and the spacious June sky overhead; the fine network and blisters of the cracking and warping white paint on the clapboarding, and the hills beyond the bulks of the village houses and trees; the woodshed stretching with its low board arches to the barn, and the milk-pans tilted to sun against the underpinning of the L, and Mrs. Bolton's pot plants in the kitchen window.

"Did you think I could be hard about such a thing as that? It was perfectly right. O Mrs. Bolton!" She stopped laughing and began to cry; she put away Mrs. Bolton's carefully offered hand, she threw herself upon the bony structure of her bosom, and buried her face sobbing in the leathery folds of her neck.

Mrs. Bolton suffered her embrace above the old dog, who fled with a cry of rheumatic apprehension from the sweep of Miss Kilburn's skirts, and then came back and snuffed at them in a vain effort to recall her.

"Well, go in and lay down by the stove," said Mrs. Bolton, with a divided interest, while she beat Miss Kilburn's back with her bony palm in sign of sympathy. But the dog went off up the lane, and stood there by the pasture bars, barking abstractedly at intervals.

IV

Miss Kilburn found that the house had been well aired for her coming, but an old earthy and mouldy smell, which it took days and nights of open doors and windows to drive out, stole back again with the first turn of rainy weather. She had fires built on the hearths and in the stoves, and after opening her trunks and scattering her dresses on beds and chairs, she spent most of the first week outside of the house, wandering about the fields and orchards to adjust herself anew to the estranged features of the place. The house she found lower-ceiled and smaller than she remembered it. The Boltons had kept it up very well, and in spite of the earthy and mouldy smell, it was conscientiously clean. There was not a speck of dust anywhere; the old yellowish-white paint was spotless; the windows shone. But there was a sort of frigidity in the perfect order and repair which repelled her, and she left her things tossed about, as if to break the ice of this propriety. In several places, within and without, she found marks of the faithful hand of Bolton in economical patches of the woodwork; but she was not sure that they had not been there eleven years before; and there were darnings in the carpets and curtains, which affected her with the same mixture of novelty and familiarity. Certain stale smells about the place (minor smells as compared with the prevalent odour) confused her; she could not decide whether she remembered them of old, or was reminded of the odours she used to catch in passing the pantry on the steamer.

Her father had never been sure that he would not return any next year or month, and the house had always been ready to

W. D. Howells

receive them. In his study everything was as he left it. His daughter looked for signs of Mr. Peck's occupation, but there were none; Mrs. Bolton explained that she had put him in a table from her own sitting-room to write at. The Judge's desk was untouched, and his heavy wooden arm-chair stood pulled up to it as if he were in it. The ranks of law-books, in their yellow sheepskin, with their red titles above and their black titles below, were in the order he had taught Mrs. Bolton to replace them in after dusting; the stuffed owl on a shelf above the mantel looked down with a clear solemnity in its gum-copal eyes, and Mrs. Bolton took it from its perch to show Miss Kilburn that there was not a moth on it, nor the sign of a moth.

Miss Kilburn experienced here that refusal of the old associations to take the form of welcome which she had already felt in the earth and sky and air outside; in everything there was a sense of impassable separation. Her dead father was no nearer in his wonted place than the trees of the orchard, or the outline of the well-known hills, or the pink of the familiar sunsets. In her rummaging about the house she pulled open a chest of drawers which used to stand in the room where she slept when a child. It was full of her own childish clothing, a little girl's linen and muslin; and she thought with a throe of despair that she could as well hope to get back into these outgrown garments, which the helpless piety of Mrs. Bolton had kept from the rag-bag, as to think of re-entering the relations of the life so long left off.

It surprised her to find how cold the Boltons were; she had remembered them as always very kind and willing; but she was so used now to the ways of the Italians and their showy affection, it was hard for her to realise that people could be both kind and cold. The Boltons seemed ashamed of their feelings, and hid them; it was the same in some degree with all the villagers when she began to meet them, and the fact slowly worked back into her consciousness, wounding its way in. People did not come to see her at once. They waited, as they told her, till she got settled, before they called, and then they did not appear very glad to have her back.

But this was not altogether the effect of their temperament. The Kilburns had made a long summer always in Hatboro', and they had always talked of it as home; but they had never passed a whole year there since Judge Kilburn first went to Congress, and they were not regarded as full neighbours or permanent citizens. Miss Kilburn, however, kept up her childhood friendships, and she and some of the ladies called one another by their Christian names, but they believed that she met people in Washington whom she liked better; the winters she spent there certainly weakened the ties between them, and when it came to those eleven years in Rome, the letters they exchanged grew rarer and rarer, till they stopped altogether. Some of the girls went away; some died; others became dead and absent to her in their marriages and household cares.

After waiting for one another, three of them came together to see her one day. They all kissed her, after a questioning glance at her face and dress, as if they wanted to see whether she had grown proud or too fashionable. But they were themselves apparently much better dressed, and certainly more richly dressed. In a place like Hatboro', where there is no dinner-giving, and evening parties are few, the best dress is a street costume, which may be worn for calls and shopping, and for church and all public entertainments. The well-to-do ladies make an effect of outdoor fashion, in which the poorest shop hand has her part; and in their turn they share her indoor simplicity. These old friends of Annie's wore bonnets and frocks of the latest style and costly material.

They let her make the advances, receiving them with blank passivity, or repelling them with irony, according to the several needs of their self-respect, and talking to one another across her. One of them asked her when her hair had begun to turn, and they each told her how thin she was, but promised her that Hatboro' air would bring her up. At the same time they feigned humility in regard to everything about Hatboro' but the air; they laughed when she said she intended now to make it her home the whole year round, and said they guessed she would be tired of it long before fall; there were plenty of summer folks that passed the winter as long as the June weather lasted. As they grew more secure of themselves, or less afraid of one another in her presence, their voices rose; they laughed loudly at nothing, and they yelled in a nervous chorus at times, each trying to make herself heard above the others.

She asked them about the social life in the village, and they told her that a good many new people had really settled there, but they did not know whether she would like them; they were not the old Hatboro' style. Annie showed them some of the things she had brought home, especially Roman views, and they said now she ought to give an evening in the church parlour with them.

"You'll have to come to our church, Annie," said Mrs. Putney. "The Unitarian doesn't have preaching once in a month, and Mr. Peck is very liberal."

"He's 'most *too* liberal for some," said Emmeline Gerrish. Of the three she had grown the stoutest, and from being a slight, light-minded girl, she had become a heavy matron, habitually censorious in her speech. She did not mean any more by it, however, than she did by her girlish frivolity, and if she was not supported in her severity, she was apt to break down and disown it with a giggle, as she now did.

"Well, I don't know about his being *too* liberal," said Mrs. Wilmington, a large red-haired blonde, with a lazy laugh. "He makes you feel that you're a pretty miserable sinner." She made a grimace of humorous disgust.

"Mr. Gerrish says that's just the trouble," Mrs. Gerrish broke in. "Mr. Peck don't put stress enough on the promises. That's what Mr. Gerrish says. You must have been surprised, Annie," she added, "to find that he'd been staying in your house."

"I was glad Mrs. Bolton invited him," answered Annie sincerely, but not instantly.

The ladies waited, with an exchange of glances, for her reply, as if they had talked the matter over beforehand, and had agreed to find out just how Annie Kilburn felt about it.

"Oh, I guess he paid his board," said Mrs. Wilmington, jocosely rejecting the implication that he had been the guest of the Boltons.

"I don't see what he expects to do with that little girl of his, without any mother, that way," said Mrs. Gerrish. "He ought to get married."

"Perhaps he will, when he's waited a proper time," suggested Mrs. Putney demurely.

"Well, his wife's been the same as dead ever since the child was born. I don't know what you call a proper time, Ellen," argued Mrs. Gerrish.

"I presume a minister feels differently about such things," Mrs. Wilmington remarked indolently.

"I don't see why a minister should feel any different from anybody else," said Mrs. Gerrish. "It's his duty to do it on his child's account. I don't see why he don't have the remains brought to Hatboro', anyway."

They debated this point at some length, and they seemed to forget Annie. She listened with more interest than her concern in the last resting-place of the minister's dead wife really inspired. These old friends of hers seemed to have lost the sensitiveness of their girlhood without having gained tenderness in its place. They treated the affair with a nakedness that shocked her. In the country and in small towns people come face to face with life, especially women. It means marrying, child-bearing, household cares and burdens, neighbourhood gossip, sickness, death, burial, and whether the corpse appeared natural. But ever so much kindness goes with their disillusion; they are blunted, but not embittered.

They ended by recalling Annie to mind, and Mrs. Putney said: "I suppose you haven't been to the cemetery yet? I They've got it all fixed up since you went away—drives laid out, and paths cut through, and everything. A good many have put up family tombs, and they've taken away the old iron fences round the lots, and put granite curbing. They mow the grass all the time. It's a perfect garden." Mrs. Putney was a small woman, already beginning to wrinkle. She had married a man whom Annie remembered as a mischievous little boy, with a sharp tongue and a nervous temperament; her father had always liked him when he came about the house, but Annie had lost sight of him in the years that make small boys and girls large ones, and he was at college when she went abroad. She had an impression of something unhappy in her friend's marriage.

"I think it's *too* much fixed up myself," said Mrs. Gerrish. She turned suddenly to Annie: "You going to have your father fetched home?"

The other ladies started a little at the question and looked at Annie; it was not that they were shocked, but they wanted to see whether she would not be so.

"No," she said briefly. She added, helplessly, "It wasn't his wish."

"I should have thought he would have liked to be buried alongside of your mother," said Mrs. Gerrish. "But the Judge always *was* a little peculiar. I presume you can have the name and the date put on the monument just the same."

Annie flushed at this intimate comment and suggestion from a woman whom as a girl she had never admitted to familiarity with her, but had tolerated her because she was such a harmless simpleton, and hung upon other girls whom she liked better.

The word monument cowed her, however. She was afraid they might begin to talk about the soldiers' monument. She answered hastily, and began to ask them about their families.

Mrs. Wilmington, who had no children, and Mrs. Putney, who had one, spoke of Mrs. Gerrish's large family. She had four children, and she refused the praises of her friends for them, though she celebrated them herself. "You ought to have seen the two little girls that Ellen lost, Annie," she said. "Ellen Putney, I don't see how you ever got over that. Those two lovely, healthy children gone, and poor little Winthrop left! I always did say it was too hard."

She had married a clerk in the principal dry-goods store, who had prospered rapidly, and was now one of the first business men of the place, and had an ambition to be a leading citizen. She believed in his fitness to deal with the questions of religion and education which he took part in, and was always quoting Mr. Gerrish. She called him Mr. Gerrish so much that other people began to call him so too. But Mrs. Putney's husband held out against it, and had the habit of returning the little man's ceremonious salutations with an easy, "Hello, Billy," "Good morning, Billy." It was his theory that this was good for Gerrish, who might otherwise have forgotten when everybody called him Billy. He was one of the old Putneys; and he was a lawyer by profession.

Mrs. Wilmington's husband had come to Hatboro' since Annie's long absence began; he had capital, and he had started a stocking-mill in Hatboro'. He was much older than his wife, whom he had married after a protracted widowerhood. She had one of the best houses and the most richly furnished in Hatboro'. She and Mrs. Putney saw Mrs. Gerrish at rare intervals, and in observance of some notable fact of their girlish friendship like the present.

In pursuance of the subject of children, Mrs. Gerrish said that she sometimes had a notion to offer to take Mr. Peck's little girl herself till he could get fixed somehow, but Mr. Gerrish would not let her. Mr. Gerrish said Mr. Peck had better get married himself if he wanted a step-mother for his little girl. Mr. Gerrish was peculiar about keeping a family to itself.

"Well, you'll think *we've* come to board with you *too*," said Mrs. Putney, in reference to Mr. Peck.

The ladies all rose, and having got upon their feet, began to shout and laugh again—like girls, they implied.

They stayed and talked a long time after rising, with the same note of unsparing personality in their talk. Where there are few public interests and few events, as in such places, there can be no small-talk, nothing of the careless touch-and-go of larger societies. Every one knows all the others, and knows the worst of them. People are not unkind; they are mutually and freely helpful; but they have only themselves to occupy their minds. Annie's friends had also to distinguish themselves to her from the rest of the villagers, and it was easiest to do this by an attitude of criticism mingled with large allowance. They ended a dissection of the community by saying that they believed there was no place like Hatboro', after all.

In the contagion of their perfunctory gaiety Annie began to scream and laugh too, as she followed them to the door, and stood talking to them while they got into Mrs. Wilmington's extension-top carry-all. She answered with deafening promises, when they put their bonnets out of the carry-all and called back to her to be sure to come soon to see them soon.

V

Mrs. Bolton made no advances with Annie toward the discussion of her friends; but when Annie asked about their families, she answered with the incisive directness of a country-bred woman. She delivered her judgments as she went about her work, the morning after the ladies' visit, while Annie sat before the breakfast-table, which she had given her leave to clear. As she passed in and out from the dining-room to the kitchen she kept talking; she raised her voice in the further room, and lowered it when she drew near again. She wore a dismal calico wrapper, which made no compromise with the gauntness of her figure; her reddish-brown hair, which grew in a fringe below her crown, was plaited into small tags or tails, pulled up and tied across the top of her head, the bare surfaces of which were curiously mottled with the dye which she sometimes put on her hair. Behind, this was gathered up into a small knob pierced with a single hair-pin; the arrangement left Mrs. Bolton's visage to the unrestricted expression of character. She did not let it express toward Annie any expectation of the confidential relations that are supposed to exist between people who have been a long time master and servant. She had never recognised her relations with the Kilburns in these terms. She was a mature Yankee single woman, of confirmed self-respect, when she first came as house-keeper to Judge Kilburn, twenty years ago, and she had not changed her nature in changing her condition by her marriage with Oliver Bolton; she was child-less, unless his comparative youth conferred a sort of adoptive maternity upon her.

Annie went into her father's study, where she had lit the fire in the Franklin-stove on her way to breakfast. It had come on to rain during the night, after the fine yesterday which Mrs. Gerrish had denounced to its face as a weather-breeder. At first it rained silently, stealthily; but toward morning Annie heard the wind rising, and when she looked out of her window after daylight she found a fierce north-easterly storm drenching and chilling the landscape. Now across the flattened and tangled grass of the lawn the elms were writhing in the gale, and swinging their long lean boughs to and fro; from another window she saw the cuffed and hustled maples ruffling their stiff masses of foliage, and shuddering in the storm. She turned away, with a sigh of the luxurious melancholy which a northeaster inspires in people safely sheltered from it, and sat down before her fire. She recalled the three women who had visited her the day before, in the better-remembered figures of their childhood and young girlhood; and their present character did not seem a broken promise. Nothing was really disappointed in it but the animal joy, the hopeful riot of their young blood, which must fade and die with the happiest fate. She perceived that what they had come to was not unjust to what they had been; and as our own fate always appears to us unaccomplished, a thing for the distant future to fulfil, she began to ask herself what was to be the natural sequence of such a temperament, such mental and moral traits, as hers. Had her life been so noble in anything but vague aspirations that she could ever reasonably expect the destiny of grand usefulness which she had always unreasonably expected? The question came home to her with such pain, in the light of what her old playmates had become, that she suddenly ceased to enjoy the misery of the storm out-of-doors, or the purring content of the fire on the hearth of the stove at her feet; the book she had taken down to read fell unopened into her lap, and she gave herself up to a half-hour of such piercing self-question as only a high-minded woman can endure when the flattering promises of youth have grown vague and few.

There is no condition of life that is wholly acceptable, but none that is not tolerable when once it establishes itself; and while Annie Kilburn had never consented to be an old maid, she had become one without great suffering. At thirty-one she could not call herself anything else; she often called herself an old maid, with the mental reservation that she was not one. She was merely unmarried; she might marry any time. Now, when she assured herself of this, as she had done many times before, she suddenly wondered if she should ever marry; she wondered if she had seemed to her friends yesterday like a person who would never marry. Did one carry such a thing in one's looks? Perhaps they, idealised her; they had not seen her since she was twenty, and perhaps they still thought of her as a young girl. It now seemed to her as if she had left her youth in Rome, as in Rome it had seemed to her that she should find it again in Hatboro'. A pang of aimless, unlocalised homesickness passed through her; she realised that she was alone in the world. She rose to escape the pang, and went to the window of the parlour which looked toward the street, where she saw the figure of a young man draped in a long indiarubber gossamer coat fluttering in the wind that pushed him along as he tacked on a southerly course; he bowed and twisted his head to escape the lash of the rain. She watched him till he turned into the lane leading to the house, and then, at a discreeter distance, she watched him through the window at the other corner, making his way up to the front door in the teeth of the gale. He seemed to have a bundle under his arm, and as he stepped into the shelter of the portico, and freed his arm to ring, she discovered that it was a bundle of books. Whether Mrs. Bolton did not hear the bell, or whether she heard it and decided that it would be absurd to leave her work for it, when Miss Kilburn, who was so much nearer, could answer it, she did not come, even at a second ring, and Annie was forced to go to the door herself, or leave the poor man dripping in the cold wind outside.

She had made up her mind, at sight of the books, that he was a canvasser for some subscription book, such as used to come in her father's time, but when she opened to him he took off his hat with a great deal of manner, and said "Miss Kilburn?" with so much insinuation of gentle disinterestedness, that it flashed upon her that it might be Mr. Peck.

"Yes," she said, with confusion, while the flash of conjecture faded away.

"Mr. Brandreth," said her visitor, whom she now saw to be much younger than Mr. Peck could be. He looked not much more than twenty-two or twenty-three; his damp hair waved and curled upon his temples and forehead, and his blue eyes lightened from a beardless and freshly shaven face. "I called this morning because I felt sure of finding you at home."

He smiled at his reference to the weather, and Annie smiled too as she again answered, "Yes?" She did not want his books, but she liked something that was cheerful and enthusiastic in him; she added, "Won't you step into the study?"

"Thanks, yes," said the young man, flinging off his gossamer, and hanging it up to drip into the pan of the hat rack. He gathered up his books from the chair where he had laid them, and held them at his waist with both hands, while he bowed her precedence beside the study door.

"I don't know," he began, "but I ought to apologise for coming on a day like this, when you were not expecting to be interrupted."

"Oh no; I'm not at all busy. But you must have had courage to brave a storm like this."

"No. The truth is, Miss Kilburn, I was very anxious to see you about a matter I have at heart—that I desire your help with."

"He wants me," Annie thought, "to give him the use of my name as a subscriber to his book"—there seemed really to be a half-dozen books in his bundle—"and he's come to me first."

"I had expected to come with Mrs. Munger—she's a great friend of mine; you haven't met her yet, but you'll like her;

she's the leading spirit in South Hatboro'—and we were coming together this morning; but she was unexpectedly called away yesterday, and so I ventured to call alone."

"I'm very glad to see you, Mr. Brandreth," Annie said. "Then Mrs. Munger has subscribed already, and I'm only second fiddle, after all," she thought.

"The truth is," said Mr. Brandreth, "I'm the factotum, or teetotum, of the South Hatboro' ladies' book club, and I've been deputed to come and see if you wouldn't like to join it."

"Oh!" said Annie, and with a thrill of dismay she asked herself how much she had let her manner betray that she had supposed he was a book agent. "I shall be very glad indeed, Mr. Brandreth."

"Mrs. Munger was sure you would," said Mr. Brandreth joyously. "I've brought some of the books with me—the last," he said; and Annie had time to get into a new social attitude toward him during their discussion of the books. She chose one, and Mr. Brandreth took her subscription, and wrote her name in the club book.

"One of the reasons," he said, "why I would have preferred to come with Mrs. Munger is that she is so heart and soul with mo in my little scheme. She could have put it before you in so much better light than I can. But she was called away so suddenly."

"I hope for no serious cause," said Annie.

"Oh no! It's just to Cambridge. Her son is one of the Freshman Nine, and he's been hit by a ball."

"Oh!" said Annie.

"Yes; it's a great pity for Mrs. Munger. But I come to you for advice as well as co-operation, Miss Kilburn. You must have met a great many English people in Rome, and heard some of them talk about it. We're thinking, some of the young people here, about getting up some outdoor theatricals, like Lady Archibald Campbell's, don't you know. You know about them?" he added, at the blankness in her face.

"I read accounts of them in the English papers. They must have been very—original. But do you think that in a community like Hatboro'—Are there enough who could—enter into the spirit?"

"Oh yes, indeed!" cried Mr. Brandreth ardently. "You've no idea what a place Hatboro' has got to be. You've not been about much yet, Miss Kilburn?"

"No," said Annie; "I haven't really been off our own place since I came. I've seen nobody but two or three old friends, and we naturally talked more about old times than anything else. But I hear that there are great changes."

"Yes," said Mr. Brandreth. "The social growth has been even greater than the business growth. You've no idea! People have come in for the winter as well as the summer. South Hatboro', where we live—you must see South Hatboro', Miss Kilburn!—is quite a famous health resort. A great many Boston doctors send their patients to us now, instead of Colorado or the Adirondacks. In fact, that's what brought *us* to Hatboro'. My mother couldn't have lived, if she had tried to stay in Melrose. One lung all gone, and the other seriously affected. And people have found out what a charming place it is for the summer. It's cool; and it's so near, you know; the gentlemen can run out every night—only an hour and a quarter from town, and expresses both ways. All very agreeable people, too; and cultivated. Mr. Fellows, the painter, makes a long summer; he bought an old farm-house, and built a studio; Miss Jennings, the flower-painter, has a little box there, too; Mr. Chapley, the publisher, of New York, has built; the Misses Clevinger, and Mrs. Valence, are all near us. There's one family from Chicago—quite nice—New England by birth, you know; and

Mrs. Munger, of course; so that there's a very pleasant variety."

"I certainly had no idea of it," said Annie.

"I knew you couldn't have," said Mr. Brandreth, "or you wouldn't have felt any doubt about our having the material for the theatricals. You see, I want to interest all the nice people in it, and make it a whole-town affair. I think it's a great pity for some of the old village families and the summer folks, as they call us, not to mingle more than they do, and Mrs. Munger thinks so too; and we've been talking you over, Miss Kilburn, and we've decided that you could do more than anybody else to help on a scheme that's meant to bring them together."

"Because I'm neither summer folks nor old village families?" asked Annie.

"Because you're both," retorted Mr. Brandreth.

"I don't see that," said Annie; "but we'll suppose the case, for the sake of argument. What do you expect me to do in theatricals, in-doors or out? I never took part in anything of the kind; I can't see an inch beyond the end of my nose without glasses; I never could learn the simplest thing by heart; I'm clumsy and awkward; I get confused."

"Oh, my dear Miss Kilburn, spare yourself! We don't expect you to take part in the play. I don't admit that you're what you say at all; but we only want you to lend us your countenance."

"Oh, is that all? And what do you expect to do with my countenance?" Annie said, with a laugh of misgiving.

"Everything. We know how much influence your name has— one of the old Hatboro' names—in the community, and all that; and we do want to interest the whole community in our scheme. We want to establish a Social Union for the work-people, don't you know, and we think it would be much nicer if it seemed to originate with the old village people."

Annie could not resist an impression in favour of the scheme. It gave definition to the vague intentions with which she had returned to Hatboro'; it might afford her a chance to make reparation for the figure on the soldiers' monument.

"I'm not sure," she began. "If I knew just what a Social Union is—"

"Well, at first," Mr. Brandreth interposed, "it will only be a reading-room, supplied with the magazines and papers, and well lighted and heated, where the work-people—those who have no families especially—could spend their evenings. Afterward we should hope to have a kitchen, and supply tea and coffee—and oysters, perhaps—at a nominal cost; and ice-cream in the summer."

"But what have your outdoor theatricals to do—But of course. You intend to give the proceeds—"

"Exactly. And we want the proceeds to be as large as possible. We propose to give our time and money to getting the thing up in the best shape, and then we want all the villagers to give their half-dollars and make it a success every way."

"I see," said Annie.

"We want it to be successful, and we want it to be distinguished; we want to make it unique. Mrs. Munger is going to give her grounds and the decorations, and there will be a supper afterward, and a little dance."

"Such things are a great deal of trouble," said Annie, with a smile, from the vantage-ground of her larger experience. "What do you propose to do—what play?"

"Well, we've about decided upon some scenes from *Romeo and Juliet*. They would be very easy to set, outdoors, don't you know, and everybody knows them, and they wouldn't be hard to do. The ballroom in the house of the Capulets could be made to open on a kind of garden terrace—Mrs. Munger has a lovely terrace in her grounds for lawn-tennis—and then we could have a minuet on the grass. You know Miss Mather introduces a minuet in that scene, and makes a great deal of it. Or, I forgot. She's come up since you went away."

"Yes; I hadn't heard of her. Isn't a minuet at Verona in the time of the Scaligeri rather—"

"Well, yes, it is, rather. But you've no idea how pretty it is. And then, you know, we could have the whole of the balcony scene, and other bits that we choose to work in—perhaps parts of other acts that would suit the scene."

"Yes, it would be charming; I can see how very charming it could be made."

"Then we may count upon you?" he asked.

"Yes, yes," she said; "but I don't really know what I'm to do."

Mr. Brandreth had risen; but he sat down again, as if glad to afford her any light he could throw upon the subject.

"How am I to 'influence people,' as you say?" she continued. "I'm quite a stranger in Hatboro'; I hardly know anybody."

"But a great many people know *you*, Miss Kilburn. Your name is associated with the history of the place, and you could do everything for us. You *won't* refuse!" cried Mr. Brandreth winningly. "For instance, you know Mrs. Wilmington."

"Oh yes; she's an old girl-friend of mine."

"Then you know how enormously clever she is. She can do anything. We want her to take an active part—the part of the Nurse. She's delightfully funny. But you know her peculiar temperament—how she hates initiative of all kinds; and we want somebody to bring Mr. Wilmington round. If we could

W. D. Howells

get them committed to the scheme, and a man like Mr. Putney—he'd make a capital Mercutio—it would go like wildfire. We want to interest the churches, too. The object is so worthy, and the theatricals will be so entirely unobjectionable in every respect. We have the Unitarians and Universalists, of course. The Baptists and Methodists will be hard to manage; but the Orthodox are of so many different shades; and I understand the new minister, Mr. Peck, is very liberal. He was here in your house, I believe."

"Yes; but I never saw him," said Annie. "He boarded with the farmer. I'm a Unitarian myself."

"Of course. It would be a great point gained if we could interest him. Every care will be taken to have the affair unobjectionable. You see, the design is to let everybody come to the theatricals, and only those remain to the supper and dance whom we invite. That will keep out the socially objectionable element—the shoe-shop hands and the straw-shop girls."

"Oh," said Annie. "But isn't the—the Social Union for just that class?"

"Yes, it's *expressly* for them, and we intend to organise a system of entertainments—lectures, concerts, readings—for the winter, and keep them interested the whole year round in it. The object is to show them that the best people in the community have their interests at heart, and wish to get on common ground with them."

"Yes," said Annie, "the object is certainly very good."

Mr. Brandreth rose again, and put out his hand. "Then you will help us?"

"Oh, I don't know about that yet."

"At least you won't hinder us?"

"Certainly not."

"Then I consider you in a very hopeful condition, Miss Kilburn, and I feel that I can safely leave you to Mrs. Munger. She is coming to see you as soon as she gets back."

Annie found herself sadder when he was gone, and she threw herself upon the old feather-cushioned lounge to enjoy a reverie in keeping with the dreary storm outside. Was it for this that she had left Rome? She had felt, as every American of conscience feels abroad, the drawings of a duty, obscure and indefinable, toward her country, the duty to come home and do something for it, be something in it. This is the impulse of no common patriotism; it is perhaps a sense of the opportunity which America supremely affords for the race to help itself, and for each member of it to help all the rest.

But from the moment Annie arrived in Hatboro' the difficulty of being helpful to anything or any one had increased upon her with every new fact that she had learned about it and the people in it. To her they seemed terribly self-sufficing. They seemed occupied and prosperous, from her front parlour window; she did not see anybody going by who appeared to be in need of her; and she shrank from a more thorough exploration of the place. She found she had fancied necessity coming to her and taking away her good works, as it were, in a basket; but till Mr. Brandreth appeared with his scheme, nothing had applied for her help She had always hated theatricals; they bored her; and yet the Social Union was a good object, and if this scheme would bring her acquainted in Hatboro' it might be the stepping-stone to something better, something really or more ideally useful. She wondered what South Hatboro' was like; she would get Mrs. Bolton's opinion, which, if severe, would be just. She would ask Mrs. Bolton about Mrs. Munger, too. She would tell Mrs. Bolton to tell Mr. Peck to call to dine. Would it be thought patronising to Mr. Peck?

The fire from the Franklin-stove diffused a drowsy comfort

through the room, the rain lashed the window-panes, and the wind shrilled in the gable. Annie fell off to sleep. When she woke up she heard Mrs. Bolton laying the table for her one o'clock dinner, and she knew it was half-past twelve, because Mrs. Bolton always laid the table just half an hour beforehand. She went out to speak to Mrs. Bolton.

There was no want of distinctness in Mrs. Bolton's opinion, but Annie felt that there was a want of perspective and proportion in it, arising from the narrowness of Mrs. Bolton's experience and her ignorance of the world; she was farm-bred, and she had always lived upon the outskirts of Hatboro', even when it was a much smaller place than now. But Mrs. Bolton had her criterions, and she believed in them firmly; in a time when agnosticism extends among cultivated people to every region of conjecture, the social convictions of Mrs. Bolton were untainted by misgiving. In the first place, she despised laziness, and as South Hatboro' was the summer home of open and avowed disoccupation, of an idleness so entire that it had to seek refuge from itself in all manner of pastimes, she held its population in a contempt to which her meagre phrase did imperfect justice. From time to time she had to stop altogether, and vent it in "Wells!" of varying accents and inflections, but all expressive of aversion, and in snorts and sniffs still more intense in purport.

Then she held that people who had nothing else to do ought at least to be exemplary in their lives, and she was merciless to the goings-on in South Hatboro', which had penetrated on the breath of scandal to the elder village. When Annie came to find out what these were, she did not think them dreadful; they were small flirtations and harmless intimacies between the members of the summer community, which in the imagination of the village blackened into guilty intrigue. On the tongues of some, South Hatboro' was another Gomorrah; Mrs. Bolton believed the worst, especially of the women.

"I hear," said Mrs. Bolton, "that them women come up here for *rest*. I don't know what they want to rest *from*; but if it's from doin' nothin' all winter long, I guess they go back to the city poot' near's tired's they come."

Perhaps Annie felt that it was useless to try to enlighten her in regard to the fatigues from which the summer sojourner in the country escapes so eagerly; the cares of giving and going to lunches and dinners; the labour of afternoon teas; the late hours and the heavy suppers of evening receptions; the drain of charity-doing and play-going; the slavery of amateur art study, and parlour readings, and musicales; the writing of invitations and acceptances and refusals; the trying on of dresses; the calls made and received. She let her talk on, and tried to figure, as well as she could from her talk, the form and magnitude of the task laid upon her by Mr. Brandreth, of reconciling Old Hatboro' to South Hatboro', and uniting them in a common enterprise.

"Mrs. Bolton," she said, abruptly leaving the subject at last, "I've been thinking whether I oughtn't to do something about Mr. Peck. I don't want him to feel that he was unwelcome to me in my house; I should like him to feel that I approved of his having been here."

As this was not a question, Mrs. Bolton, after the fashion of country people, held her peace, and Annie went on—

"Does he never come to see you?"

"Well, he was here last night," said Mrs. Bolton.

"Last *night*!" cried Annie. "Why in the world didn't you let me know?"

"I didn't know as you wanted to know," began Mrs. Bolton, with a sullen defiance mixed with pleasure in Annie's reproach. "He was out there in my settin'-room with his little girl."

"But don't you see that if you didn't let me know he was here it would look to him as if I didn't wish to meet him—as if I had told you that you were not to introduce him?"

Probably Mrs. Bolton believed too that a man's mind was agile enough for these conjectures; but she said she did not suppose he would take it in that way; she added that he stayed longer than she expected, because the little girl seemed to like it so much; she always cried when she had to go away.

"Do you mean that she's attached to the place?" demanded Annie.

"Well, yes, she is," Mrs. Bolton admitted. "And the cat."

Annie had a great desire to tell Mrs. Bolton that she had behaved very stupidly. But she knew Mrs. Bolton would not stand that, and she had to content herself with saying, severely, "The next time he comes, let me know without fail, please. What is the child like?" she asked.

"Well, I guess it must favour the mother, if anything. It don't seem to take after him any."

"Why don't you have it here often, then," asked Annie, "if it's so much attached to the place?"

"Well I didn't know as you wanted to have it round," replied Mrs. Bolton bluntly.

Annie made a "Tchk!" of impatience with her obtuseness, and asked, "Where is Mr. Peck staying?"

"Well, he's staying at Mis' Warner's till he can get settled."

"Is it far from here?"

"It's down in the north part of the village—Over the Track."

"Is Mr. Bolton at home?"

"Yes, he is," said Mrs. Bolton, with the effect of not intending to deny it.

"Then I want him to hitch up—now—at once—right away—and go and get the child and bring her here to dinner with me." Annie got so far with her severity, feeling that it was needed to mask a proceeding so romantic, perhaps so silly. She added timidly, "Can he do it?"

"I d'know but what he can," said Mrs. Bolton, dryly, and whatever her feeling really was in regard to the matter, her manner gave no hint of it. Annie did not know whether Bolton was going on her errand or not, from Mrs. Bolton, but in ten or twelve minutes she saw him emerge from the avenue into the street, in the carry-all, tightly curtained against the storm. Half an hour later he returned, and his wife set down in the library a shabbily dressed little girl, with her cheeks bright and her hair curling from the weather, and staring at Annie, and rather disposed to cry. She said hastily, "Bring in the cat, Mrs. Bolton; we're going to have the cat to dinner with us."

This inspiration seemed to decide the little girl against crying. The cat was equipped with a doily, and actually provided with dinner at a small table apart; the child did not look at it as Annie had expected she would, but remained with her eyes fastened on Annie herself: She did not stir from the spot where Mrs. Bolton had put her down, but she let Annie take her up and arrange her in a chair, with large books graduated to the desired height under her, and made no sign of satisfaction or disapproval. Once she looked round, when Mrs. Bolton finally went out after bringing in the last dish for dinner, and then fastened her eyes on Annie again, twisting her head shyly round to follow her in every gesture and expression as Annie fitted on a napkin under her chin, cut up her meat, poured her milk, and buttered her bread. She answered nothing to the chatter which Annie tried to make lively and entertaining, and made no sound but that of a broken and suppressed breathing. Annie had forgotten to ask her name of Mrs. Bolton, and she asked it in vain of the child herself, with a great variety of

W. D. Howells

circumlocution; she was so unused to children that she was ashamed to invent any pet name for her; she called her, in what she felt to be a stiff and school-mistressly fashion, "Little Girl," and talked on at her, growing more and more nervous herself without perceiving that the child's condition was approaching a climax. She had taken off her glasses, from the notion that they embarrassed her guest, and she did not see the pretty lips beginning to curl, nor the searching eyes clouding with tears; the storm of sobs that suddenly burst upon her astounded her.

"Mrs. Bolton! Mrs. Bolton!" she screamed, in hysterical helplessness. Mrs. Bolton rushed in, and with an instant perception of the situation, caught the child to her bony breast, and fled with it to her own room, where Annie heard its wails die gradually away amid murmurs of comfort and reassurance from Mrs. Bolton.

She felt like a great criminal and a great fool; at the same time she was vexed with the stupid child which she had meant so well by, and indignant with Mrs. Bolton, whose flight with it had somehow implied a reproach of her behaviour. When she could govern herself, she went out to Mrs. Bolton's room, where she found the little one quiet enough, and Mrs. Bolton tying on the long apron in which she cleared up the dinner and washed the dishes.

"I guess she'll get along now," she said, without the critical tone which Annie was prepared to resent. "She was scared some, and she felt kind of strange, I presume."

"Yes, and I behaved like a simpleton, dressing up the cat, I suppose," answered Annie. "But I thought it would amuse her."

"You can't tell how children will take a thing. I don't believe they like anything that's out of the common—well, not a great deal."

There was a leniency in Mrs. Bolton's manner which encouraged Annie to go on and accuse herself more and more, and then an unresponsive blankness that silenced her. She went back to her own rooms; and to get away from her shame, she began to write a letter.

It was to a friend in Rome, and from the sense we all have that a letter which is to go such a great distance ought to be a long letter, and from finding that she had really a good deal to say, she let it grow so that she began apologising for its length half a dozen pages before the end. It took her nearly the whole afternoon, and she regained a little of her self-respect by ridiculing the people she had met.

VI

Toward five o'clock Annie was interrupted by a knock at her door, which ought to have prepared her for something unusual, for it was Mrs. Bolton's habit to come and go without knocking. But she called "Come in!" without rising from her letter, and Mrs. Bolton entered with a stranger. The little girl clung to his forefinger, pressing her head against his leg, and glancing shyly up at Annie. She sprang up, and, "This is Mr. Peck, Miss Kilburn," said Mrs. Bolton.

"How do you do?" said Mr. Peck, taking the hand she gave him.

He was gaunt, without being tall, and his clothes hung loosely about him, as if he had fallen away in them since they were made. His face was almost the face of the caricature American: deep, slightly curved vertical lines enclosed his mouth in their parenthesis; a thin, dust-coloured beard fell from his cheeks and chin; his upper lip was shaven. But instead of the slight frown of challenge and self-assertion which marks this face in the type, his large blue eyes, set near together, gazed sadly from under a smooth forehead, extending itself well up toward the crown, where his dry hair dropped over it.

"I am very glad to see you, Mr. Peck," said Annie; "I've wanted to tell you how pleased I am that you found shelter in my old home when you first came to Hatboro'."

Mr. Peck's trousers were short and badly kneed, and his long coat hung formlessly from his shoulders; she involuntarily took a patronising tone toward him which was not habitual with her.

"Thank you," he said, with the dry, serious voice which seemed the fit vocal expression of his presence; "I have been afraid that it seemed like an intrusion to you."

"Oh, not the least," retorted Annie. "You were very welcome. I hope you're comfortably placed where you are now?"

"Quite so," said the minister.

"I'd heard so much of your little girl from Mrs. Bolton, and her attachment to the house, that I ventured to send for her to-day. But I believe I gave her rather a bad quarter of an hour, and that she liked the place better under Mrs. Bolton's *regime*."

She expected some deprecatory expression of gratitude from him, which would relieve her of the lingering shame she felt for having managed so badly, but he made none.

"It was my fault. I'm not used to children, and I hadn't taken the precaution to ask her name—"

"Her name is Idella," said the minister.

Annie thought it very ugly, but, with the intention of saying something kind, she said, "What a quaint name!"

"It was her mother's choice," returned the minister. "Her own name was Ella, and my mother's name was Ida; she combined the two."

"Oh!" said Annie. She abhorred those made-up names in which the New England country people sometimes indulge their fancy, and Idella struck her as a particularly repulsive invention; but she felt that she must not visit the fault upon the little creature. "Don't you think you could give me another trial some time, Idella?" She stooped down and took the child's unoccupied hand, which she let her keep, only twisting her face away to hide it in her father's pantaloon leg. "Come now, won't you give me a forgiving little kiss?" Idella looked round, and Annie made bold to gather her up.

Idella broke into a laugh, and took Annie's cheeks between her hands.

"Well, I declare!" said Mrs. Bolton. "You never can tell what that child will do next.'

"I never can tell what I will do next myself," said Annie. She liked the feeling of the little, warm, soft body in her arms, against her breast, and it was flattering to have triumphed where she had seemed to fail so desperately. They had all been standing, and she now said, "Won't you sit down, Mr. Peck?" She added, by an impulse which she instantly thought ill-advised, "There is something I would like to speak to you about."

"Thank you," said Mr. Peck, seating himself beyond the stove. "We must be getting home before a great while. It is nearly tea-time."

"I won't detain you unduly," said Annie.

Mrs. Bolton left them at her hint of something special to say to the minister. Annie could not have had the face to speak of Mr. Brandreth's theatricals in that grim presence; and as it was, she resolved to put forward their serious object. She began abruptly: "Mr. Peck, I've been asked to interest myself for a Social Union which the ladies of South Hatboro' are trying to establish for the operatives. I suppose you haven't heard anything of the scheme?"

"No, I hadn't," said Mr. Peck.

He was one of those people who sit very high, and he now

seemed taller and more impressive than when he stood.

"It is certainly a-very good object," Annie resumed; and she went on to explain it at second-hand from Mr. Brandreth as well as she could. The little girl was standing in her lap, and got between her and Mr. Peck, so that she had to look first around one side of her and then another to see how he was taking it.

He nodded his head, and said gravely, "Yes," and "Yes," and "Yes," at each significant point of her statement. At the end he asked: "And are the means forthcoming? Have they raised the money for renting and furnishing the rooms?"

"Well, no, they haven't yet, or not quite, as I understand."

"Have they tried to interest the working people themselves in it? If they are to value its benefits, it ought to cost them something—self-denial, privation even."

"Yes, I know," Annie began.

"I'm not satisfied," the minister pursued, "that it is wise to provide people with even harmless amusements that take them much away from their homes. These things are invented by well-to-do people who have no occupation, and think that others want pastimes as much as themselves. But what working people want is rest, and what they need are decent homes where they can take it. Besides, unless they help to support this union out of their own means, the better sort among them will feel wounded by its existence, as a sort of superfluous charity."

"Yes, I see," said Annie. She saw this side of the affair with surprise. The minister seemed to have thought more about such matters than she had, and she insensibly receded from her first hasty generalisation of him, and paused to reapproach him on another level. The little girl began to play with her glasses, and accidentally knocked them from her nose. The minister's face and figure became a blur, and in the purblindness to

W. D. Howells

which she was reduced she had a moment of clouded volition in which she was tempted to renounce, and even oppose, the scheme for a Social Union, in spite of her promise to Mr. Brandreth. But she remembered that she was a consistent and faithful person, and she said: "The ladies have a plan for raising the money, and they've applied to me to second it—to use my influence somehow among the villagers to get them interested; and the working people can help too if they choose. But I'm quite a stranger amongst those I'm expected to influence, and I don't at all know how they will take it." The minister listened, neither prompting nor interrupting. "The ladies' plan is to have an entertainment at one of the cottages, and charge an admission, and devote the proceeds to the union." She paused. Mr. Peck still remained silent, but she knew he was attentive. She pushed on. "They intend to have a—a representation, in the open air, of one of Shakespeare's plays, or scenes from one—"

"Do you wish me," interrupted the minister, "to promote the establishment of this union? Is that why you speak to me of it?"

"Why, I don't know *why* I speak to you of it," she replied with a laugh of embarrassment, to which he was cold, apparently. "I certainly couldn't ask you to take part in an affair that you didn't approve."

"I don't know that I disapprove of it. Properly managed, it might be a good thing."

"Yes, of course. But I understand why you might not sympathise with that part of it, and that is why I told you of it," said Annie.

"What part?"

"The—the—theatricals."

"Why not?" asked the minister.

"I know—Mrs. Bolton told me you were very liberal," Annie faltered on; "but I didn't expect you as a—But of course—"

"I read Shakespeare a great deal," said Mr. Peck. "I have never been in the theatre; but I should like to see one of his plays represented where it could cause no one to offend."

"Yes," said Annie, "and this would be by amateurs, and there could be no *possible* 'offence in it.' I wished to know how the general idea would strike you. Of course the ladies would be only too glad of your advice and co-operation. Their plan is to sell tickets to every one for the theatricals, and to a certain number of invited persons for a supper, and a little dance afterward on the lawn."

"I don't know if I understand exactly," said the minister.

Annie repeated her statement more definitely, and explained, from Mr. Brandreth, as before, that the invitations were to be given so as to eliminate the shop-hand element from the supper and dance.

Mr. Peck listened quietly. "That would prevent my taking part in the affair," he said, as quietly as he had listened.

"Of course—dancing," Annie began.

"It is not that. Many people who hold strictly to the old opinions now allow their children to learn dancing. But I could not join at all with those who were willing to lay the foundations of a Social Union in a social disunion—in the exclusion of its beneficiaries from the society of their benefactors."

He was not sarcastic, but the grotesqueness of the situation as he had sketched it was apparent. She remembered now that she had felt something incongruous in it when Mr. Brandreth exposed it, but not deeply.

The minister continued gently: "The ladies who are trying to get up this Social Union proceed upon the assumption that working people can neither see nor feel a slight; but it is a great mistake to do so."

Annie had the obtuseness about those she fancied below her which is one of the consequences of being brought up in a superior station. She believed that there was something to say on the other side, and she attempted to say it.

"I don't know that you could call it a slight exactly. People can ask those they prefer to a social entertainment."

"Yes—if it is for their own pleasure."

"But even in a public affair like this the work-people would feel uncomfortable and out of place, wouldn't they, if they stayed to the supper and the dance? They might be exposed to greater suffering among those whose manners and breeding were different, and it might be very embarrassing all round. Isn't there that side to be regarded?"

"You beg the question," said the minister, as unsparingly as if she were a man. "The point is whether a Social Union beginning in social exclusion could ever do any good. What part do these ladies expect to take in maintaining it? Do they intend to spend their evenings there, to associate on equal terms with the shoe-shop and straw-shop hands?"

"I don't suppose they do, but I don't know," said Annie dryly; and she replied by helplessly quoting Mr. Brandreth: "They intend to organise a system of lectures, concerts, and readings. They wish to get on common ground with them."

"They can never get on common ground with them in that way," said the minister. "No doubt they think they want to do them good; but good is from the heart, and there is no heart in what they propose. The working people would know that at once."

"Then you mean to say," Annie asked, half alarmed and half amused, "that there can be no friendly intercourse with the poor and the well-to-do unless it is based upon social equality?"

"I will answer your question by asking another. Suppose you were one of the poor, and the well-to-do offered to be friendly with you on such terms as you have mentioned, how should you feel toward them?"

"If you make it a personal question—"

"It makes itself a personal question," said the minister dispassionately.

"Well, then, I trust I should have the good sense to see that social equality between people who were better dressed, better taught, and better bred than myself was impossible, and that for me to force myself into their company was not only bad taste, but it was foolish, I have often heard my father say that the great superiority of the American practice of democracy over the French ideal was that it didn't involve any assumption of social equality. He said that equality before the law and in politics was sacred, but that the principle could never govern society, and that Americans all instinctively recognised it. And I believe that to try to mix the different classes would be un-American."

Mr. Peck smiled, and this was the first break in his seriousness. "We don't know what is or will be American yet. But we will suppose you are quite right. The question is, how would you feel toward the people whose company you wouldn't force yourself into?"

"Why, of course," Annie was surprised into saying, "I suppose I shouldn't feel very kindly toward them."

"Even if you knew that they felt kindly toward you?"

"I'm afraid that would only make the matter worse," she said, with an uneasy laugh.

The minister was silent on his side of the stove.

"But do I understand you to say," she demanded, "that there can be no love at all, no kindness, between the rich and the poor? God tells us all to love one another."

"Surely," said the minister. "Would you suffer such a slight as your friends propose, to be offered to any one you loved?"

She did not answer, and he continued, thoughtfully: "I suppose that if a poor person could do a rich person a kindness which cost him some sacrifice, he might love him. In that case there could be love between the rich and the poor."

"And there could be no love if a rich man did the same?"

"Oh yes," the minister said—"upon the same ground. Only, the rich man would have to make a sacrifice first that he would really feel."

"Then you mean to say that people can't do any good at all with their money?" Annie asked.

"Money is a palliative, but it can't cure. It can sometimes create a bond of gratitude perhaps, but it can't create sympathy between rich and poor."

"But *why* can't it?"

"Because sympathy—common feeling—the sense of fraternity—can spring only from like experiences, like hopes, like fears. And money cannot buy these."

He rose, and looked a moment about him, as if trying to recall something. Then, with a stiff obeisance, he said, "Good evening," and went out, while she remained daunted and bewildered, with the child in her arms, as unconscious of having kept it as he of having left it with her.

Mrs. Bolton must have reminded him of his oversight, for after being gone so long as it would have taken him to walk to her parlour and back, he returned, and said simply, "I forgot Idella."

He put out his hands to take her, but she turned perversely from him, and hid her face in Annie's neck, pushing his hands away with a backward reach of her little arm.

"Come, Idella!" he said. Idella only snuggled the closer.

Mrs. Bolton came in with the little girl's wraps; they were very common and poor, and the thought of getting her something prettier went through Annie's mind.

At sight of Mrs. Bolton the child turned from Annie to her older friend.

"I'm afraid you have a woman-child for your daughter, Mr. Peck," said Annie, remotely hurt at the little one's fickleness.

Neither Mr. Peck nor Mrs. Bolton smiled, and with some vague intention of showing him that she could meet the poor on common ground by sharing their labours, she knelt down and helped Mrs. Bolton tie on and button on Idella's things.

VII

Next morning the day broke clear after the long storm, and Annie woke in revolt against the sort of subjection in which she had parted from Mr. Peck. She felt the need of showing Mrs. Bolton that, although she had been civil to him, she had no sympathy with his ideas; but she could not think of any way to formulate her opposition, and all she could say in offence was, "Does Mr. Peck usually forget his child when he starts home?"

"I don't know as he does," answered Mrs. Bolton simply. "He's rather of an absent-minded man, and I suppose he's like other men when he gets talking."

"The child's clothes were disgracefully shabby!" said Annie, vexed that her attack could come to no more than this.

"I presume," said Mrs. Bolton, "that if he kept more of his money for himself, he could dress her better."

"Oh, that's the way with these philanthropists," said Annie, thinking of Hollingsworth, in *The Blithedale Romance*, the only philanthropist whom she had really ever known, "They are always ready to sacrifice the happiness and comfort of any one to the general good."

Mrs. Bolton stood a moment, and then went out without replying; but she looked as offended as Annie could have wished. About ten o'clock the bell rang, and she came gloomily into the study, and announced that Mrs. Munger was in the parlour.

Annie had already heard an authoritative rustling of skirts, and she was instinctively prepared for the large, vigorous woman who turned upon her from the picture she had been looking at on the wall, and came toward her with the confident air of one sure they must be friends. Mrs. Munger was dressed in a dark, firm woollen stuff, which communicated its colour, if not its material, to the matter-of-fact bonnet which she wore on her plainly dressed hair. In one of her hands, which were cased in driving gloves of somewhat insistent evidence, she carried a robust black silk sun-umbrella, and the effect of her dress otherwise might be summarised in the statement that where other women would have worn lace, she seemed to wear leather. She had not only leather gloves, and a broad leather belt at her waist, but a leather collar; her watch was secured by a leather cord, passing round her neck, and the stubby tassel of her umbrella stick was leather: she might be said to be in harness. She had a large, handsome face, no longer fresh, but with an effect of exemplary cleanness, and a pair of large grey eyes that suggested the notion of being newly washed, and that now looked at Annie with the assumption of fully understanding her.

"Ah, Miss Kilburn!" she said, without any of the wonted preliminaries of introduction and greeting. "I should have come long ago to see you, but I've been dispersed over the four quarters of the globe ever since you came, my dear. I got home last night on the nine o'clock train, in the last agonies of that howling tempest. Did you ever know anything like it? I see your trees have escaped. I wonder they weren't torn to shreds."

Annie took her on her own ground of ignoring their past non-acquaintance. "Yes, it was awful. And your son—how did you leave him? Mr. Brandreth—"

"Oh yes, poor little man! I found him waiting for me at home last night, and he told me he had been here. He was blowing about in the storm all day. Such a spirit! There was nothing serious the matter; the bridge of the nose was all right; merely the cartilage pushed aside by the ball."

She had passed so lightly from Mr. Brandreth's heroic spirit to her son's nose that Annie, woman as she was, and born to these bold bounds over sequence, was not sure where they had arrived, till Mrs. Munger added: "Jim's used to these things. I'm thankful it wasn't a finger, or an eye. What is *that*?" She jumped from her chair, and swooped upon the Spanish-Roman water-colour Annie had stood against some books on the table, pending its final disposition.

"It's only a Guerra," said Annie. "My things are all scattered about still; I have scarcely tried to get into shape yet."

Mrs. Munger would not let her interpose any idea of there being a past between them. She merely said: "You knew the Herricks at Rome, of course. I'm in hopes I shall get them here when they come back. I want you to help me colonise Hatboro' with the right sort of people: it's so easy to get the wrong sort! But, so far, I think we've succeeded beyond our wildest dreams. It's easy enough to get nice people together at the seaside; but inland! No; it's only a very few nice people who will come into the country for the summer; and we propose to make Hatboro' a winter colony too; that gives us agreeable invalids, you know; it gave us the Brandreths. He told you of our projected theatricals, I suppose?"

"Yes," said Annie non-committally, "he did."

"I know just how you feel about it, my dear," said Mrs. Munger. "'Been there myself,' as Jim says. But it grows upon you. I'm glad you didn't refuse outright;" and Mrs. Munger looked at her with eyes of large expectance.

"No, I didn't," said Annie, obliged by this expectance to say something. "But to tell you the truth, Mrs. Munger, I don't see how I'm to be of any use to you or to Mr. Brandreth."

"Oh, take a cab and go about, like Boots and Brewer, you know, for the Veneerings." She said this as if she knew about the humour rather than felt it. "We are placing all our hopes of bringing round the Old Hatborians in you."

"I'm afraid you're mistaken about my influence," said Annie. "Mr. Brandreth spoke of it, and I had an opportunity of trying it last night, and seeing just what it amounted to."

"Yes?" Mrs. Munger prompted, with an increase of expectance in her large clear eyes, and of impartiality in her whole face.

"Mr. Peck was here," said Annie reluctantly, "and I tried it on him."

"Yes?" repeated Mrs. Munger, as immutably as if she were sitting for her photograph and keeping the expression.

Annie broke from her reluctance with a sort of violence which carried her further than she would have gone otherwise. She ridiculed Mr. Peck's appearance and manner, and laughed at his ideas to Mrs. Munger. She had not a good conscience in it, but the perverse impulse persisted in her. There seemed no other way in which she could assert herself against him.

Mrs. Munger listened judicially, but she seemed to take in only what Mr. Peck had thought of the dance and supper; at the end she said, rather vacantly, "What nonsense!"

"Yes; but I'm afraid he thinks it's wisdom, and for all practical purposes it amounts to that. You see what my 'influence' has done at the outset, Mrs. Munger. He'll never give way on such a point."

"Oh, very well, then," said Mrs. Munger, with the utmost lightness and indifference, "we'll drop the idea of the invited supper and dance."

"Do you think that would be well?" asked Annie.

W. D. Howells

"Yes; why not? It's only an idea. I don't think you've made at all a bad beginning. It was very well to try the idea on some one who would be frank about it, and wouldn't go away and talk against it," said Mrs. Munger, rising. "I want you to come with me, my dear."

"To see Mr. Peck? Excuse me. I don't think I could," said Annie.

"No; to see some of his parishioners," said Mrs. Munger. "His deacons, to begin with, or his deacons' wives."

This seemed so much less than calling on Mr. Peck that Annie looked out at Mrs. Munger's basket-phaeton at her gate, and knew that she would go with very little more urgency.

"After all, you know, you're not one of his congregation; he may yield to them," said Mrs. Munger. "We must *have* him— if only because he's hard to get. It'll give us an idea of what we've got to contend with."

It had a very practical sound; it was really like meeting the difficulties on their own ground, and it overcame the question of taste which was rising in Annie's mind. She demurred a little more upon the theory of her uselessness; but Mrs. Munger insisted, and carried her off down the village street.

The air sparkled full of sun, and a breeze from the south-west frolicked with the twinkling leaves of the overarching elms, and made their shadows dance on the crisp roadway, packed hard by the rain, and faced with clean sand, which crackled pleasantly under Mrs. Munger's phaeton wheels. She talked incessantly. "I think we'll go first to Mrs. Gerrish's, and then to Mrs. Wilmington's. You know them?"

"Oh yes; they were old girl friends."

"Then you know why I go to Mrs. Gerrish's first. She'll care a great deal, and Mrs. Wilmington won't care at all. She's a delicious creature, Mrs. Wilmington—don't you think? That large, indolent nature; Mr. Brandreth says she makes him think of 'the land in which it seemed always afternoon.'"

Annie remembered Lyra Goodman as a long, lazy, red-haired girl who laughed easily; and she could not readily realise her in the character of a Titian-esque beauty with a gift for humorous dramatics, which she had filled out into during the years of her absence from Hatboro'; but she said "Oh yes," in the necessity of polite acquiescence, and Mrs. Munger went on talking—

"She's the only one of the Old Hatboro' people, so far as I know them, who has any breadth of view. Whoa!" She pulled up suddenly beside a stout, short lady in a fashionable walking dress, who was pushing an elegant perambulator with one hand, and shielding her complexion with a crimson sun-umbrella in the other.

"Mrs. Gerrish!" Mrs. Munger called; and Mrs. Gerrish, who had already looked around at the approaching phaeton, and then looked away, so as not to have seemed to look, stopped abruptly, and after some exploration of the vicinity, discovered where the voice came from.

"Oh, Mrs. Munger!" she called back, bridling with pleasure at being greeted in that way by the chief lady of South Hatboro', and struggling to keep up a dignified indifference at the same time. "Why, Annie!" she added.

"Good morning, Emmeline," said Annie; she annexed some irrelevancies about the weather, which Mrs. Munger swept away with business-like robustness.

"We were driving down to your house to find you. I want to see the principal ladies of your church, and talk with them about our Social Union. You've heard about it?"

"Well, nothing very particular," said Mrs. Gerrish; she had probably heard nothing at all. After a moment she asked,

W. D. Howells

"Have you seen Mrs. Wilmington yet?"

"No, I haven't," cried Mrs. Munger. "The fact is, I wanted to talk it over with you and Mr. Gerrish first."

"Oh!" said Mrs. Gerrish, brightening. "Well, I was just going right there. I guess he's in.'

"Well, we shall meet there, then. Sorry I can't offer you a *seat*. But there's nothing but the rumble, and that wouldn't hold you *all*."

Mrs. Munger called this back after starting her pony. Mrs. Gerrish did not understand, and screamed, "*What?*"

Mrs. Munger repeated her joke at the top of her voice.

"Oh, I can walk!" Mrs. Gerrish yelled at the top of hers. Both the ladies laughed at their repartee.

"She's as jealous of Mrs. Wilmington as a cat," Mrs. Munger confided to Annie as they drove away; "and she's just as pleased as Punch that I've spoken to her first. Mrs. Wilmington won't mind. She's so delightfully indifferent, it really renders her almost superior; you might forget that she was a village person. But this has been an immense stroke. I don't know," she mused, "whether I'd better let her get there first and prepare her husband, or do it myself. No; I'll let *her*. I'll stop here at Gates's."

She stopped at the pavement in front of a provision store, and a pale, stout man, in the long over-shirt of his business, came out to receive her orders. He stood, passing his hand through the top of a barrel of beans, and listened to Mrs. Munger with a humorous, patient smile.

"Mr. Gates, I want you to send me up a leg of lamb for dinner—a large one."

"Last year's, then," suggested Gates.

"No; *this* year's," insisted Mrs. Munger; and Gates gave way with the air of pacifying a wilful child, which would get, after all, only what he chose to allow it.

"All right, ma'am; a large leg of this year's lamb—grown to order. Any peas, spinnage, cucumbers, sparrowgrass?"

"Southern, I suppose?" said Mrs. Munger.

"Well, not if you want to call 'em native," said Gates.

"Yes, I'll take two bunches of asparagus, and some peas."

"Any strawberries?—natives?" suggested Gates.

"Nonsense!"

"Same thing; natives of Norfolk."

"You had better be honest with *me*, Mr. Gates," said Mrs. Munger. "Yes, I'll take a couple of boxes."

"All right! Want 'em nice, and the biggest ones at the bottom of the box?"

"Yes, I do."

"That's what I thought. Some customers wants the big ones on top; but I tell 'em it's all foolishness; just vanity." Gates laughed a dry, hacking little laugh at his drollery, and kept his eyes on Annie. She smiled at last, with permissive recognition, and Gates came forward. "Used to know your father pretty well; but I can't keep up with the young folks any more." He was really not many years older than Annie; he rubbed his right hand on the inside of his long shirt, and gave it her to shake. "Well, you haven't been about much for the last nine or ten years, that's a fact."

"Eleven," said Annie, trying to be gay with the hand-shaking, and wondering if this were meeting the lower classes on common ground, and what Mr. Peck would think of it.

"That so?" queried Gates. "Well, I declare! No wonder you've grown!" He hacked out another laugh, and stood on the curb-stone looking at Annie a moment. Then he asked, "Anything else, Mrs. Munger?"

"No; that's all. Tell me, Mr. Gates, how *do* Mr. Peck and Mr. Gerrish get on?" asked Mrs. Munger in a lower tone.

"Well," said Gates, "he's workin' round—the deacon's workin' round gradually, I guess. I guess if Mr. Peck was to put in a little more brimstone, the deacon'd be all right. He's a great hand for brimstone, you know, the deacon is."

Mrs. Munger laughed again, and then she said, with a proselyting sigh, "It's a pity you couldn't all find your way into the Church."

"Well, may be it *would* be a good thing," said Gates, as Mrs. Munger gathered up her reins and chirped to her pony.

"He isn't a member of Mr. Peck's church," she explained to Annie; "but he's one of the society, and his wife's very devout Orthodox. He's a great character, we think, and he'll treat you very well, if you keep on the right side of him. They say he cheats awfully in the weight, though."

VIII

Mrs. Munger drove across the street, and drew up before a large, handsomely ugly brick dry-goods store, whose showy windows had caught Annie's eye the day she arrived in Hatboro'.

"I see Mrs. Gerrish has got here first," Mrs. Munger said, indicating the perambulator at the door, and she dismounted and fastened her pony with a weight, which she took from the front of the phaeton. On either door jamb of the store was a curved plate of polished metal, with the name GERRISH cut into it in black letters; the sills of the wide windows were of metal, and bore the same legend. At the threshold a very prim, ceremonious little man, spare and straight, met Mrs. Munger with a ceremonious bow, and a solemn "How do you do, ma'am I how do you do? I hope I see you well," and he put a small dry hand into the ample clasp of Mrs. Munger's gauntlet.

"Very well indeed, Mr. Gerrish. Isn't it a lovely morning? You know Miss Kilburn, Mr. Gerrish."

He took Annie's hand into his right and covered it with his left, lifting his eyes to look her in the, face with an old-merchant-like cordiality.

"Why, yes, indeed! Delighted to see her. Her father was one of my best friends. I may say that I owe everything that I am to Squire Kilburn; he advised me to stick to commerce when I

W. D. Howells

once thought of studying law. Glad to welcome you back to Hatboro', Miss Kilburn. You see changes on the surface, no doubt, but you'll find the genuine old feeling here. Walk right back, ladies," he continued, releasing Annie's hand to waft them before him toward the rear of the store. "You'll find Mrs. Gerrish in my room there—my Growlery, as I call it." He seemed to think he had invented the name. "And Mrs. Gerrish tells me that you've really come back," he said, leaning decorously toward Annie as they walked, "with the intention of taking up your residence permanently among us. You will find very few places like Hatboro'."

As he spoke, walking with his hands clasped behind him, he glanced to right and left at the shop-girls on foot behind the counter, who dropped their eyes under their different bangs as they caught his glance, and bridled nervously. He denied them the use of chewing-gum; he permitted no conversation, as he called it, among them; and he addressed no jokes or idle speeches to them himself. A system of grooves overhead brought to his counting-room the cash from the clerks in wooden balls, and he returned the change, and kept the accounts, with a pitiless eye for errors. The women were afraid of him, and hated him with bitterness, which exploded at crises in excesses of hysterical impudence.

His store was an example of variety, punctuality, and quality. Upon the theory, for which he deserved the credit, of giving to a country place the advantages of one of the great city establishments, he was gradually gathering, in their fashion, the small commerce into his hands. He had already opened his bazaar through into the adjoining store, which he had bought out, and he kept every sort of thing desired or needed in a country town, with a tempting stock of articles before unknown to the shopkeepers of Hatboro'. Everything was of the very quality represented; the prices were low, but inflexible, and cash payments, except in the case of some rich customers of unimpeachable credit, were invariably exacted; at the same time every reasonable facility for the exchange or return of goods was afforded. Nothing could exceed the justice and fidelity of his dealing with the public. He had even some effects of generosity in his dealing with his dependants; he furnished them free seats in the churches of their different persuasions, and he closed every night at six o'clock, except Saturday, when the shop hands were paid off, and made their purchases for the coming week.

He stepped lightly before Annie and Mrs. Munger, and pushed open the ground-glass door of his office for them. It was like a bank parlour, except for Mrs. Gerrish sitting in her husband's leather-cushioned swivel chair, with her last-born in her lap; she greeted the others noisily, without trying to rise.

"You see we are quite at home here," said Mr. Gerrish.

"Yes, and very snug you are, too," said Mrs. Munger, taking one half of the leather lounge, and leaving the other half to Annie. "I don't wonder Mrs. Gerrish likes to visit you here."

Mr. Gerrish laughed, and said to his wife, who moved provisionally in her chair, seeing he had none, "Sit still, my dear; I prefer my usual perch." He took a high stool beside a desk, and gathered a ruler in his hand.

"Well, I may as well begin at the beginning," said Mrs. Munger, "and I'll try to be short, for I know that these are business hours."

"Take all the time you want, Mrs. Munger," said Mr. Gerrish affably. "It's my idea that a good business man's business can go on without him, when necessary."

"Of course!" Mrs. Munger sighed. "If everybody had your *system*, Mr. Gerrish!" She went on and succinctly expounded the scheme of the Social Union. "I suppose I can't deny that the idea occurred to *me*," she concluded, "but we can't hope to develop it without the co-operation of the ladies of Old Hatboro', and I've come, first of all, to Mrs. Gerrish."

Mr. Gerrish bowed his acknowledgments of the honour done his wife, with a gravity which she misinterpreted.

"I think," she began, with her censorious manner and accent, "that these people have too much done for them *now*. They're perfectly spoiled. Don't you, Annie?"

Mr. Gerrish did not give Annie time to answer. "I differ with you, my dear," he cut in. "It is my opinion—Or I don't know but you wish to confine this matter entirely to the ladies?" he suggested to Mrs. Munger.

"Oh, I'm only too proud and glad that you feel interested in the matter!" cried Mrs. Munger. "Without the gentlemen's practical views, we ladies are such feeble folk—mere conies in the rocks."

"I am as much opposed as Mrs. Gerrish—or any one—to acceding to unjust demands on the part of my clerks or other employees," Mr. Gerrish began.

"Yes, that's what I mean," said his wife, and broke down with a giggle.

He went on, without regarding her: "I have always made it a rule, as far as business went, to keep my own affairs entirely in my own hands. I fix the hours, and I fix the wages, and I fix all the other conditions, and I say plainly, 'If you don't like them, 'don't come,' or 'don't stay,' and I never have any difficulty."

"I'm sure," said Mrs. Munger, "that if all the employers in the country would take such a stand, there would soon be an end of labour troubles. I think we're too concessive."

"And I do too, Mrs. Munger!" cried Mrs. Gerrish, glad of the occasion to be censorious and of the finer lady's opinion at the same time. "That's what I meant. Don't you, Annie?"

"I'm afraid I don't understand exactly," Annie replied.

Mr. Gerrish kept his eye on Mrs. Munger's face, now arranged for indefinite photography, as he went on. "That is exactly what I say to them. That is what I said to Mr. Marvin one year ago, when he had that trouble in his shoe shop. I said, 'You're too concessive.' I said, 'Mr. Marvin, if you give those fellows an inch, they'll take an ell. Mr. Marvin,' said I, 'you've got to begin by being your own master, if you want to be master of anybody else. You've got to put your foot down, as Mr. Lincoln said; and as *I* say, you've got to *keep* it down.'"

Mrs. Gerrish looked at the other ladies for admiration, and Mrs. Munger said, rapidly, without disarranging her face—

"Oh yes. And how much *misery* could be saved in such cases by a little firmness at the outset!"

"Mr. Marvin differed with me," said Mr. Gerrish sorrowfully. "He agreed with me on the main point, but he said that too many of his hands had been in his regiment, and he couldn't lock them out. He submitted to arbitration. And what is arbitration?" asked Mr. Gerrish, levelling his ruler at Mrs. Munger. "It is postponing the evil day."

"Exactly," said Mrs. Munger, without winking.

"Mr. Marvin," Mr. Gerrish proceeded, "may be running very smoothly now, and sailing before the wind all—all—nicely; but I tell *you* his house is built upon the *sand*," He put his ruler by on the desk very softly, and resumed with impressive quiet: "I never had any trouble but once. I had a porter in this store who wanted his pay raised. I simply said that I made it a rule to propose all advances of salary myself, and I should submit to no dictation from any one. He told me to go to—a place that I will not repeat, and I told him to walk out of my store. He was under the influence of liquor at the time, I suppose. I understand that he is drinking very hard. He does nothing to support his family whatever, and from all that I can gather, he bids fair to fill a drunkard's grave inside of six months."

Mrs. Munger seized her opportunity. "Yes; and it is just such cases as this that the Social Union is designed to meet. If this man had some such place to spend his evenings—and bring his family if he chose—where he could get a cup of good coffee for the same price as a glass of rum—Don't you see?"

She looked round at the different faces, and Mr. Gerrish slightly frowned, as if the vision of the Social Union interposing between his late porter and a drunkard's grave, with a cup of good coffee, were not to his taste altogether; but he said: "Precisely so! And I was about to make the remark that while I am very strict—and obliged to be—with those under me in business, *no* one is more disposed to promote such objects as this of yours."

"I was *sure* you would approve of it," said Mrs. Munger. "That is why I came to you—to you and Mrs. Gerrish—first," said Mrs. Munger. "I was sure you would see it in the right light." She looked round at Annie for corroboration, and Annie was in the social necessity of making a confirmatory murmur.

Mr. Gerrish ignored them both in the more interesting work of celebrating himself. "I may say that there is not an institution in this town which I have not contributed my humble efforts to—to—establish, from the drinking fountain in front of this store, to the soldiers' monument on the village green."

Annie turned red; Mrs. Munger said shamelessly, "That beautiful monument!" and looked at Annie with eyes full of gratitude to Mr. Gerrish.

"The schools, the sidewalks, the water-works, the free library, the introduction of electricity, the projected system of drainage, and *all* the various religious enterprises at various times, I am proud—I am humbly proud—that I have been allowed to be the means of doing—sustaining—"

He lost himself in the labyrinths of his sentence, and Mrs. Munger came to his rescue: "I fancy Hatboro' wouldn't be

Hatboro' without *you*, Mr. Gerrish! And you *don't* think that Mr. Peck's objection will be seriously felt by other leading citizens?"

"*What* is Mr. Peck's objection?" demanded Mr. Gerrish, perceptibly bristling up at the name of his pastor.

"Why, he talked it over with Miss Kilburn last night, and he objected to an entertainment which wouldn't be open to all— to the shop hands and everybody." Mrs. Munger explained the point fully. She repeated some things that Annie had said in ridicule of Mr. Peck's position regarding it. "If you *do* think that part would be bad or impolitic," Mrs. Munger concluded, "we could drop the invited supper and the dance, and simply have the theatricals."

She bent upon Mr. Gerrish a face of candid deference that filled him with self-importance almost to bursting.

"No!" he said, shaking his head, and "No!" closing his lips abruptly, and opening them again to emit a final "No!" with an explosive force which alone seemed to save him. "Not at all, Mrs. Munger; not on any account! I am surprised at Mr. Peck, or rather I am *not* surprised. He is not a practical man—not a man of the world; and I should have much preferred to hear that he objected to the dancing and the play; I could have understood that; I could have gone with him in that to a certain extent, though I can see no harm in such things when properly conducted. I have a great respect for Mr. Peck; I was largely instrumental in getting him here; but he is altogether wrong in this matter. We are not obliged to go out into the highways and the hedges until the bidden guests have—er— declined."

"Exactly," said Mrs. Munger. "I never thought of that."

Mrs. Gerrish shifted her baby to another knee, and followed her husband with her eyes, as he dismounted from his stool and began to pace the room.

"I came into this town a poor boy, without a penny in my pocket, and I have made my own way, every inch of it, unaided and alone. I am a thorough believer in giving every one an equal chance to rise and to—get along; I would not throw an obstacle in anybody's way; but I do not believe—I do *not* believe—in pampering those who have not risen, or have made no effort to rise."

"It's their wastefulness, in nine cases out of ten, that keeps them down," said Mrs. Gerrish.

"I don't care *what* it is, I don't *ask* what it is, that keeps them down. I don't expect to invite my clerks or Mrs. Gerrish's servants into my parlour. I will meet them at the polls, or the communion table, or on any proper occasion; but a man's home is *sacred*. I will not allow my wife or my children to associate with those whose—whose—whose idleness, or vice, or whatever, has kept them down in a country where—where everybody stands on an equality; and what I will not do myself, I will not ask others to do. I make it a rule to do unto others as I would have them do unto me. It is all nonsense to attempt to introduce those one-ideaed notions into—put them in practice."

"Yes," said Mrs. Munger, with deep conviction, "that is my own feeling, Mr. Gerrish, and I'm glad to have it corroborated by your experience. Then you *wouldn't* drop the little invited dance and supper?"

"I will tell you how I feel about it, Mrs. Munger," said Mr. Gerrish, pausing in his walk, and putting on a fine, patronising, gentleman-of-the-old-school smile. "You may put me down for any number of tickets—five, ten, fifteen—and you may command me in anything I can do to further the objects of your enterprise, if you will *keep* the invited supper and dance. But I should not be prepared to do anything if they are dropped."

"What a comfort it is to meet a person who knows his own

mind!" exclaimed Mrs. Munger.

"Got company, Billy?" asked a voice at the door; and it added, "Glad to see *you* here, Mrs. Gerrish."

"Ah, Mr. Putney! Come in. Hope I see you well, sir!" cried Mr. Gerrish. "Come in!" he repeated, with jovial frankness. "Nobody but friends here."

"I don't know about that," said Mr. Putney, with whimsical perversity, holding the door ajar. "I see that arch-conspirator from South Hatboro'," he said, looking at Mrs. Munger.

He showed himself, as he stood holding the door ajar, a lank little figure, dressed with reckless slovenliness in a suit of old-fashioned black; a loose neck-cloth fell stringing down his shirt front, which his unbuttoned waistcoat exposed, with its stains from the tobacco upon which his thin little jaws worked mechanically, as he stared into the room with flamy blue eyes; his silk hat was pushed back from a high, clear forehead; he had yesterday's stubble on his beardless cheeks; a heavy moustache and imperial gave dash to a cast of countenance that might otherwise have seemed slight and effeminate.

"Yes; but I'm in charge of Miss Kilburn, and you needn't be afraid of me. Come in. We wish to consult you," cried Mrs. Munger. Mrs. Gerrish cackled some applausive incoherencies.

Putney advanced into the room, and dropped his burlesque air as he approached Annie.

"Miss Kilburn, I must apologise for not having called with Mrs. Putney to pay my respects. I have been away; when I got back I found she had stolen a march on me. But I'm going to make Ellen bring me at once. I don't think I've been in your house since the old Judge's time. Well, he was an able man, and a good man; I was awfully fond of the old Judge, in a boy's way."

"Thank you," said Annie, touched by something gentle and honest in his words.

"He was a Christian gentleman," said Mr. Gerrish, with authority.

Putney said, without noticing Mr. Gerrish, "Well, I'm glad you've come back to the old place, Miss Kilburn—I almost said Annie."

"I shouldn't have minded, Ralph," she retorted.

"Shouldn't you? Well, that's right." Putney continued, ignoring the laugh of the others at Annie's sally: "You'll find Hatboro' pretty exciting, after Rome, for a while, I suppose. But you'll get used to it. It's got more of the modern improvements, I'm told, and it's more public-spirited—more snap to it. I'm told that there's more enterprise in Hatboro', more real *crowd* in South Hatboro' alone, than there is in the Quirinal and the Vatican put together."

"You had better come and live at South Hatboro', Mr. Putney; that would be just the atmosphere for you," said Mrs. Munger, with aimless hospitality. She said this to every one.

"Is it about coming to South Hatboro' you want to consult me?" asked Putney.

"Well, it is, and it isn't," she began.

"Better be honest, Mrs. Munger," said Putney. "You can't do anything for a client who won't be honest with his attorney. That's what I have to continually impress upon the reprobates who come to me. I say, 'It don't matter what you've done; if you expect me to get you off, you've got to make a clean breast of it.' They generally do; they see the sense of it."

They all laughed, and Mr. Gerrish said, "Mr. Putney is one of Hatboro's privileged characters, Miss Kilburn."

"Thank you, Billy," returned the lawyer, with mock-tenderness. "Now, Mrs. Munger, out with it!"

"You'll have to tell him sooner or later, Mrs. Munger!" said Mrs. Gerrish, with overweening pleasure in her acquaintance with both of these superior people. "He'll get it out of you anyway." Her husband looked at her, and she fell silent.

Mrs. Munger swept her with a tolerant smile as she looked up at Putney. "Why, it's really Miss Kilburn's affair," she began; and she laid the case before the lawyer with a fulness that made Annie wince.

Putney took a piece of tobacco from his pocket, and tore off a morsel with his teeth. "Excuse me, Annie! It's a beastly habit. But it's saved me from something worse. *You* don't know what I've been; but anybody in Hatboro' can tell you. I made my shame so public that it's no use trying to blink the past. You don't have to be a hypocrite in a place where everybody's seen you in the gutter; that's the only advantage I've got over my fellow-citizens, and of course I abuse it; that's nature, you know. When I began to pull up I found that tobacco helped me; I smoked and chewed both; now I only chew. Well," he said, dropping the pathetic simplicity with which he had spoken, and turning with a fierce jocularity from the shocked and pitying look in Annie's face to Mrs. Munger, "what do you propose to do? Brother Peck's head seems to be pretty level, in the abstract."

"Yes," said Mrs. Munger, willing to put the case impartially; "and I should be perfectly willing to drop the invited dance and supper, if it was thought best, though I must say I don't at all agree with Mr. Peck in principle. I don't see what would become of society."

"You ought to be in politics, Mrs. Munger," said Putney. "Your readiness to sacrifice principle to expediency shows what a reform will be wrought when you ladies get the suffrage. What does Brother Gerrish think?"

W. D. Howells

"No, no," said Mrs. Munger. "We want an impartial opinion."

"I always think as Brother Gerrish thinks," said Putney. "I guess you better give up the fandango; hey, Billy?"

"No, sir; no, Mr. Putney,' answered the merchant nervously. "I can't agree with you. And I will tell you why, sir."

He gave his reasons, with some abatement of pomp and detail, and with the tremulous eagerness of a solemn man who expects a sarcastic rejoinder. "It would be a bad precedent. This town is full now of a class of persons who are using every opportunity to—to abuse their privileges. And this would be simply adding fuel to the f.ame."

"Do you really think so, Billy ?" asked the lawyer, with cool derision. "Well, we all abuse our privileges at every opportunity, of course; I was just saying that I abused mine; and I suppose those fellows would abuse theirs if you happened to hurt their wives' and daughters' feelings. And how are you going to manage? Aren't you afraid that they will hang around, after the show, indefinitely, unless you ask all those who have not received invitations to the dance and supper to clear the grounds, as they do in the circus when the minstrels are going to give a performance not included in the price of admission? Mind, I don't care anything about your Social Union."

"Oh, but *surely*!" cried Mrs. Munger, "you *must* allow that it's a good object."

"Well, perhaps it is, if it will keep the men away from the rum-holes. Yes, I guess it is. You won't sell liquor?"

"We expect to furnish coffee at cost price," said Mrs. Munger, smiling at Putney's joke.

"And good navy-plug too, I hope. But you see it would be rather awkward, don't you? You see, Annie?"

"Yes, I see," said Annie. "I hadn't thought of that part before."

"And you didn't agree with Brother Peck on general principles? There we see the effect of residence abroad," said Putney. "The uncorrupted—or I will say the uninterrupted—Hatborian has none of those aristocratic predilections of yours, Annie. He grows up in a community where there is neither poverty nor richness, and where political economy can show by the figures that the profligate shop hands get nine-tenths of the profits, and starve on 'em, while the good little company rolls in luxury on the other tenth. But you've got used to something different over there, and of course Brother Peck's ideas startled you. Well, I suppose I should have been just so myself."

"Mr. Putney has never felt just right about the working-men since he lost the boycotters' case," said Mr. Gerrish, with a snicker.

"Oh, come now, Billy, why did you give me away?" said Putney, with mock suffering. "Well, I suppose I might as well own up, Mrs. Munger; it's no use trying to keep it from *you*; you know it already. Yes, Annie, I defended some poor devils here for combining to injure a non-union man—for doing once just what the big manufacturing Trusts do every day of the year with impunity; and I lost the case. I expected to. I told 'em they were wrong, but I did my best for 'em. 'Why, you fools,' said I—that's the way I talk to 'em, Annie; I call 'em pet names; they like it; they're used to 'em; they get 'em every day in the newspapers—'you fools,' said I, 'what do you want to boycott for, when you can *vote*? What do you want to break the laws for, when you can *make* 'em? You idiots, you,' said I, 'what do you putter round for, persecuting non-union men, that have as good a right to earn their bread as you, when you might make the whole United States of America a Labour Union?' Of course I didn't say that in court."

"Oh, how delicious you are, Mr. Putney!" said Mrs. Munger.

W. D. Howells

"Glad you like me, Mrs. Munger," Putney replied.

"Yes, you're delightful," said the lady, recovering from the effects of the drollery which they had all pretended to enjoy, Mr. Gerrish, and Mrs. Gerrish by his leave, even more than the others. "But you're not candid. All this doesn't help us to a conclusion. Would you give up the invited dance and supper, or wouldn't you? That's the question."

"And no shirking, hey?" asked Putney.

"No shirking."

Putney glanced through a little transparent space in the ground-glass windows framing the room, which Mr. Gerrish used for keeping an eye on his sales-ladies to see that they did not sit down.

"Hello!" he exclaimed. "There's Dr. Morrell. Let's put the case to him." He opened the door and called down the store, "Come in here, Doc!"

"What?" called back an amused voice; and after a moment steps approached, and Dr. Morrell hesitated at the open door. He was a tall man, with a slight stoop; well dressed; full bearded; with kind, boyish blue eyes that twinkled in fascinating friendliness upon the group. "Nobody sick here, I hope?"

"Walk right in, sir! come in, Dr. Morrell," said Mr. Gerrish. "Mrs. Munger and Mrs. Gerrish you know. Present you to Miss Kilburn, who has come to make her home among us after a prolonged residence abroad. Dr. Morrell, Miss Kilburn."

"No, there's nobody sick here, in one sense," said Putney, when the doctor had greeted the ladies. "But. we want your advice all the same. Mrs. Munger is in a pretty bad way morally, Doc."

"Don't you mind Mr. Putney, doctor!" screamed Mrs. Gerrish.

Putney said, with respectful recognition of the poor woman's attempt to be arch, "I'll try to keep within the bounds of truth in stating the case, Mrs. Gerrish."

He went on to state it, with so much gravity and scrupulosity, and with so many appeals to Mrs. Munger to correct him if he were wrong, that the doctor was shaking with laughter when Putney came to an end with unbroken seriousness. At each repetition of the facts, Annie's relation to them grew more intolerable; and she suspected Putney of an intention to punish her. "Well, what do you say?" he demanded of the doctor.

"Ha, ha, ha! ah, ha, ha." laughed the doctor, shutting his eyes and throwing back his head.

"Seems to consider it a *laughing* matter," said Putney to Mrs. Munger.

"Yes; and that is all your fault," said Mrs. Munger, trying, with the ineffectiveness of a large woman, to pout.

"No, no, I'm not laughing." began the doctor.

"Smiling, perhaps," suggested Putney.

The doctor went off again. Then, "I beg—I *beg* your pardon, Mrs. Munger," he resumed. "But it isn't a professional question, you know; and I—I really couldn't judge—have any opinion on such a matter."

"No shirking," said Putney. "That's what Mrs. Munger said to me."

"Of course not," gurgled the doctor. "You ladies will know what to do. I'm sure *I* shouldn't," he added.

"Well, I must be going," said Putney. "Sorry to leave you in this fix, Doc." He flashed out of the door, and suddenly came back to offer Annie his hand. "I beg your pardon, Annie. I'm going to make Ellen bring me round. Good morning." He bowed cursorily to the rest.

"Wait—I'll go with you, Putney," said the doctor.

Mrs. Munger rose, and Annie with her. "We must go too," she said. "We've taken up Mr. Gerrish's time most unconscionably," and now Mr. Gerrish did not urge her to remain.

"Well, good-bye," said Mrs. Gerrish, with a genteel prolongation of the last syllable.

Mr. Gerrish followed his guests down the store, and even out upon the sidewalk, where he presided with unheeded hospitality over the superfluous politeness of Putney and Dr. Morrell in putting Mrs. Munger and Annie into the phaeton. Mrs. Munger attempted to drive away without having taken up her hitching weight.

"I suppose that there isn't a post in this town that my wife hasn't tried to pull up in that way," said Putney gravely.

The doctor doubled himself down with another fit of laughing.

Annie wanted to laugh too, but she did not like his laughing. She questioned if it were not undignified. She felt that it might be disrespectful. Then she asked herself why he should respect her.

IX

"That was a great success," said Mrs. Munger, as they drove away. Annie said nothing, and she added, "Don't you think so?"

"Well, I confess," said Annie, "I don't see how, exactly. Do you mean with regard to Mr. Gerrish?"

"Oh no; I don't care anything about him," said Mrs. Munger, touching her pony with the tip of her whip-lash. "He's an odious little creature, and I knew that he would go for the dance and supper because Mr. Peck was opposed to them. He's one of the anti-Peck party in his church, and that is the reason I spoke to him. But I meant the other gentlemen. You saw how they took it."

"I saw that they both made fun of it," said Annie.

"Yes; that's just the point. It's so fortunate they were frank about it. It throws a new light on it; and if that's the way nice people are going to look at it, why, we must give up the idea. I'm quite prepared to do so. But I want to see Mrs. Wilmington first."

"Mrs. Munger," said Annie uneasily, "I would rather not see Mrs. Wilmington with you on this subject; I should be of no use."

"My dear, you would be of the *greatest* use," persisted Munger,

W. D. Howells

and she laid her arm across Annie's lap, as if to prevent her jumping out of the phaeton. "As Mrs. Wilmington's old friend, you will have the greatest influence with her."

"But I don't know that I wish to influence her in favour of the supper and dance; I don't know that I believe in them," said Annie, cowed and troubled by the affair.

"That doesn't make the slightest difference," said Mrs. Munger impartially. "All you will have to do is to keep still. I will put the case to her."

She checked the pony before the bar which the flagman at the railroad crossing had let down, while a long freight train clattered deafeningly by, and then drove bumping and jouncing across the tracks. "I suppose you remember what 'Over the Track' means in Hatboro'?"

"Oh yes," said Annie, with a smile. "Social perdition at the least. You don't mean that Mrs. Wilmington lives 'Over the Track'?"

"Yes. It isn't so bad as it used to be, socially. Mr. Wilmington has built a very fine house on this side, and there are several pretty Queen Anne cottages going up."

They drove along under the elms which here stood somewhat at random about the wide, grassless street, between the high, windowy bulks of the shoe shops and hat shops. The dust gradually freed itself from the cinders about the tracks, and it hardened into a handsome, newly made road beyond the houses of the shop hands. They passed some open lots, and then, on a pleasant rise of ground, they came to a stately residence, lifted still higher on its underpinning of granite blocks. It was built in a Boston suburban taste of twenty years ago, with a lofty mansard-roof, and it was painted the stone-grey colour which was once esteemed for being so quiet. The lawn before it sloped down to the road, where it ended smoothly at the brink of a neat stone wall. A black asphalt path curved from the steps by which you mounted from the street to the steps by which you mounted to the heavy portico before the massive black walnut doors.

The ladies were shown into the music-room, from which the notes of a piano were sounding when they rang, and Mrs. Wilmington rose from the instrument to meet them. A young man who had been standing beside her turned away. Mrs. Wilmington was dressed in a light morning dress with a Watteau fall, whose delicate russets and faded reds and yellows heightened the richness of her complexion and hair.

"Why, Annie," she said, "how glad I am to see you! And you too, Mrs. Munger. How *vurry* nice!" Her words took value from the thick mellow tones of her voice, and passed for much more than they were worth intrinsically. She moved lazily about and got them into chairs, and was not resentful when Mrs. Munger broke out with "How hot you have it!" "Have we? We had the furnace lighted yesterday, and we've been in all the morning, and so we hadn't noticed. Jack, won't you shut the register?" she drawled over her shoulder. "This is my nephew, Mr. Jack Wilmington, Miss Kilburn. Mr. Wilmington and Mrs. Munger are old friends."

The young fellow bowed silently, and Annie instantly took a dislike to him, his heavy jaw, long eyes, and low forehead almost hidden under a thick bang. He sat down cornerwise on a chair, and listened, with a scornful thrust of his thick lips, to their talk.

Mrs. Munger was not abashed by him. She opened her budget with all her robust authority, and once more put Annie to shame. When she came to the question of the invited supper and dance, and having previously committed Mrs. Wilmington in favour of the general scheme, asked her what she thought of that part, Mr. Jack Wilmington answered for her—

"I should think you had a right to do what you please about it.

It's none of the hands' business if you don't choose to ask them."

"Yes, that's what any one would think—in the abstract," said Mrs. Munger.

"Now, little boy," said Mrs. Wilmington, with indolent amusement, putting out a silencing hand in the direction of the young man, "don't you be so fast. You let your aunty speak for herself. I don't know about not letting the hands stay to the dance and supper, Mrs. Munger. You know I might feel 'put upon.' I used to be one of the hands myself. Yes, Annie, there was a time after you went away, and after father died, when I actually fell so low as to work for an honest living."

"I think I heard, Lyra," said Annie; "but I had forgotten." The fact, in connection with what had been said, made her still more uncomfortable.

"Well, I didn't work very hard, and I didn't have to work long. But I was a hand, and there's no use trying to deny it. As Mr. Putney says, he and I have our record, and we don't have to make any pretences. And the question is, whether I ought to go back on my fellow-hands."

"Oh, but Mrs. *Wilmington*!" said Mrs. Munger, with intense deprecation, "that's such a very different thing. You were not brought up to it; it was just temporary; and besides—"

"And besides, there was Mr. Wilmington, I know. He was very opportune. I might have been a hand at this moment if Mr. Wilmington had not come along and invited me to be a head—the head of his house. But I don't know, Annie, whether I oughtn't to remember my low beginnings."

"I suppose we all like to be consistent," answered Annie aimlessly, uneasily.

"Yes," Mrs. Munger broke in; "but they were not your

beginnings, Mrs. Wilmington; they were your incidents—your accidents."

"It's very pretty of you to say so, Mrs. Munger," drawled Mrs. Wilmington. "But I guess I must oppose the little invited dance and supper, on principle. We all like to be consistent, as Annie says—even if we're inconsistent in the attempt," she added, with a laugh.

"Very well, then," exclaimed Mrs. Munger, "we'll *drop* them. As I said to Miss Kilburn on our way here, 'if Mrs. Wilmington is opposed to them, we'll drop them.'"

"Oh, am I such an influential person?" said Mrs. Wilmington, with a shrug. "It's rather awful—isn't it, Annie?"

"Not at all!" Mrs. Munger answered for Annie. "We've just been talking the matter over with Mr. Putney and Dr. Morrell, and they're both opposed. You're merely the straw that breaks the camel's back, Mrs. Wilmington."

"Oh, *thank* you! That's a great relief."

"Well—and now the question is, will you take the part of the Nurse or not in the dramatics?" asked Mrs. Munger, returning to business.

"Well, I must think about that, and I must ask Mr. Wilmington. Jack," she called over her shoulder to the young man at the window, "do you think your uncle would approve of me as Juliet's Nurse?"

"You'd better ask him," growled the young fellow.

"Well," said Mrs. Wilmington, with another laugh, "I'll think it over, Mrs. Munger."

"Thank you," said Mrs. Munger. "And now we must really be going," she added, pulling out her watch by its leathern guard.

W. D. Howells

"Not till you've had lunch," said Mrs. Wilmington, rising with the ladies. "You must stay. Annie, I shall not excuse you."

"Well," said Mrs. Munger, complying without regard to Annie, "all this diplomacy is certainly very exhausting."

"Lunch will be on the table in one moment," returned Mrs. Wilmington, as the ladies sat down again provisionally. "Will you join us, Jack?"

"No; I'm going to the office," said the nephew, bowing himself out of the room.

"Jack's learning to be superintendent," said Mrs. Wilmington, lifting her teasing voice to make him hear her in the hall, "and he's been spending the whole morning here."

In the richly appointed dining-room—a glitter of china and glass and a mass of carven oak—the table was laid for two.

"Put another plate, Norah," said Mrs. Wilmington carelessly.

There was bouillon in teacups, chicken cutlets in white sauce, and luscious strawberries.

"*What* a cook!" cried Mrs. Munger, over the cutlets.

"Yes, she's a treasure; I don't deny it," said Mrs. Wilmington.

X

By the end of May most of the summer folk had come to their cottages in South Hatboro'. One after another the ladies called upon Annie. They all talked to her of the Social Union, and it seemed to be agreed that it was fully in train, though what was really in train was the entertainment to be given at Mrs. Munger's for the benefit of the Union; the Union always dropped out of the talk as soon as the theatricals were mentioned.

When Annie went to return these visits she scarcely recognised even the shape of the country, once so familiar to her, of which the summer settlement had possessed itself. She found herself in a strange world—a world of colonial and Queen Anne architecture, where conscious lines and insistent colours contributed to an effect of posing which she had never seen off the stage. But it was not a very large world, and after the young trees and hedges should have grown up and helped to hide it, she felt sure that it would be a better world. In detail it was not so bad now, but the whole was a violent effect of porches, gables, chimneys, galleries, loggias, balconies, and jalousies, which nature had not yet had time to palliate.

Mrs. Munger was at home, and wanted her to spend the day, to drive out with her, to stay to lunch. When Annie would not do any of these things, she invited herself to go with her to call at the Brandreths'. But first she ordered her to go out with her to see the place where they intended to have the theatricals: a pretty bit of natural boscage—white birches, pines, and

W. D. Howells

oaks—faced by a stretch of smooth turf, where a young man in a flannel blazer was painting a tennis-court in the grass. Mrs. Munger introduced him as her Jim, and the young fellow paused from his work long enough to bow to her: his nose now seemed in perfect repair.

Mr. Brandreth met them at the door of his mother's cottage. It was a very small cottage on the outside, with a good deal of stained glass *en evidence* in leaded sashes; where the sashes were not leaded and the glass not stained, the panes were cut up into very large ones, with little ones round them. Everything was very old-fashioned inside. The door opened directly into a wainscoted square hall, which had a large fireplace with gleaming brass andirons, and a carved mantel carried to the ceiling. It was both baronial and colonial in its decoration; there was part of a suit of imitation armour under a pair of moose antlers on one wall, and at one side of the fireplace there was a spinning-wheel, with a tuft of flax ready to be spun. There were Japanese swords on the lowest mantel-shelf, together with fans and vases; a long old flint-lock musket stretched across the panel above. Mr. Brandreth began to show things to Annie, and to tell how little they cost, as soon as the ladies entered. His mother's voice called from above, "Now, Percy, you stop till *I* get there!" and in a moment or two she appeared from behind a *portiere* in one corner. Before she shook hands with the ladies, or allowed any kind of greeting, she pulled the *portiere* aside, and made Annie admire the snug concealment of the staircase. Then she made her go upstairs and see the chambers, and the second-hand colonial bedsteads, and the andirons everywhere, and the old chests of drawers and their brasses; and she told her some story about each, and how Percy picked it up and had it repaired. When they came down, the son took Annie in hand again and walked her over the ground-floor, ending with the kitchen, which was in the taste of an old New England kitchen, with hard-seated high-backed chairs, and a kitchen table with curiously turned legs, which he had picked up in the hen-house of a neighbouring farmer for a song. There was an authentic crane in the dining-room fireplace, which he had found in a heap of scrap-iron at a blacksmith's shop, and had got for next to nothing. The sideboard he had got at an old second-hand shop in the North End; and he believed it was an heirloom from the house of one of the old ministers of the North End Church. Everything, nearly, in the Brandreth cottage was an heirloom, though Annie could not remember afterward any object that had been an heirloom in the Brandreth family.

When she went back with Mr. Brandreth to the hall, which seemed to be also the drawing-room, she found that Mrs. Brandreth had lighted the fire on the hearth, though it was rather a warm day without, for the sake of the effect. She was sitting in the chimney-seat, and shielding her face from the blaze with an old-fashioned feather hand-screen.

"Now don't you think we have a lovely little home?" she demanded.

Mrs. Munger began to break out in its praise, but she shook the screen silencingly at her.

"No, no! I want Miss Kilburn's unbiassed opinion. Don't you speak, Mrs. Munger! Now haven't we?"

Mrs. Brandreth made Annie assent to the superiority of her cottage in detail. She recapitulated the different facts of the architecture and furnishing, from each of which she seemed to acquire personal merit, and she insisted that Percy should show some of them again. "We think it's a little picture," she concluded, and once more Annie felt obliged to murmur her acquiescence.

At last Mrs. Munger said that she must go to lunch, and was going to take Annie with her; Annie said she must lunch at home; and then Mrs. Brandreth pressed them both to stay to lunch with her. "You shall have a cup of tea out of a piece of real Satsuma," she said; but they resisted. "I don't believe," she added, apparently relieved by their persistence, and losing a little anxiety of manner, "that Percy's had any chance to consult you on a very important point about your theatricals, Miss Kilburn."

"Oh, that will do some other time, mother," said Mr. Brandreth.

"No, no! Now! And you can have Mrs. Munger's opinion too. You know Miss Sue Northwick is going to be Juliet?"

"No!" shouted Mrs. Munger. "I thought she had refused positively. When did she change her mind?"

"She's just sent Percy a note. We were talking it over when you came, and Percy was going over to tell you."

"Then it is *sure* to be a success," said Mrs. Munger, with a solemnity of triumph.

"Yes, but Percy feels that it complicates one point more than ever—"

"It's a question that always comes up in amateur dramatics," said Mr. Brandreth, with reluctance, "and it always will; and of course it's particularly embarrassing in *Romeo and Juliet*. If they don't show any affection—it's very awkward and stiff; and if—"

"I never approved of those liberties on the stage," said Mrs. Brandreth. "I tell Percy that it's my principal objection to it. I can't make it seem nice. But he says that it's essential to the effect. Now *I* say that they might just incline their heads toward each other without *actually*, you know. But Percy is afraid that it won't do, especially in the parting scene on the balcony—so passionate, you know—it won't do simply to— They must *act* like lovers. And it's such a great point to get Miss Sue Northwick to take the part, that he mustn't risk losing her by anything that might seem—"

"Yes," said Mrs. Munger, with deep concern.

Mr. Brandreth looked very unhappy. "It's an embarrassing point. We can't change the play, and so the difficulty must be met and disposed of at once."

He did not look at either of the ladies, but Mrs. Munger referred the matter to Annie with a glance of impartiality. His mother also turned her eyes upon Annie. "Percy thought that you must have seen so much of amateur dramatics in Europe that you could tell him just how to do."

"Perhaps you could consult Miss Northwick herself," said Annie dryly, after a moment of indignation, and another of amusement.

"I thought of that," said Mrs. Brandreth; "but as Percy's to be Romeo—You see he wishes the play to be a success artistically; but if it's to succeed socially, he must have Miss Northwick, and she might resign at the first suggestion of—"

"Bessie Chapley would certainly have been better. She's so outspoken you could have put the case right to her," said Mrs. Munger.

"Yes," said Mr. Brandreth gloomily.

"But we shall find out a way. Why, you can settle it at rehearsal!"

"Perhaps at rehearsal," said Mr. Brandreth, with a pensive absence of mind.

Mrs. Munger crushed his hand and his mother's in her leathern grasp, and took Annie away with her. "It isn't lunch-time yet," she explained, when they were out of earshot, "but I saw she was simply killing you, and so I made the excuse. She has no mercy. There's time enough for you to make your calls before lunch, and then you can come home with me."

W. D. Howells

Annie suggested that this would not do after refusing Mrs. Brandreth.

"Why, it would never have done to *accept*!" Mrs. Munger cried. "They didn't dream of it!" At the next place she said: "This is the Clevingers'. *They're* some of our all-the-year-round people too." She opened the door without ringing, and let herself noisily in. "This is the way we run in, without ceremony, everywhere. It's quite one family. That's the charm of the place. We expect to take each other as we find them."

Her freedom did not find the ladies off their guard anywhere. At all the houses there was a skurrying of feet and a flashing of skirts out of the room or up the stairs, and there was an interval for a thorough study of the features of the room before the hostess came in, with the effect of coming in just as she was. She had naturally always made some change in her dress, and Annie felt that she had not really liked being run in upon. Everywhere they talked to her about the theatricals; and they talked across her to Mrs. Munger, about one another, pretty freely.

"Well, that's all there is of us at present," said Mrs. Munger, coming down the main road with her from the last place, "and you see just what we are. It's a neighbourhood where everybody's just adapted to everybody else. It's not a mere mush of concession, as Emerson says; people are perfectly outspoken; but there's the greatest good feeling, and no vulgar display, or lavish expenditure, or—anything."

Annie walked slowly homeward. She was tired, and she was now aware of having been extremely bored by the South Hatboro' people. She was very censorious of them, as we are of other people when we have reason to be discontented with ourselves. They were making a pretence of simplicity and unconventionality; but they had brought each her full complement of servants with her, and each was apparently giving herself in the summer to the unrealities that occupied her during the winter. Everywhere Annie had found the affectation of intellectual interests, and the assumption that these were the highest interests of life: there could be no doubt that culture was the ideal of South Hatboro', and several of the ladies complained that in the summer they got behind with their reading, or their art, or their music. They said it was even more trouble to keep house in the country than it was in town; sometimes your servants would not come with you; or, if they did, they were always discontented, and you did not know what moment they would leave you.

Annie asked herself how her own life was in any wise different from that of these people. It had received a little more light into it, but as yet it had not conformed itself to any ideal of duty. She too was idle and vapid, like the society of which her whole past had made her a part, and she owned to herself, groaning in spirit, that it was no easier to escape from her tradition at Hatboro' than it was at Rome.

When she reached her own house again, Mrs. Bolton called to her from the kitchen threshold as she was passing the corner on her way to the front door: "Mis' Putney's b'en here. I guess you'll find a note from her on the parlour table."

Annie fired in resentment of the uncouthness. It was Mrs. Bolton's business to come into the parlour and give her the note, with a respectful statement of the facts. But she did not tell her so; it would have been useless.

Mrs. Putney's note was an invitation to a family tea for the next evening.

XI

Putney met Annie at the door, and led her into the parlour beside the hall. He had a little crippled boy on his right arm, and he gave her his left hand. In the parlour he set his burden down in a chair, and the child drew up under his thin arms a pair of crutches that stood beside it. His white face had the eager purity and the waxen translucence which we see in sufferers from hip-disease.

"This is our Winthrop," said his father, beginning to talk at once. "We receive the company and do the honours while mother's looking after the tea. We only keep one undersized girl," he explained more directly to Annie, "and Ellen has to be chief cook and bottlewasher herself. She'll be in directly. Just lay off your bonnet anywhere."

She was taking in the humility of the house and its belongings while she received the impression of an unimagined simplicity in its life from his easy explanations. The furniture was in green terry, the carpet a harsh, brilliant tapestry; on the marble-topped centre table was a big clasp Bible and a basket with a stereoscope and views; the marbleised iron shelf above the stove-pipe hole supported two glass vases and a French clock under a glass bell; through the open door, across the oil-cloth of the hallway, she saw the white-painted pine balusters of the steep, cramped stairs. It was clear that neither Putney nor his wife had been touched by the aesthetic craze; the parlour was in the tastelessness of fifteen years before; but after the decoration of South Hatboro', she found a delicious repose in it. Her eyes dwelt with relief on the wall-paper of French grey, sprigged with small gilt flowers, and broken by a few cold engravings and framed photographs.

Putney himself was as little decorated as the parlour. He had put on a clean shirt, but the bulging bosom had broken away from its single button, and showed two serrated edges of ragged linen; his collar lost itself from time to time under the rise of his plastron scarf band, which kept escaping from the stud that ought to have held it down behind. His hair was brushed smoothly across a forehead which looked as innocent and gentle as the little boy's.

"We don't often give these festivities," he went on, "but you don't come home once in twelve years every day, Annie. I can't tell you how glad I am to see you in our house; and Ellen's just as excited as the rest of us; she was sorry to miss you when she called."

"You're very kind, Ralph. I can't tell *you* what a pleasure it was to come, and I'm not going to let the trouble I'm giving spoil my pleasure."

"Well, that's right," said Putney. "*We* sha'n't either." He took out a cigar and put it into his mouth. "It's only a dry smoke. Ellen makes me let up on my chewing when we have company, and I must have something in my mouth, so I get a cigar. It's a sort of compromise. I'm a terribly nervous man, Annie; you can't imagine. If it wasn't for the grace of God, I think I should fly to pieces sometimes. But I guess that's what holds me together—that and Winthy here. I dropped him on the stairs out there, when I was drunk, one night. I saw you looking at them; I suppose you've been told; it's all right. I presume the Almighty knows what He's about; but sometimes He appears to save at the spigot and waste at the bung-hole, like the rest of us. He let me cripple my boy to reform me."

"Don't, Ralph!" said Annie, with a voice of low entreaty. She turned and spoke to the child, and asked him if he would not

W. D. Howells

come to see her.

"What?" he asked, breaking with a sort of absent-minded start from his intentness upon his father's words.

She repeated her invitation.

"Thanks!" he said, in the prompt, clear little pipe which startles by its distinctness and decision on the lips of crippled children. "I guess father'll bring me some day. Don't you want I should go out and tell mother she's here?" he asked his father.

"Well, if you want to, Winthrop," said his father.

The boy swung himself lightly out of the room on his crutches, and his father turned to her. "Well, how does Hatboro' strike you, anyway, Annie? You needn't mind being honest with me, you know."

He did not give her a chance to say, and she was willing to let him talk on, and tell her what he thought of Hatboro' himself. "Well, it's like every other place in the world, at every moment of history—it's in a transition state. The theory is, you know, that most places are at a standstill the greatest part of the time; they haven't begun to move, or they've stopped moving; but I guess that's a mistake; they're moving all the while. I suppose Rome itself was in a transition state when you left?"

"Oh, very decidedly. It had ceased to be old and was becoming new."

"Well, that's just the way with Hatboro'. There is no old Hatboro' any more; and there never was, as your father and mine could tell us if they were here. They lived in a painfully transitional period, poor old fellows! But, for all that, there is a difference. They lived in what was really a New England village, and we live now in a sprawling American town; and by American of course I mean a town where at least one-third of the people are raw foreigners or rawly extracted natives. The old New England ideal characterises them all, up to a certain point, socially; it puts a decent outside on most of 'em; it makes 'em keep Sunday, and drink on the sly. We got in the Irish long ago, and now they're part of the conservative element. We got in the French Canadians, and some of them are our best mechanics and citizens. We're getting in the Italians, and as soon as they want something better than bread and vinegar to eat, they'll begin going to Congress and boycotting and striking and forming pools and trusts just like any other class of law-abiding Americans. There used to be some talk of the Chinese, but I guess they've pretty much blown over. We've got Ah Lee and Sam Lung here, just as they have everywhere, but their laundries don't seem to increase. The Irish are spreading out into the country and scooping in the farms that are not picturesque enough for the summer folks. You can buy a farm anywhere round Hatboro' for less than the buildings on it cost. I'd rather the Irish would have the land than the summer folks. They make an honest living off it, and the other fellows that come out to roost here from June till October simply keep somebody else from making a living off it, and corrupt all the poor people in sight by their idleness and luxury. That's what I tell 'em at South Hatboro'. They don't like it, but I guess they believe it; anyhow they have to hear it. They'll tell you in self-defence that J. Milton Northwick is a practical farmer, and sells his butter for a dollar a pound. He's done more than anybody else to improve the breeds of cattle and horses; and he spends fifteen thousand a year on his place. It can't return him five; and that's the reason he's a curse and a fraud."

"Who *is* Mr. Northwick, Ralph?" Annie interposed. "Everybody at South Hatboro' asked me if I'd met the Northwicks."

"He's a very great and good man," said Putney. "He's worth a million, and he runs a big manufacturing company at Ponkwasset Falls, and he owns a fancy farm just beyond South Hatboro'. He lives in Boston, but he comes out here early enough to dodge his tax there, and let poorer people pay it. He's got miles of cut stone wall round his place, and conservatories and gardens and villas and drives inside of it, and he keeps up the town roads outside at his own expense. Yes, we feel it such an honour and advantage to have J. Milton in Hatboro' that our assessors practically allow him to fix the amount of tax here himself. People who can pay only a little at the highest valuation are assessed to the last dollar of their property and income; but the assessors know that this wouldn't do with Mr. Northwick. They make a guess at his income, and he always pays their bills without asking for abatement; they think themselves wise and public-spirited men for doing it, and most of their fellow-citizens think so too. You see it's not only difficult for a rich man to get into the kingdom of heaven, Annie, but he makes it hard for other people.

"Well, as I was saying, socially, the old New England element is at the top of the heap here. That's so everywhere. The people that are on the ground first, it don't matter much who they are, have to manage pretty badly not to leave their descendants in social ascendency over all newer comers for ever. Why, I can see it in my own case. I can see that I was a sort of fetich to the bedevilled fancy of the people here when I was seen drunk in the streets every day, just because I was one of the old Hatboro' Putneys; and when I began to hold up, there wasn't a man in the community that wasn't proud and flattered to help me. Curious, isn't it? It made me sick of myself and ashamed of them, and I just made up my mind, as soon as I got straight again, I'd give all my help to the men that hadn't a tradition. That's what I've done, Annie. There isn't any low, friendless rapscallion in this town that hasn't got me for his friend—and Ellen. We've been in all the strikes with the men, and all their fool boycottings and kicking over the traces generally. Anybody else would have been turned out of respectable society for one-half that I've done, but it tolerates me because I'm one of the old Hatboro' Putneys. You're one of the old Hatboro' Kilburns, and if you want to have a mind of your own and a heart of your own, all you've got to do is to have it. They'll like it; they'll think it's original. That's the reason South Hatboro' got after you with that

Social Union scheme. They were right in thinking you would have a great deal of influence. I was sorry you had to throw it against Brother Peck."

Annie felt herself jump at this climax, as if she had been touched on an exposed nerve. She grew red, and tried to be angry, but she was only ashamed and tempted to lie out of the part she had taken. "Mrs. Munger," she said, "gave that a very unfair turn. I didn't mean to ridicule Mr. Peck. I think he was perfectly sincere. The scheme of the invited dance and supper has been entirely given up. And I don't care for the project of the Social Union at all."

"Well, I'm glad to hear it," said Putney, indifferently, and he resumed his analysis of Hatboro'—

"We've got all the modern improvements here, Annie. I suppose you'd find the modern improvements, most of 'em, in Sheol: electric light, Bell telephone, asphalt sidewalks, and city water—though I don't know about the water; and I presume they haven't got a public library or an opera-house—perhaps they *have* got an opera-house in Sheol: you see I use the Revised Version, it don't sound so much like swearing. But, as I was saying—"

Mrs. Putney came in, and he stopped with the laugh of a man who knows that his wife will find it necessary to account for him and apologise for him.

The ladies kissed each other. Mrs. Putney was dressed in the black silk of a woman who has one silk; she was red from the kitchen, but all was neat and orderly in the hasty toilet which she must have made since leaving the cook-stove. A faint, mixed perfume of violet sachet and fricasseed chicken attended her.

"Well, as you were saying, Ralph?" she suggested.

"Oh, I was just tracing a little parallel between Hatboro' and

Sheol," replied her husband.

Mrs. Putney made a *tchk* of humorous patience, and laughed toward Annie for sympathy. "Well, then, I guess you needn't go on. Tea's ready. Shall we wait for the doctor?"

"No; doctors are too uncertain. We'll wait for him while we're eating. That's what fetches him the soonest. I'm hungry. Ain't you, Win?"

"Not so very," said the boy, with his queer promptness. He stood resting himself on his crutches at the door, and he now wheeled about, and led the way out to the living-room, swinging himself actively forward. It seemed that his haste was to get to the dumb-waiter in the little china closet opening off the dining-room, which was like the papered inside of a square box. He called to the girl below, and helped pull it up, as Annie could tell by the creaking of the rope, and the light jar of the finally arriving crockery. A half-grown girl then appeared, and put the dishes on at the places indicated with nods and looks by Mrs. Putney, who had taken her place at the table. There was a platter of stewed fowl, and a plate of high-piled waffles, sweltering in successive courses of butter and sugar. In cut-glass dishes, one at each end of the table, there were canned cherries and pine-apple. There was a square of old-fashioned soda biscuit, not broken apart, which sent up a pleasant smell; in the centre of the table was a shallow vase of strawberries.

It was all very good and appetising; but to Annie it was pathetically old-fashioned, and helped her to realise how wholly out of the world was the life which her friends led.

"Winthrop," said Putney, and the father and mother bowed their heads.

The boy dropped his over his folded hands, and piped up clearly: "Our Father, which art in heaven, help us to remember those who have nothing to eat. Amen!"

"That's a grace that Win got up himself," his father explained, beginning to heap a plate with chicken and mashed potato, which he then handed to Annie, passing her the biscuit and the butter. "We think it suits the Almighty about as well as anything."

"I suppose you know Ralph of old, Annie?" said Mrs. Putney. "The only way he keeps within bounds at all is by letting himself perfectly loose."

Putney laughed out his acquiescence, and they began to talk together about old times. Mrs. Putney and Annie recalled the childish plays and adventures they had together, and one dreadful quarrel. Putney told of the first time he saw Annie, when his father took him one day for a call on the old judge, and how the old judge put him through his paces in American history, and would not admit the theory that the battle of Bunker's Hill could have been fought on Breed's Hill. Putney said that it was years before it occurred to him that the judge must have been joking: he had always thought he was simply ignorant.

"I used to set a good deal by the battle of Bunker's Hill," he continued. "I thought the whole Revolution and subsequent history revolved round it, and that it gave us all liberty, equality, and fraternity at a clip. But the Lord always finds some odd jobs to look after next day, and I guess He didn't clear 'em all up at Bunker's Hill."

Putney's irony and piety were very much of a piece apparently, and Annie was not quite sure which this conclusion was. She glanced at his wife, who seemed satisfied with it in either case. She was waiting patiently for him to wake up to the fact that he had not yet given her anything to eat; after helping Annie and the boy, he helped himself, and pending his wife's pre-occupation with the tea, he forgot her.

"Why didn't you throw something at me," he roared, in grief and self-reproach. "There wouldn't have been a loose piece of crockery on this side of the table if I hadn't got my tea in time."

"Oh, I was listening to Annie's share in the conversation," said Mrs. Putney; and her husband was about to say something in retort of her thrust when a tap on the front door was heard.

"Come in, come in, Doc!" he shouted. "Mrs. Putney's just been helped, and the tea is going to begin."

Dr. Morrell's chuckle made answer for him, and after time enough to put down his hat, he came in, rubbing his hands and smiling, and making short nods round the table. "How d'ye do, Mrs. Putney? How d'ye do, Miss Kilburn? Winthrop?" He passed his hand over the boy's smooth hair and slipped into the chair beside him.

"You see, the reason why we always wait for the doctor in this formal way," said Putney, "is that he isn't in here more than seven nights of the week, and he rather stands on his dignity. Hand round the doctor's plate, my son," he added to the boy, and he took it from Annie, to whom the boy gave it, and began to heap it from the various dishes. "Think you can lift that much back to the doctor, Win?"

"I guess so," said the boy coolly.

"What is flooring Win at present," said his father, "and getting him down and rolling him over, is that problem of the robin that eats half a pint of grasshoppers and then doesn't weigh a bit more than he did before."

"When he gets a little older," said the doctor, shaking over his plateful, "he'll be interested to trace the processes of his father's thought from a guest and half a peck of stewed chicken, to a robin and half a pint of—"

"Don't, doctor!" pleaded Mrs. Putney. "He won't have the least trouble if he'll keep to the surface."

Putney laughed impartially, and said: "Well, we'll take the doctor out and weigh him when he gets done. We expected Brother Peck here this evening," he explained to Dr. Morrell. "You're our sober second thought—Well," he broke off, looking across the table at his wife with mock anxiety. "Anything wrong about that, Ellen?"

"Not as far as I'm concerned, Mrs. Putney," interposed the doctor. "I'm glad to be here on any terms. Go on, Putney."

"Oh, there isn't anything more. You know how Miss Kilburn here has been round throwing ridicule on Brother Peck, because he wants the shop-hands treated with common decency, and my idea was to get the two together and see how she would feel."

Dr. Morrell laughed at this with what Annie thought was unnecessary malice; but he stopped suddenly, after a glance at her, and Putney went on—

"Brother Peck pleaded another engagement. Said he had to go off into the country to see a sick woman that wasn't expected to live. You don't remember the Merrifields, do you, Annie? Well, it doesn't matter. One of 'em married West, and her husband left her, and she came home here and got a divorce; I got it for her. She's the one. As a consumptive, she had superior attractions for Brother Peck. It isn't a case that admits of jealousy exactly, but it wouldn't matter to Brother Peck anyway. If he saw a chance to do a good action, he'd wade through blood."

"Now look here, Ralph," said Mrs. Putney, "there's such a thing as letting yourself *too* loose."

"Well, *gore*, then," said Putney, buttering himself a biscuit.

The boy, who had kept quiet till now, seemed reached by this last touch, and broke into a high, crowing laugh, in which they all joined except his father.

"Gore suits Winthy, anyway," he said, beginning to eat his biscuit. "I met one of the deacons from Brother Peck's last parish, in Boston, yesterday. He asked me if we considered Brother Peck anyways peculiar in Hatboro', and when I said we thought he was a little too luxurious, the deacon came out with a lot of things. The way Brother Peck behaved toward the needy in that last parish of his made it simply uninhabitable to the standard Christian. They had to get rid of him somehow— send him away or kill him. Of course the deacon said they didn't want to *kill* him."

"Where was his last parish?" asked the doctor.

"Down on the Maine coast somewhere. Penobscotport, I believe."

"And was he indigenous there?"

"No, I believe not; he's from Massachusetts. Farm-boy and then mill-hand, I understand. Self-helped to an education; divinity student with summer intervals of waiting at table in the mountain hotels probably. Drifted down Maine way on his first call and stuck; but I guess he won't stick here very long. Annie's friend Mr. Gerrish is going to look after Brother Peck before a great while." He laughed, to see her blush, and went on. "You see, Brother Gerrish has got a high ideal of what a Christian minister ought to be; he hasn't said much about it, but I can see that Brother Peck doesn't come up to it. Well, Brother Gerrish has got a good many ideals. He likes to get anybody he can by the throat, and squeeze the difference of opinion out of 'em."

"There, now, Ralph," his wife interposed, "you let Mr. Gerrish alone. *You* don't like people to differ with you, either. Is your cup out, doctor?"

"Thank you," said the doctor, handing it up to her. "And you mean Mr. Gerrish doesn't like Mr. Peck's doctrine?" he asked of Putney.

"Oh, I don't know that he objects to his doctrine; he can't very well; it's 'between the leds of the Bible,' as the Hard-shell Baptist said. But he objects to Brother Peck's walk and conversation. He thinks he walks too much with the poor, and converses too much with the lowly. He says he thinks that the pew-owners in Mr. Peck's church and the people who pay his salary have some rights to his company that he's bound to respect."

The doctor relished the irony, but he asked, "Isn't there something to say on that side?"

"Oh yes, a good deal. There's always something to say on both sides, even when one's a wrong side. That's what makes it all so tiresome—makes you wish you were dead." He looked up, and caught his boy's eye fixed with melancholy intensity upon him. "I hope you'll never look at both sides when you grow up, Win. It's mighty uncomfortable. You take the right side, and stick to that. Brother Gerrish," he resumed, to the doctor, "goes round taking the credit of Brother Peck's call here; but the fact is he opposed it. He didn't like his being so indifferent about the salary. Brother Gerrish held that the labourer was worthy of his hire, and if he didn't inquire what his wages were going to be, it was a pretty good sign that he wasn't going to earn them."

"Well, there was some logic in that," said the doctor, smiling as before.

"Plenty. And now it worries Brother Gerrish to see Brother Peck going round in the same old suit of clothes he came here in, and dressing his child like a shabby little Irish girl. He says that he who provideth not for those of his own household is worse than a heathen. That's perfectly true. And he would like to know what Brother Peck does with his money, anyway. He would like to insinuate that he loses it at poker, I guess; at any rate, he can't find out whom he gives it to, and he certainly doesn't spend it on himself."

"From your account of Mr. Peck." said the doctor, "I should think Brother Gerrish might safely object to him as a certain kind of sentimentalist."

"Well, yes, he might, looking at him from the outside. But when you come to talk with Brother Peck, you find yourself sort of frozen out with a most unexpected, hard-headed cold-bloodedness. Brother Peck is plain common-sense itself. He seems to be a man without an illusion, without an emotion."

"Oh, not so bad as that!" laughed the doctor.

"Ask Miss Kilburn. She's talked with him, and she hates him."

"No, I don't, Ralph," Annie began.

"Oh, well, then, perhaps he only made you hate yourself," said Putney. There was something charming in his mockery, like the teasing of a brother with a sister; and Annie did not find the atonement to which he brought her altogether painful. It seemed to her really that she was getting off pretty easily, and she laughed with hearty consent at last.

Winthrop asked solemnly, "How did he do that?"

"Oh, I can't tell exactly, Winthrop," she said, touched by the boy's simple interest in this abstruse point. "He made me feel that I had been rather mean and cruel when I thought I had only been practical. I can't explain; but it wasn't a comfortable feeling, my dear."

"I guess that's the trouble with Brother Peck," said Putney. "He doesn't make you feel comfortable. He doesn't flatter you up worth a cent. There was Annie expecting him to take the most fervent interest in her theatricals, and her Social Union, and coo round, and tell her what a noble woman she was, and beg her to consider her health, and not overwork herself in doing good; but instead of that he simply showed her that she was a moral Cave-Dweller, and that she was living in a Stone

Age of social brutalities; and of course she hated him."

"Yes, that was the way, Winthrop," said Annie; and they all laughed with her.

"Now you take them into the parlour, Ralph," said his wife, rising, "and tell them how he made *you* hate him."

"I shouldn't like anything better," replied Putney. He lifted the large ugly kerosene lamp that had been set on the table when it grew dark during tea, and carried it into the parlour with him. His wife remained to speak with her little helper, but she sent Annie with the gentlemen.

"Why, there isn't a great deal of it—more spirit than letter, so to speak," said Putney, when he put down the lamp in the parlour. "You know how I like to go on about other people's sins, and the world's wickedness generally; but one day Brother Peck, in that cool, impersonal way of his, suggested that it was not a wholly meritorious thing to hate evil. He went so far as to say that perhaps we could not love them that despitefully used us if we hated their evil so furiously. He said it was a good deal more desirable to understand evil than to hate it, for then we could begin to cure it. Yes, Brother Peck let in a good deal of light on me. He rather insinuated that I must be possessed by the very evils I hated, and that was the reason I was so violent about them. I had always supposed that I hated other people's cruelty because I was merciful, and their meanness because I was magnanimous, and their intolerance because I was generous, and their conceit because I was modest, and their selfishness because I was disinterested; but after listening to Brother Peck a while I came to the conclusion that I hated these things in others because I was cruel myself, and mean, and bigoted, and conceited, and piggish; and that's why I've hated Brother Peck ever since—just like you, Annie. But he didn't reform me, I'm thankful to say, any more than he did you. I've gone on just the same, and I suppose I hate more infernal scoundrels and loathe more infernal idiots to-day than ever; but I perceive that I'm no part of the power that makes

W. D. Howells

for righteousness as long as I work that racket; and now I sin with light and knowledge, anyway. No, Annie," he went on, "I can understand why Brother Peck is not the success with women, and feminine temperaments like me, that his virtues entitle him to be. What we feminine temperaments want is a prophet, and Brother Peck doesn't prophesy worth a cent. He doesn't pretend to be authorised in any sort of way; he has a sneaking style of being no better than you are, and of being rather stumped by some of the truths he finds out. No, women like a good prophet about as well as they do a good doctor. Now if you, if you could unite the two functions, Doc—"

"Sort of medicine-man?" suggested Morrell.

"Exactly! The aborigines understood the thing. Why, I suppose that a real live medicine-man could go through a community like this and not leave a sinful soul nor a sore body in it among the ladies—perfect faith cure."

"But what did you say to Mr. Peck, Ralph?" asked Annie. "Didn't you attempt any defence?"

"No," said Putney. "He had the advantage of me. You can't talk back at a man in the pulpit."

"Oh, it was a sermon?"

"I suppose the other people thought so. But I knew it was a private conversation that he was publicly holding with me."

Putney and the doctor began to talk of the nature and origin of evil, and Annie and the boy listened. Putney took high ground, and attributed it to Adam. "You know, Annie," he explained, "I don't believe this; but I like to get a scientific man that won't quite deny Scripture or the good old Bible premises, and see him suffer. Hello! you up yet, Winthrop? I guess I'll go through the form of carrying you to bed, my son."

When Mrs. Putney rejoined them, Annie said she must go,

and Mrs. Putney went upstairs with her, apparently to help her put on her things, but really to have that talk before parting which guest and hostess value above the whole evening's pleasure. She showed Annie the pictures of the little girls that had died, and talked a great deal about their sickness and their loveliness in death. Then they spoke of others, and Mrs. Putney asked Annie if she had seen Lyra Wilmington lately. Annie told of her call with Mrs. Munger, and Mrs. Putney said: "I *like* Lyra, and I always did. I presume she isn't very happily married; he's too old; there couldn't have been any love on her part. But she would be a better woman than she is if she had children. Ralph says," added Mrs. Putney, smiling, "that he knows she would be a good mother, she's such a good aunt."

Annie put her two hands impressively on the hands of her friend folded at her waist. "Ellen, what *does* it mean?"

"Nothing more than what you saw, Annie. She must have—or she *will* have—some one to amuse her; to be at her beck and call; and it's best to have it all in the family, Ralph says."

"But isn't it—doesn't he think it's—odd?"

"It makes talk."

They moved a little toward the door, holding each other's hands. "Ellen, I've had a *lovely* time!"

"And so have I, Annie. I thought you'd like to meet Dr. Morrell."

"Oh yes, indeed!"

"And I can't tell you what a night this has been for Ralph. He likes you so much, and it isn't often that he has a chance to talk to two such people as you and Dr. Morrell."

"How brilliant he is!" Annie sighed.

"Yes, he's a very able man. It's very fortunate for Hatboro' to have such a doctor. He and Ralph are great cronies. I never feel uneasy now when Ralph's out late—I know he's been up at the doctor's office, talking. I—"

Annie broke in with a laugh. "I've no doubt Dr. Morrell is all you say, Ellen, but I meant Ralph when I spoke of brilliancy. He has a great future, I'm sure."

Mrs. Putney was silent for a moment. "I'm satisfied with the present, so long as Ralph—" The tears suddenly gushed out of her eyes, and ran down over the fine wrinkles of her plump little cheeks.

"Not quite so much loud talking, please," piped a thin, high voice from a room across the stairs landing.

"Why, dear little soul!" cried Annie. "I forgot he'd gone to bed."

"Would you like to see him?" asked his mother.

She led the way into the room where the boy lay in a low bed near a larger one. His crutches lay beside it. "Win sleeps in our room yet. He can take care of himself quite well. But when he wakes in the night he likes to reach out and touch his father's hand."

The child looked mortified.

"I wish I could reach out and touch *my* father's hand when I wake in the night," said Annie.

The cloud left the boy's face. "I can't remember whether I said my prayers, mother, I've been thinking so."

"Well, say them over again, to me."

The men's voices sounded in the hall below, and the ladies

found them there. Dr. Morrell had his hat in his hand.

"Look here, Annie," said Putney, "*I* expected to walk home with you, but Doc Morrell says he's going to cut me out. It looks like a put-up job. I don't know whether you're in it or not, but there's no doubt about Morrell."

Mrs. Putney gave a sort of gasp, and then they all shouted with laughter, and Annie and the doctor went out into the night. In the imperfect light which the electrics of the main street flung afar into the little avenue where Putney lived, and the moon sent through the sidewalk trees, they struck against each other as they walked, and the doctor said, "Hadn't you better take my arm, Miss Kilburn, till we get used to the dark?"

"Yes, I think I had, decidedly," she answered; and she hurried to add: "Dr. Morrell, there is something I want to ask you. You're their physician, aren't you?"

"The Putneys? Yes."

"Well, then, you can tell me—"

"Oh no, I can't, if you ask me as their physician," he interrupted.

"Well, then, as their friend. Mrs. Putney said something to me that makes me very unhappy. I thought Mr. Putney was out of all danger of his—trouble. Hasn't he perfectly reformed? Does he ever—"

She stopped, and Dr. Morrell did not answer at once. Then he said seriously: "It's a continual fight with a man of Putney's temperament, and sometimes he gets beaten. Yes, I guess you'd better know it."

"Poor Ellen!"

"They don't allow themselves to be discouraged. As soon as

he's on his feet they begin the fight again. But of course it prevents his success in his profession, and he'll always be a second-rate country lawyer."

"Poor Ralph! And so brilliant as he is! He could be anything."

"We must be glad if he can be something, as it is."

"Yes, and how happy they seem together, all three of them! That child worships his father; and how tender Ralph is of him! How good he is to his wife; and how proud she is of him! And that awful shadow over them all the time! I don't see how they live!"

The doctor was silent for a moment, and finally said: "They have the peace that seems to come to people from the presence of a common peril, and they have the comfort of people who never blink the facts."

"I think Ralph is terrible. I wish he'd let other people blink the facts a little."

"Of course," said the doctor, "it's become a habit with him now, or a mania. He seems to speak of his trouble as if mentioning it were a sort of conjuration to prevent it. I wouldn't venture to check him in his way of talking. He may find strength in it.'

"It's all terrible!"

"But it isn't by any means hopeless."

"I'm so glad to hear you say so. You see a great deal of them, I believe?"

"Yes," said the doctor, getting back from their seriousness, with apparent relief. "Pretty nearly every day. Putney and I consider the ways of God to man a good deal together. You can imagine that in a place like Hatboro' one would make the most of such a friend. In fact, anywhere."

"Yes, of course," Annie assented. "Dr. Morrell," she added, in that effect of continuing the subject with which one breaks away from it, "do you know much about South Hatboro'?"

"I have some patients there."

"I was there this morning—"

"I heard of you. They all take a great interest in your theatricals."

"In *my* theatricals? Really this is too much! Who has made them my theatricals, I should like to know? Everybody at South Hatboro' talked as if I had got them up."

"And haven't you?"

"No. I've had nothing to do with them. Mr. Brandreth spoke to me about them a week ago, and I was foolish enough to go round with Mrs. Munger to collect public opinion about her invited dance and supper; and now it appears that I have invented the whole affair."

"I certainly got that impression," said the doctor, with a laugh lurking under his gravity.

"Well, it's simply atrocious," said Annie. "I've nothing at all to do with either. I don't even know that I approve of their object."

"Their object?"

"Yes. The Social Union."

"Oh! Oh yes. I had forgot about the object," and now the doctor laughed outright.

"It seems to have dropped into the background with every-body," said Annie, laughing too.

"You like the unconventionality of South Hatboro'?" suggested the doctor, after a little silence.

"Oh, very much," said Annie. "I was used to the same thing abroad. It might be an American colony anywhere on the Continent."

"I suppose," said the doctor musingly, "that the same condi-tions of sojourn and disoccupation *would* produce the same social effects anywhere. Then you must feel quite at home in South Hatboro'!"

"Quite! It's what I came back to avoid. I was sick of the life over there, and I wanted to be of some use here, instead of wasting all my days."

She stopped, resolved not to go on if he took this lightly, but the doctor answered her with sufficient gravity: "Well?"

"It seemed to me that if I could be of any use in the world anywhere, I could in the place where I was born, and where my whole childhood was spent. I've been at home a month now, the most useless person in Hatboro'. I did catch at the first thing that offered—at Mr. Brandreth and his ridiculous Social Union and theatricals, and brought all this trouble on myself. I talked to Mr. Peck about them. You know what his views are?"

"Only from Putney's talk," said the doctor.

"He didn't merely disapprove of the dance and supper, but he had some very peculiar notions about the relations of the different classes in general," said Annie; and this was the point she had meant circuitously to lead up to when she began to speak of South Hatboro', though she theoretically despised all sorts of feminine indirectness.

"Yes?" said the doctor. "What notions?"

"Well, he thinks that if you have money, you *can't* do good with it."

"That's rather odd," said Dr. Morrell.

"I don't state it quite fairly. He meant that you can't make any kindness with it between yourself and the—the poor."

"That's odd too."

"Yes," said Annie anxiously. "You can impose an obligation, he says, but you can't create sympathy. Of course Ralph exaggerates what I said about him in connection with the invited dance and supper, though I don't justify what I did say; and if I'd known then, as I do now, what his history had been, I should have been more careful in my talk with him. I should be very sorry to have hurt his feelings, and I suppose people who've come up in that way are sensitive?"

She suggested this, and it was not the reassurance she was seeking to have Dr. Morrell say, "Naturally."

She continued with an effort: "I'm afraid I didn't respect his sincerity, and I ought to have done that, though I don't at all agree with him on the other points. It seems to me that what he said was shocking, and perfectly—impossible."

"Why, what was it?" asked the doctor.

"He said there could be no real kindness between the rich and poor, because all their experiences of life were different. It amounted to saying that there ought not to *be* any wealth. Don't you think so?"

"Really, I've never thought about it," returned Dr. Morrell. After a moment he asked, "Isn't it rather an abstraction?"

W. D. Howells

"Don't say that!" said Annie nervously. "It's the *most* concrete thing in the world!"

The doctor laughed with enjoyment of her convulsive emphasis; but she went on: "I don't think life's worth living if you're to be shut up all your days to the intelligence merely of your own class."

"Who said you were?"

"Mr. Peck."

"And what was your inference from the fact? That there oughtn't to be any classes?"

"Of course it won't do to say that. There *must* be social differences. Don't you think so?"

"I don't know," said Dr. Morrell. "I never thought of it in that light before. It's a very curious question." He asked, brightening gaily after a moment of sober pause, "Is that the whole trouble?"

"Isn't it enough?"

"No; I don't think it is. Why didn't you tell him that you didn't want any gratitude?".

"Not *want* any?" she demanded.

"Oh!" said Dr. Morrell, "I didn't know but you thought it was enough to *give.*"

Annie believed that he was making fun of her, and she tried to make her resentful silence dignified; but she only answered sadly: "No; it isn't enough for me. Besides, he made me see that you can't give sympathy where you can't receive it."

"Well, that *is* bad," said the doctor, and he laughed again.

"Excuse me," he added. "I see the point. But why don't you forget it?"

"Forget it!"

"Yes. If you can't help it, why need you worry about it?"

She gave a kind of gasp of astonishment. "Do you really think that would be right?" She edged a little away from Dr. Morrell, as if with distrust.

"Well, no; I can't say that I do," he returned thoughtfully, without seeming to have noticed her withdrawal. "I don't suppose I was looking at the moral side. It's rather out of my way to do that. If a physician let himself get into the habit of doing that, he might regard nine-tenths of the diseases he has to treat as just penalties, and decline to interfere."

She fancied that he was amused again, rather than deeply concerned, and she determined to make him own his personal complicity in the matter if she could. "Then you *do* feel sympathy with your patients? You find it necessary to do so?"

The doctor thought a moment. "I take an interest in their diseases."

"But you want them to get well?"

"Oh, certainly. I'm bound to do all I can for them as a physician."

"Nothing more?"

"Yes; I'm sorry for them—for their families, if it seems to be going badly with them."

"And—and as—as—Don't you care at all for your work as a part of what every one ought to do for others—as humanity, philan—" She stopped the offensive word.

"Well, I can't say that I've looked at it in that light exactly," he answered. "I suspect I'm not very good at generalising my own relations to others, though I like well enough to speculate in the abstract. But don't you think Mr. Peck has overlooked one important fact in his theory? What about the people who have grown rich from being poor, as most Americans have? They have the same experiences, and why can't they sympathise with those who have remained poor?"

"I never thought of that. Why didn't I ask him that?" She lamented so sincerely that the doctor laughed again. "I think that Mr. Peck—"

"Oh no! oh no!" said the doctor, in an entreating, coaxing tone, expressive of a satiety with the subject that he might very well have felt; and he ended with another laugh, in which, after a moment of indignant self-question, she joined him.

"Isn't that delicious?" he exclaimed; and she involuntarily slowed her pace with his.

The spicy scent of sweet-currant blossoms hung in the dewy air that wrapped one of the darkened village houses. From a syringa bush before another, as they moved on, a denser perfume stole out with the wild song of a cat-bird hidden in it; the music and the odour seemed braided together. The shadows of the trees cast by the electrics on the walks were so thick and black that they looked palpable; it seemed as if she could stoop down and lift them from the ground. A broad bath of moonlight washed one of the house fronts, and the white-painted clapboards looked wet with it.

They talked of these things, of themselves, and of their own traits and peculiarities; and at her door they ended far from Mr. Peck and all the perplexities he had suggested.

She had told Dr. Morrell of some things she had brought home with her, and had said she hoped he would find time to come and see them. It would have been stiff not to do it, and she believed she had done it in a very off-hand, business-like way. But she continued to question whether she had.

W. D. Howells

XII

Miss Northwick called upon Annie during the week, with excuses for her delay and for coming alone. She seemed to have intentions of being polite; but she constantly betrayed her want of interest in Annie, and disappointed an expectation of refinement which her physical delicacy awakened. She asked her how she ever came to take up the Social Union, and answered for her that of course it had the attraction of the theatricals, and went on to talk of her sister's part in them. The relation of the Northwick family to the coming entertainment, and an impression of frail mottled wrists and high thin cheeks, and an absence of modelling under affluent drapery, was the main effect of Miss Northwick's visit.

When Annie returned it, she met the younger sister, whom she found a great beauty. She seemed very cold, and of a *hauteur* which she subdued with difficulty; but she was more consecutively polite than her sister, and Annie watched with fascination her turns of the head, her movements of leopard swiftness and elasticity; the changing lights of her complexion; the curves of her fine lips, the fluttering of her thin nostrils.

A very new basket phaeton stood glittering at Annie's door when she got home, and Mrs. Wilmington put her head out of the open parlour window.

"How d'ye do, Annie?" she drawled, in her tender voice. "Won't you come in? You see I'm in possession. I've just got my new phaeton, and I drove up at once to crush you with it.

Isn't it a beauty?"

"You're too late, Lyra," said Annie. "I've just come from the Northwicks, and another crushing beauty has got in ahead of your phaeton."

"Oh, *poor* Annie!" Lyra began to laugh with agreeable intelligence. "*Do* come in and tell me about it!"

"Why is that girl going to take part in the theatricals? She doesn't care to please any one, does she?"

"I didn't know that people took part in theatricals for that, Annie. I thought they wanted to please themselves and mortify others. *I* do. But then I may be different. Perhaps Miss Northwick wants to please Mr. Brandreth."

"Do you mean it, Lyra?" demanded Annie, arrested on her threshold by the charm of this improbability.

"Well, I don't know; they're opposites. But, upon second thoughts, you needn't come in, Annie. I want you to take a drive with me, and try my new phaeton," said Lyra, coming out.

Annie now looked at it with that irresolution of hers, and Lyra commanded: "Get right in. We'll go down to the Works. You've never met my husband yet; have you, Annie?"

"No, I haven't, Lyra. I've always just missed him somehow. He seems to have been perpetually just gone to town, or not got back."

"Well, he's really at home now. And I don't mean at the house, which isn't home to him, but the Works. You've never seen the Works either, have you?"

"No, I haven't."

"Well, then, we'll just go round there, and kill two birds with one stone. I ought to show off my new phaeton to Mr. Wilmington first of all; he gave it to me. It would be kind of conjugal, or filial, or something. You know Mr. Wilmington and I are not exactly contemporaries, Annie?"

"I heard he was somewhat your senior," said Annie reluctantly.

Lyra laughed. "Well, I always say we were born in the same century, *any*way."

They came round into the region of the shops, and Lyra checked her pony in front of her husband's factory. It was not imposingly large, but, as Mrs. Wilmington caused Annie to observe, it was as big as the hat shops and as ugly as the shoe shops.

The structure trembled with the operation of its industry, and as they mounted the wooden steps to the open outside door, an inner door swung ajar for a moment, and let out a roar mingled of the hum and whirl and clash of machinery and fragments of voice, borne to them on a whiff of warm, greasy air. "Of course it doesn't smell very nice," said Lyra.

She pushed open the door of the office, and finding its first apartment empty, led the way with Annie to the inner room, where her husband sat writing at a table.

"George, I want to introduce you to Miss Kilburn."

"Oh yes, yes, yes,' said her husband, scrambling to his feet, and coming round to greet Annie. He was a small man, very bald, with a serious and wrinkled forehead, and rather austere brows; but his mouth had a furtive curl at one corner, which, with the habit he had of touching it there with the tip of his tongue, made Annie think of a cat that had been at the cream. "I've been hoping to call with Mrs. Wilmington to pay my respects; but I've been away a great deal this season, and— and—We're all very happy to have you home again, Miss

Kilburn. I've often heard my wife speak of your old days together at Hatboro'."

They fenced with some polite feints of interest in each other, the old man standing beside his writing-table, and staying himself with a shaking hand upon it.

Lyra interrupted them. "Well, I think now that Annie is here, we'd better not let her get away without showing her the Works."

"Oh—oh—decidedly! I'll go with you, with great pleasure. Ah!" He bustled about, putting the things together on his table, and then reaching for the Panama hat on a hook behind it. There was something pathetic in his eagerness to do what Lyra bade him, and Annie fancied in him the uneasy consciousness which an elderly husband might feel in the presence of those who met him for the first time with his young wife. At the outer office door they encountered Jack Wilmington.

"I'll show them through," he said to his uncle; and the old man assented with, "Well, perhaps you'd better, Jack," and went back to his room.

The Wilmington Stocking-Mills spun their own threads, and the first room was like what Annie had seen before in cotton factories, with a faint smell of oil from the machinery, and a fine snow of fluff in the air, and catching to the white-washed walls and the foul window sashes. The tireless machines marched back and forth across the floor, and the men who watched them with suicidal intensity ran after them barefooted when they made off with a broken thread, spliced it, and then escaped from them to their stations again. In other rooms, where there was a stunning whir of spindles, girls and women were at work; they looked after Lyra and her nephew from under cotton-frowsed bangs; they all seemed to know her, and returned her easy, kindly greetings with an effect of liking. From time to time, at Lyra's bidding, the young fellow explained to Annie some curious feature of the processes; in the room where the stockings were knitted she tried to understand the machinery that wrought and seemed to live before her eyes. But her mind wandered to the men and women who were operating it, and who seemed no more a voluntary part of it than all the rest, except when Jack Wilmington curtly ordered them to do this or that in illustration of some point he was explaining. She wear.ed herself, as people do in such places, in expressing her wonder at the ingenuity of the machinery; it was a relief to get away from it all into the room, cool and quiet, where half a dozen neat girls were counting and stamping the stockings with different numbers. "Here's where *I* used to work," said Lyra, "and here's where I first met Mr. Wilmington. The place is *full* of romantic associations. The stockings are all one *size*, Annie; but people like to wear different numbers, and so we try to gratify them. Which number do *you* wear? Or don't you wear the Wilmington machine-knit? *I* don't. Well, they're not *dreams* exactly, Annie, when all's said and done for them."

When they left the mill she asked Annie to come home to tea with her, saying, as if from a perception of her dislike for the young fellow, that Jack was going to Boston.

They had a long evening together, after Mr. Wilmington took himself off after tea to his study, as he called it, and remained shut in there. Annie was uneasily aware of him from time to time, but Lyra had apparently no more disturbance from his absence than from his presence, which she had managed with a frank acceptance of everything it suggested. She talked freely of her marriage, not as if it were like others, but for what it was. She showed Annie over the house, and she ended with a display of the rich dresses which he was always buying her, and which she never wore, because she never went anywhere.

Annie said she thought she would at least like to go to the seaside somewhere during the summer, but "No," Lyra said; "it would be too much trouble, and you know, Annie, I always did hate *trouble*. I don't want the care of a cottage, and I don't want to be poked into a hotel, so I stay in Hatboro'." She said that she had always been a village girl, and did not miss the interests of a larger life, as she caught glimpses of them in South Hatboro', or want the bother of them. She said she studied music a little, and confessed that she read a good deal, novels mostly, though the library was handsomely equipped with well-bound general literature.

At moments it all seemed no harm; at others, the luxury in which this life was so contentedly sunk oppressed Annie like a thick, close air. Yet she knew that Lyra was kind to many of the poor people about her, and did a great deal of good, as the phrase is, with the superfluity which it involved no self-denial to give from. But Mr. Peck had given her a point of view, and though she believed she did not agree with him, she could not escape from it.

Lyra told her much about people in Hatboro', and characterised them all so humorously, and she seemed so good-natured, in her ridicule which spared nobody.

She shrieked with laughter about Mr. Brandreth when Annie told her of his mother's doubt whether his love-making with Miss Northwick ought to be tacit or explicit in the kissing and embracing between Romeo and Juliet.

"Don't you think, Annie, we'd better refer him to Mr. Peck? I *should* like to hear Mr. Brandreth and Mr. Peek discussing it. I must tell Jack about it. I might get him to ask Sue Northwick, and get her ideas."

"Has Mr. Wilmington known the Northwicks long?" Annie asked.

"He used to go to their Boston house when he was at Harvard."

"Oh, then," said Annie, "perhaps *he* accounts for her playing Juliet; though, as Tybalt, I don't see exactly how he—"

"Oh, it's at the rehearsals, you know, that the fun is, and then it don't matter what part you have."

Annie lay awake a long time that night. She was sure that she ought not to like Lyra if she did not approve of her, and that she ought not to have gone home to tea with her and spent the evening with her unless she fully respected her. But she had to own to herself that she did like her, and enjoyed hearing her soft drawl. She tried to think how Jack Wilmington's having gone to Boston for the evening made it somehow less censurable for her to spend it with Lyra, even if she did not approve of her. As she drowsed, this became perfectly clear.

XIII

In the process of that expansion from a New England village to an American town of which Putney spoke, Hatboro' had suffered one kind of deterioration which Annie could not help noticing. She remembered a distinctly intellectual life, which might still exist in its elements, but which certainly no longer had as definite expression. There used to be houses in which people, maiden aunts and hale grandmothers, took a keen interest in literature, and read the new books and discussed them, some time after they had ceased to be new in the publishing centres, but whilst they were still not old. But now the grandmothers had died out, and the maiden aunts had faded in, and she could not find just such houses anywhere in Hatboro'. The decay of the Unitarians as a sect perhaps had something to do with the literary lapse of the place: their highly intellectualised belief had favoured taste in a direction where the more ritualistic and emotional religions did not promote it: and it is certain that they were no longer the leading people.

It would have been hard to say just who these leading people were. The old political and juristic pre-eminence which the lawyers had once enjoyed was a tradition; the learned professions yielded in distinction to the growing wealth and plutocratic influence of the prosperous manufacturers; the situation might be summed up in the fact that Colonel Marvin of the shoe interest and Mr. Wilmington now filled the place once held by Judge Kilburn and Squire Putney. The social life in private houses had undoubtedly shrunk; but it had expanded in the direction of church sociables, and it had become much more ecclesiastical in every way, without becoming more religious. As formerly, some people were acceptable, and some were not; but it was, as everywhere else, more a question of money; there was an aristocracy and a commonalty, but there was a confusion and a more ready convertibility in the materials of each.

The social authority of such a person as Mrs. Gerrish was not the only change that bewildered Annie, and the effort to extend her relations with the village people was one from which she shrank till her consciousness had more perfectly adjusted itself to the new conditions. Meanwhile Dr. Morrell came to call the night after their tea at the Putneys', and he fell into the habit of coming several nights in the week, and staying late. Sometimes he was sent for at her house by sick people, and he must have left word at his office where he was to be found.

He had spent part of his student life in Europe, and he looked back to his travel there with a fondness that the Old World inspires less and less in Americans. This, with his derivation from one of the unliterary Boston suburbs, and his unambitious residence in a place like Hatboro', gave her a sense of provinciality in him. On his part, he apparently found it droll that a woman of her acquaintance with a larger life should be willing to live in Hatboro' at all, and he seemed incredulous about her staying after summer was over. She felt that she mystified him, and sometimes she felt the pursuit of a curiosity which was a little too like a psychical diagnosis. He had a way of sitting beside her table and playing with her paper-cutter, while he submitted with a quizzical smile to her endeavours to turn him to account. She did not mind his laughing at her eagerness (a woman is willing enough to join a man in making fun of her femininity if she believes that he respects her), and she tried to make him talk about Hatboro', and tell her how she could be of use among the working people. She would have liked very much to know whether he gave his medical service gratis among them, and whether he found it a pleasure and a privilege to do so. There was one moment when she would have liked to ask him to let her be at the charges of his more indigent patients, but with the words behind her lips she perceived that it would not do. At the best, it would be taking his opportunity from him and making it hers. She began to see that one ought to have a conscience about doing good.

She let the chance of proposing this impossibility go by; and after a little silence Dr. Morrell seemed to revert, in her interest, to the economical situation in Hatboro'.

"You know that most of the hands in the hat-shops are from the farms around; and some of them own property here in the village. I know the owner of three small houses who's always worked in the shops. You couldn't very well offer help to a landed proprietor like that?"

"No," said Annie, abashed in view of him.

"I suppose you ought to go to a factory town like Fall River, if you really wanted to deal with overwork and squalor."

"I'm beginning to think there's no such thing anywhere," she said desperately.

The doctor's eyes twinkled sympathetically. "I don't know whether Benson earned his three houses altogether in the hat-shops. He 'likes a good horse,' as he says; and he likes to trade it for a better; I know that from experience. But he's a great friend of mine. Well, then, there are more women than men in the shops, and they earn more. I suppose that's rather disappointing too."

"It is, rather."

"But, on the other hand, the work only lasts eight months of the year, and that cuts wages down to an average of a dollar a day."

"Ah!" cried Annie. "There's some hope in *that*! What do they do when the work stops?"

"Oh, they go back to their country-seats."

"All?"

"Perhaps not all."

"I *thought* so!"

"Well, you'd better look round among those that stay."

Even among these she looked in vain for destitution; she could find that in satisfactory degree only in straggling veterans of the great army of tramps which once overran country places in the summer.

She would have preferred not to see or know the objects of her charity, and because she preferred this she forced herself to face their distasteful misery. Mrs. Bolton had orders to send no one from the door who asked for food or work, but to call Annie and let her judge the case. She knew that it was folly, and she was afraid it was worse, but she could not send the homeless creatures away as hungry or poor as they came. They filled her gentlewoman's soul with loathing; but if she kept beyond the range of the powerful corporeal odour that enveloped them, she could experience the luxury of pity for them. The filthy rags that caricatured them, their sick or sodden faces, always frowsed with a week's beard, represented typical poverty to her, and accused her comfortable state with a poignant contrast; and she consoled herself as far as she could with the superstition that in meeting them she was fulfilling a duty sacred in proportion to the disgust she felt in the encounter.

The work at the hat-shops fell off after the spring orders, and did not revive till the beginning of August. If there was less money among the hands and their families who remained than there was in time of full work, the weather made less demand upon their resources. The children lived mostly out-of-doors, and seemed to have always what they wanted of the season's fruit and vegetables. They got these too late from the decaying lots at the provision stores, and too early from the nearest orchards; and Dr. Morrell admitted that there was a good deal of sickness, especially among the little ones, from this diet. Annie wondered whether she ought not to offer herself as a nurse among them; she asked him whether she could not be of use in that way, and had to confess that she knew nothing about the prevailing disease.

"Then, I don't think you'd better undertake it," he said. "There are too many nurses there already, such as they are. It's the dull time in most of the shops, you know, and the women have plenty of leisure. There are about five volunteer nurses for every patient, not counting the grandmothers on both sides. I think they would resent any outside aid."

"Ah, I'm always on the outside! But can't I send—I mean carry—them anything nourishing, any little dishes—"

"Arrowroot is about all the convalescents can manage." She made a note of it. "But jelly and chicken broth are always relished by their friends."

"Dr. Morrell, I must ask you not to turn me into ridicule, if you please. I cannot permit it."

"I beg your pardon—I do indeed, Miss Kilburn. I didn't mean to ridicule you. I began seriously, but I was led astray by remembering what becomes of most of the good things sent to sick people."

"I know," she said, breaking into a laugh. "I have eaten lots of them for my father. And is arrowroot the only thing?"

The doctor reflected gravely. "Why, no. There's a poor little life now and then that might be saved by the sea-air. Yes, if you care to send some of my patients, with a mother and a grandmother apiece, to the seaside—"

"Don't say another word, doctor," cried Annie. "You make me *so* happy! I will—I will send their whole families. And you won't, you *won't* let a case escape, will you, doctor?" It was a break in the iron wall of uselessness which had closed her in; she behaved like a young girl with an invitation to a ball.

When the first patient came back well from the seaside her rejoicing overflowed in exultation before the friends to whom she confessed her agency in the affair. Putney pretended that he could not see what pleasure she could reasonably take in restoring the child to the sort of life it had been born to; but that was a matter she would not consider, theoretically or practically.

She began to go outside of Dr. Morrell's authority; she looked up two cases herself, and, upon advising with their grand-mothers, sent them to the seaside, and she was at the station when the train came in with the young mother and the still younger aunt of one of the sick children. She did not see the baby, and the mother passed her with a stare of impassioned reproach, and fell sobbing on the neck of her husband, waiting for her on the platform. Annie felt the blood drop back upon her heart. She caught at the girlish aunt, who was looking about her with a sense of the interest which attached to herself as a party to the spectacle.

"Oh, Rebecca, where is the child?"

"Well, there, Miss Kilburn, I'm *ril* sorry to tell you, but I guess the sea-air didn't do it a great deal of good, if any. I tell Maria she'll see it in the right light after a while, but of course she can't, first off. Well, there! *Somebody's* got to look after it. You'll excuse *me*, Miss Kilburn."

Annie saw her run off to the baggage-car, from which the baggage-man was handing out a narrow box. The ground reeled under her feet; she got the public depot carriage and drove home.

She sent for Dr. Morrell, and poured out the confession of her error upon him before he could speak. "I am a murderess," she ended hysterically. "Don't deny it!"

"I think you can be got off on the ground of insanity, Miss Kilburn, if you go on in this way," he answered.

Her desperation broke in tears. "Oh, what shall I do—what shall I do? I've killed the child!"

"Oh no, you haven't," he retorted. "I know the case. The only hope for it was the sea-air; I was going to ask you to send it—"

She took down her handkerchief and gave him a piercing look. "Dr. Morrell, if you are lying to me—"

"I'm not lying, Miss Kilburn," he answered. "You've done a very unwarrantable thing in both of the cases that you sent to the seaside on your own responsibility. One of them I certainly shouldn't have advised sending, but it's turned out well. You've no more credit for it, though, than for this that died; and you won't think I'm lying, perhaps, when I say you're equally to blame in both instances."

"I—I beg your pardon," she faltered, with dawning comfort in his severity. "I didn't mean—I didn't intend to say—"

"I know it," said Dr. Morrell, allowing himself to smile. "Just remember that you blundered into doing the only thing left to be done for Mrs. Savor's child; and—don't try it again. That's all."

He smiled once more, and at some permissive light in her face, he began even to laugh.

"You—you're horrible!"

"Oh no, I'm not," he gasped. "All the tears in the world wouldn't help; and my laughing hurts nobody. I'm sorry for you, and I'm sorry for the mother; but I've told you the truth—I have indeed; and you *must* believe me."

The child's father came to see her the next night. "Rebecca she seemed to think that you felt kind of bad, may be, because Maria wouldn't speak to you when she first got off the cars yesterday, and I don't say she done exactly right, myself. The way I look at it, and the way I tell Maria *she'd* ought to, is like this: You done what you done for the best, and we wa'n't *obliged* to take your advice anyway. But of course Maria she'd kind of set her heart on savin' it, and she can't seem to get over it right away." He talked on much longer to the same effect, tilted back in his chair, and looking down, while he covered and uncovered one of his knees with his straw hat. He had the usual rustic difficulty in getting away, but Annie was glad to keep him, in her gratitude for his kindness. Besides, she could not let him go without satisfying a suspicion she had.

"And Dr. Morrell—have you seen him for Mrs. Savor—have you—" She stopped, for shame of her hypocrisy.

"No, 'm. We hain't seen him *sence*. I guess she'll get along."

It needed this stroke to complete her humiliation before the single-hearted fellow.

"I—I suppose," she stammered out, "that you—your wife, wouldn't like me to come to the—I can understand that; but oh! if there is anything I can do for you—flowers—or my carriage—or helping anyway—"

Mr. Savor stood up. "I'm much obliged to *you*, Miss Kilburn; but we thought we hadn't better wait, well not a great while, and—the funeral was this afternoon. Well, I wish you good evening."

She met the mother, a few days after, in the street; with an impulse to cross over to the other side she advanced straight upon her.

"Mrs. Savor! What can I say to you?"

"Oh, I don't presume but what you meant for the best, Miss Kilburn. But I guess I shall know what to do next time. I kind of felt the whole while that it was a resk. But it's all right now."

Annie realised, in her resentment of the poor thing's uncouth sorrow, that she had spoken to her with the hope of getting, not giving, comfort.

"Yes, yes," she confessed. "I was to blame." The bereaved mother did not gainsay her, and she felt that, whatever was the justice of the case, she had met her present deserts.

She had to bear the discredit into which the seaside fell with the mothers of all the other sick children. She tried to bring Dr. Morrell once to the consideration of her culpability in the case of those who might have lived if the case of Mrs. Savor's baby had not frightened their mothers from sending them to the seaside; but he refused to grapple with the problem. She was obliged to believe him when he said he should not have advised sending any of the recent cases there; that the disease was changing its character, and such a course could have done no good.

"Look here, Miss Kilburn," he said, after scanning her face sharply, "I'm going to leave you a little tonic. I think you're rather run down."

"Well," she said passively.

XIV

It was in her revulsion from the direct beneficence which had proved so dangerous that Annie was able to give herself to the more general interests of the Social Union. She had not the courage to test her influence for it among the workpeople whom it was to entertain and elevate, and whose co-operation Mr. Peck had thought important; but she went about among the other classes, and found a degree of favour and deference which surprised her, and an ignorance of what lay so heavy on her heart which was still more comforting. She was nowhere treated as the guilty wretch she called herself; some who knew of the facts had got them wrong; and she discovered what must always astonish the inquirer below the pretentious surface of our democracy—an indifference and an incredulity concerning the feelings of people of lower station which could not be surpassed in another civilisation. Her concern for Mrs. Savor was treated as a great trial for Miss Kilburn; but the mother's bereavement was regarded as something those people were used to, and got over more easily than one could imagine.

Annie's mission took her to the ministers of the various denominations, and she was able to overcome any scruples they might have about the theatricals by urging the excellence of their object. As a Unitarian, she was not prepared for the liberality with which the matter was considered; the Episcopalians of course were with her; but the Universalist minister himself was not more friendly than the young Methodist preacher, who volunteered to call with her on the pastor of the Baptist church, and help present the affair in the right light;

she had expected a degree of narrow-mindedness, of bigotry, which her sect learned to attribute to others in the militant period before they had imbibed so much of its own tolerance.

But the recollection of what had passed with Mr. Peck remained a reproach in her mind, and nothing that she accomplished for the Social Union with the other ministers was important. In her vivid reveries she often met him, and combated his peculiar ideas, while she admitted a wrong in her own position, and made every expression of regret, and parted from him on the best terms, esteemed and complimented in high degree; in reality she saw him seldom, and still more rarely spoke to him, and then with a distance and conscious-ness altogether different from the effects dramatised in her fancy. Sometimes during the period of her interest in the sick children of the hands, she saw him in their houses, or coming and going outside; but she had no chance to speak with him, or else said to herself that she had none, because she was ashamed before him. She thought he avoided her; but this was probably only a phase of the impersonality which seemed characteristic of him in everything. At these times she felt a strange pathos in the lonely man whom she knew to be at odds with many of his own people, and she longed to interpret herself more sympathetically to him, but actually confronted with him she was sensible of something cold and even hard in the nimbus her compassion cast about him. Yet even this added to the mystery that piqued her, and that loosed her fancy to play, as soon as they parted, in conjecture about his past life, his marriage, and the mad wife who had left him with the child he seemed so ill-fitted to care for. Then, the next time they met she was abashed with the recollection of having unwarrantably romanced the plain, simple, homely little man, and she added an embarrassment of her own to that shyness of his which kept them apart.

Except for what she had heard Putney say, and what she learned casually from the people themselves, she could not have believed he ever did anything for them. He came and went so elusively, as far as Annie was concerned, that she knew of his presence in the houses of sickness and death usually by his little girl, whom she found playing about in the street before the door with the children of the hands. She seemed to hold her own among the others in their plays and their squabbles; if she tried to make up to her, Idella smiled, but she would not be approached, and Annie's heart went out to the little mischief in as helpless goodwill as toward the minister himself.

She used to hear his voice through the summer-open windows when he called upon the Boltons, and wondered if some accident would not bring them together, but she had to send for Mrs. Bolton at last, and bid her tell Mr. Peck that she would like to see him before he went away, one night. He came, and then she began a parrying parley of preliminary nothings before she could say that she supposed he knew the ladies were going on with their scheme for the establishment of the Social Union; he admitted vaguely that he had heard something to that effect, and she added that the invited dance and supper had been given up.

He remained apparently indifferent to the fact, and she hurried on: "And I ought to say, Mr. Peck, that nearly every one— every one whose opinion you would value—agreed with you that it would have been extremely ill-advised, and—and shocking. And I'm quite ashamed that I should not have seen it from the beginning; and I hope—I hope you will forgive me if I said things in my—my excitement that must have—I mean not only what I said to you, but what I said to others; and I assure you that I regret them, and—"

She went on and repeated herself at length, and he listened patiently, but as if the matter had not really concerned either of them personally. She had to conclude that what she had said of him had not reached him, and she ended by confessing that she had clung to the Social Union project because it seemed the only thing in which her attempts to do good were not mischievous.

Mr. Peck's thin face kindled with a friendlier interest than it had shown while the question at all related to himself, and a light of something that she took for humorous compassion came into his large, pale blue eyes. At least it was intelligence; and perhaps the woman nature craves this as much as it is supposed to crave sympathy; perhaps the two are finally one.

"I want to tell you something, Mr. Peck—an experience of mine," she said abruptly, and without trying to connect it obviously with what had gone before, she told him the story of her ill-fated beneficence to the Savors. He listened intently, and at the end he said: "I understand. But that is sorrow you have caused, not evil; and what we intend in goodwill must not rest a burden on the conscience, no matter how it turns out. Otherwise the moral world is no better than a crazy dream, without plan or sequence. You might as well rejoice in an evil deed because good happened to come of it."

"Oh, I *thank* you!" she gasped. "You don't know what a load you have lifted from me!"

Her words feebly expressed the sense of deliverance which overflowed her heart. Her strength failed her like that of a person suddenly relieved from some great physical stress or peril; but she felt that he had given her the truth, and she held fast by it while she went on.

"If you knew, or if any one knew, how difficult it, is, what a responsibility, to do the least thing for others! And once it seemed so simple! And it seems all the more difficult, the more means you have for doing good. The poor people seem to help one another without doing any harm, but if *I* try it—"

"Yes," said the minister, "it is difficult to help others when we cease to need help ourselves. A" man begins poor, or his father or grandfather before him—it doesn't matter how far back he begins—and then he is in accord and full understanding with all the other poor in the world; but as he prospers he withdraws from them and loses their point of view. Then when he offers help, it is not as a brother of those who need it, but a patron, an agent of the false state of things in which want is possible; and his help is not an impulse of the love that ought to bind us all together, but a compromise proposed by iniquitous social conditions, a peace-offering to his own guilty consciousness of his share in the wrong."

"Yes," said Annie, too grateful for the comfort he had given her to question words whose full purport had not perhaps reached her. "And I assure you, Mr. Peck, I feel very differently about these things since I first talked with you. And I wish to tell you, in justice to myself, that I had no idea then that—that—you were speaking from your own experience when you—you said how working people looked at things. I didn't know that you had been—that is, that—"

"Yes," said the minister, coming to her relief, "I once worked in a cotton-mill. Then," he continued, dismissing the personal concern, "it seems to me that I saw things in their right light, as I have never been able to see them since—"

"And how brutal," she broke in, "how cruel and vulgar, what I said must have seemed to you!"

"I fancied," he continued evasively, "that I had authority to set myself apart from my fellow-workmen, to be a teacher and guide to the true life. But it was a great error. The true life was the life of work, and no one ever had authority to turn from it. Christ Himself came as a labouring man."

"That is true," said Annie; and his words transfigured the man who spoke them, so that her heart turned reverently toward him. "But if you had been meant to work in a mill all your life," she pursued, "would you have been given the powers you have, and that you have just used to save me from despair?"

The minister rose, and said, with a sigh: "No one was meant to work in a mill all his life. Good night."

She would have liked to keep him longer, but she could not think how, at once. As he turned to go out through the Boltons' part of the house, "Won't you go out through my door?" she asked, with a helpless effort at hospitality.

"Oh, if you wish," he answered submissively.

When she had closed the door upon him she went to speak with Mrs. Bolton. She was in the kitchen mixing flour to make bread, and Annie traced her by following the lamp-light through the open door. It discovered Bolton sitting in the outer doorway, his back against one jamb and his stocking-feet resting against the base of the other.

"Mrs. Bolton," Annie began at once, making herself free of one of the hard kitchen chairs, "how is Mr. Peck getting on in Hatboro'?"

"I d'know as I know just what you mean, Miss Kilburn," said Mrs. Bolton, on the defensive.

"I mean, is there a party against him in his church? Is he unpopular?"

Mrs. Bolton took some flour and sprinkled it on her bread-board; then she lifted the mass of dough out of the trough before her, and let it sink softly upon the board.

"I d'know as you can say he's unpoplah. He ain't poplah with some. Yes, there's a party—the Gerrish party."

"Is it a strong one?"

"It's pretty strong."

"Do you think it will prevail?"

"Well, most o' folks don't know *what* they want; and if there's some folks that know what they *don't* want, they can generally

W. D. Howells

keep from havin' it."

Bolton made a soft husky prefatory noise of protest in his throat, which seemed to stimulate his wife to a more definite assertion, and she cut in before he could speak—

"*I* should say that unless them that stood Mr. Peck's friends first off, and got him here, done something to keep him, his enemies wa'n't goin' to take up his cause."

Annie divined a personal reproach for Bolton in the apparent abstraction.

"Oh, now, you'll see it'll all come out right in the end, Pauliny," he mildly opposed. "There ain't any such great feelin' about Mr. Peck; nothin' but what'll work itself off perfec'ly natural, give it time. It's goin' to come out all right."

"Yes, at the day o' jedgment," Mrs. Bolton assented, plunging her fists into the dough, and beginning to work a contempt for her husband's optimism into it.

"Yes, an' a good deal before," he returned. "There's always somethin' to objec' to every minister; we ain't any of us perfect, and Mr. Peck's got his failin's; he hain't built up the church quite so much as some on 'em expected but what he would; and there's some that don't like his prayers; and some of 'em thinks he ain't doctrinal enough. But I guess, take it all round, he suits pretty well. It'll come out all right, Pauliny. You'll see."

A pause ensued, of which Annie felt the awfulness. It seemed to her that Mrs. Bolton's impatience with this intolerable hopefulness must burst violently. She hastened to interpose. "I think the trouble is that people don't fully understand Mr. Peck at first. But they do finally."

"Yes; take time," said Bolton.

"Take eternity, I guess, for some," retorted his wife. "If you think William B. Gerrish is goin' to work round with time—" She stopped for want of some sufficiently rejectional phrase, and did not go on.

"The way I look at it," said Bolton, with incorrigible courage, "is like this: When it comes to anything like askin' Mr. Peck to resign, it'll develop his strength. You can't tell how strong he is without you try to git red of him. I 'most wish it would come, once, fair and square."

"I'm sure you're right, Mr. Bolton," said Annie. "I don't believe that your church would let such a man go when it really came to it. Don't they all feel that he has great ability?"

"Oh, I guess they appreciate him as far forth as ability goes. Some on 'em complains that he's a little *too* intellectial, if anything. But I tell 'em it's a good fault; it's a thing that can be got over in time."

Mrs. Bolton had ceased to take part in the discussion. She finished kneading her dough, and having fitted it into two baking-pans and dusted it with flour, she laid a clean towel over both. But when Annie rose she took the lamp from the mantel-shelf, where it stood, and held it up for her to find her way back to her own door.

Annie went to bed with a spirit lightened as well as chastened, and kept saying over the words of Mr. Peck, so as to keep fast hold of the consolation they had given her. They humbled her with, a sense of his wisdom and insight; the thought of them kept her awake. She remembered the tonic that Dr. Morrell had left with her, and after questioning whether she really needed it now, she made sure by getting up and taking it.

XV

The spring had filled and flushed into summer. Bolton had gone over the grass on the slope before the house, and it was growing thick again, dark green above the yellow of its stubble, and the young generation of robins was foraging in it for the callow grasshoppers. Some boughs of the maples were beginning to lose the elastic upward lift of their prime, and to hang looser and limper with the burden of their foliage. The elms drooped lower toward the grass, and swept the straggling tops left standing in their shade.

The early part of September had been fixed for the theatricals. Annie refused to have anything to do with them, and the preparations remained altogether with Brandreth. "The minuet," he said to her one afternoon, when he had come to report to her as a co-ordinate authority, "is going to be something exquisite, I assure you. A good many of the ladies studied it in the Continental times, you know, when we had all those Martha Washington parties—or, I forgot you were out of the country—and it will be done perfectly. We're going to have the ball-room scene on the tennis-court just in front of the evergreens, don't you know, and then the balcony scene in the same place. We have to cut some of the business between Romeo and Juliet, because it's too long, you know, and some of it's too—too passionate; we couldn't do it properly, and we've decided to leave it out. But we sketch along through the play, and we have Friar Laurence coming with Juliet out of his cell onto the tennis-court and meeting Romeo; so that tells the story of the marriage. You can't imagine what a Mercutio Mr.

Putney makes; he throws himself into it heart and soul, especially where he fights with Tybalt and gets killed. I give him lines there out of other scenes too; the tennis-court sets that part admirably; they come out of a street at the side. I think the scenery will surprise you, Miss Kilburn. Well, and then we have the Nurse and Juliet, and the poison scene—we put it into the garden, on the tennis-court, and we condense the different acts so as to give an idea of all that's happened, with Romeo banished, and all that. Then he comes back from Mantua, and we have the tomb scene set at one side of the tennis-court just opposite the street scene; and he fights with Paris; and then we have Juliet come to the door of the tomb— it's a liberty, of course; but we couldn't arrange the light inside—and she stabs herself and falls on Romeo's body, and that ends the play. You see, it gives a notion of the whole action, and tells the story pretty well. I think you'll be pleased."

"I've no doubt I shall," said Annie. "Did you make the adaptation yourself, Mr. Brandreth?"

"Well, yes, I did," Mr. Brandreth modestly admitted. "It's been a good deal of work, but it's been a pleasure too. You know how that is, Miss Kilburn, in your charities."

"*Don't* speak of my charities, Mr. Brandreth. I'm not a charitable person."

"You won't get people to believe *that*" said Mr. Brandreth. "Everybody knows how much good you do. But, as I was saying, my idea was to give a notion of the whole play in a series of passages or tableaux. Some of my friends think I've succeeded so well in telling the story, don't you know, without a change of scene, that they're urging me to publish my arrangement for the use of out-of-door theatricals."

"I should think it would be a very good idea," said Annie. "I suppose Mr. Chapley would do it?"

"Well, I don't know—I don't know," Mr. Brandreth answered, with a note of trouble in his voice. "I'm afraid not," he added sadly. "Miss Kilburn, I've been put in a very unfair position by Miss Northwick's changing her mind about Juliet, after the part had been offered to Miss Chapley. I've been made the means of a seeming slight to Miss Chapley, when, if it hadn't been for the cause, I'd rather have thrown up the whole affair. She gave up the part instantly when she heard that Miss Northwick wished to change her mind, but all the same I know—."

He stopped, and Annie said encouragingly: "Yes, I see. But perhaps she doesn't really care."

"That's what she said," returned Mr. Brandreth ruefully. "But I don't know. I have never spoken of it with her since I went to tell her about it, after I got Miss Northwick's note."

"Well, Mr. Brandreth, I think you've really been victimised; and I don't believe the Social Union will ever be worth what it's costing."

"I was sure you would appreciate—would understand;" and Mr. Brandreth pressed her hand gratefully in leave-taking.

She heard him talking with some one at the gate, whose sharp, "All right, my son!" identified Putney.

She ran to the door to welcome him.

"Oh, you're *both* here!' she rejoiced, at sight of Mrs. Putney too.

"I can send Ellen home," suggested Putney.

"Oh *no*, indeed!" said Annie, with single-mindedness at which she laughed with Mrs. Putney. "Only it seemed too good to have you both," she explained, kissing Mrs. Putney. "I'm so glad to see you!"

"Well, what's the reason?" Putney dropped into a chair and began to rock nervously. "Don't be ashamed: we're *all* selfish. Has Brandreth been putting up any more jobs on you?"

"No, no! Only giving me a hint of his troubles and sorrows with those wretched Social Union theatricals. Poor young fellow! I'm sorry for him. He is really very sweet and unselfish. I like him."

"Yes, Brandreth is one of the most lady-like fellows I ever saw," said Putney. "That Juliet business has pretty near been the death of him. I told him to offer Miss Chapley some other part—Rosaline, the part of the young lady who was dropped; but he couldn't seem to see it. Well, and how come on the good works, Annie?"

"The good works! Ralph, tell me: *do* people think me a charitable person? Do they suppose I've done or can do any good whatever?" She looked from Putney to his wife, and back again with comic entreaty.

"Why, aren't you a charitable person? Don't you do any good?" he asked.

"No!" she shouted. "Not the least in the world!"

"It is pretty rough," said Putney, taking out a cigar for a dry smoke; "and nobody will believe me when I report what you say, Annie. Mrs. Munger is telling round that she don't see how you can live through the summer at the rate you're going. She's got it down pretty cold about your taking Brother Peck's idea of the invited dance and supper, and joining hands with him to save the vanity of the self-respecting poor. She says that your suppression of that one unpopular feature has done more than anything else to promote the success of the Social Union. You ought to be glad Brother Peck is coming to the show."

"To the theatricals?"

Putney nodded his head. "That's what he says. I believe Brother Peck is coming to see how the upper classes amuse themselves when they really try to benefit the lower classes."

Annie would not laugh at his joke. "Ralph," she asked, "is it true that Mr. Peck is so unpopular in his church? Is he really going to be turned out—dismissed?"

"Oh, I don't know about that. But they'll bounce him if they can."

"And can nothing be done? Can't his friends unite?"

"Oh, they're united enough now; what they're afraid of is that they're not numerous enough. Why don't you buy in, Annie, and help control the stock? That old Unitarian concern of yours isn't ever going to get into running order again, and if you owned a pew in Ellen's church you could have a vote in church meeting, after a while, and you could lend Brother Peck your moral support now."

"I never liked that sort of thing, Ralph. I shouldn't believe with your people."

"Ellen's people, please. *I* don't believe with them either. But I always vote right. Now you think it over."

"No, I shall not think it over. I don't approve of it. If I should take a pew in your church it would be simply to hear Mr. Peck preach, and contribute toward his—"

"Salary? Yes, that's the way to look at it in the beginning. I knew you'd work round. Why, Annie, in a year's time you'll be trying to *buy* votes for Brother Peck."

"I should *never* vote," she retorted. "And I shall keep myself out of all temptation by not going to your church."

"Ellen's church," Putney corrected.

She went the next Sunday to hear Mr. Peck preach, and Putney, who seemed to see her the moment she entered the church, rose, as the sexton was showing her up the aisle, and opened the door of his pew for her with ironical welcome.

"You can always have a seat with us, Annie," he mocked, on their way out of the church together.

"Thank you, Ralph," she answered boldly. "I'm going to speak to the sexton for a pew."

XVI

A wire had been carried from the village to the scene of the
play at South Hatboro', and electric globes fizzed and hissed
overhead, flooding the open tennis-court with the radiance of
sharper moonlight, and stamping the thick velvety shadows of
the shrubbery and tree-tops deep into the raw green of the
grass along its borders.

The spectators were seated on the verandas and terraced turf at
the rear of the house, and they crowded the sides of the court
up to a certain point, where a cord stretched across it kept
them from encroaching upon the space intended for the
action. Another rope enclosed an area all round them, where
chairs and benches were placed for those who had tickets. After
the rejection of the exclusive feature of the original plan, Mrs.
Munger had liberalised more and more: she caused it to be
known that all who could get into her grounds would be
welcome on the outside of that rope, even though they did not
pay anything; but a large number of tickets had been sold to
the hands, as well as to the other villagers, and the area within
the rope was closely packed. Some of the boys climbed the
neighbouring trees, where from time to time the town
authorities threatened them, but did not really dislodge them.

Annie, with other friends of Mrs. Munger, gained a reserved
seat on the veranda through the drawing-room windows; but
once there, she found herself in the midst of a sufficiently
mixed company.

"How do, Miss Kilburn? That you? Well, I declare!" said a voice that she seemed to know, in a key of nervous excitement. Mrs. Savor's husband leaned across his wife's lap and shook hands with Annie. "William thought I better come," Mrs. Savor seemed called upon to explain. "I got to do *something*. Ain't it just too cute for anything the way they got them screens worked into the shrubbery down they-ar? It's like the cycloraymy to Boston; you can't tell where the ground ends and the paintin' commences. Oh, I do want 'em to *begin*!"

Mr. Savor laughed at his wife's impatience, and she said playfully: "What you laughin' at? I guess you're full as excited as what I be, when all's said and done."

There were other acquaintances of Annie's from Over the Track, in the group about her, and upon the example of the Savors they all greeted her. The wives and sweethearts tittered with self-derisive expectation; the men were gravely jocose, like all Americans in unwonted circumstances, but they were respectful to the coming performance, perhaps as a tribute to Annie. She wondered how some of them came to have those seats, which were reserved at an extra price; she did not allow for that self-respect which causes the American workman to supply himself with the best his money can buy while his money lasts.

She turned to see who was on her other hand. A row of three small children stretched from her to Mrs. Gerrish, whom she did not recognise at first. "Oh, Emmeline!" she said; and then, for want of something else, she added, "Where is Mr. Gerrish? Isn't he coming?"

"He was detained at the store," said Mrs. Gerrish, with cold importance; "but he will be here. May I ask, Annie," she pursued solemnly, "how you got here?"

"How did I get here? Why, through the windows. Didn't you?"

"May I ask who had charge of the arrangements?"

"I don't know, I'm sure," said Annie. "I suppose Mrs. Munger."

A burst of music came from the dense shadow into which the group of evergreens at the bottom of the tennis-court deepened away from the glister of the electrics. There was a deeper hush; then a slight jarring and scraping of a chair beyond Mrs. Gerrish, who leaned across her children and said, "He's come, Annie—right through the parlour window!" Her voice was lifted to carry above the music, and all the people near were able to share the fact that righted Mrs. Gerrish in her own esteem.

From the covert of the low pines in the middle of the scene Miss Northwick and Mr. Brandreth appeared hand in hand, and then the place filled with figures from other apertures of the little grove and through the artificial wings at the sides, and walked the minuet. Mr. Fellows, the painter, had helped with the costumes, supplying some from his own artistic properties, and mediavalising others; the Boston costumers had been drawn upon by the men; and they all moved through the stately figures with a security which discipline had given them. The broad solid colours which they wore took the light and shadow with picturesque effectiveness; the masks contributed a sense of mystery novel in Hatboro', and kept the friends of the dancers in exciting doubt of their identity; the strangeness of the audience to all spectacles of the sort held its judgment in suspense. The minuet was encored, and had to be given again, and it was some time before the applause of the repetition allowed the characters to be heard when the partners of the minuet began to move about arm in arm, and the drama properly began. When the applause died away it was still not easy to hear; a boy in one of the trees called, "Louder!" and made some of the people laugh, but for the rest they were very orderly throughout.

Toward the end of the fourth act Annie was startled by a child dashing itself against her knees, and breaking into a gurgle of shy laughter as children do.

"Why, you little witch!" she said to the uplifted face of Idella Peck. "Where is your father?"

"Oh, somewhere," said the child, with entire ease of mind.

"And your hat?" said Annie, putting her hand on the curly bare head—"where's your hat?"

"On the ground."

"On the ground—where?"

"Oh, I don't know," said Idella lightly, as if the pursuit bored her.

Annie pulled her up on her lap. "Well, now, you stay here with me, if you please, till your papa or your hat comes after you."

"My—hat—can't—come—after—me!" said the child, turning back her head, so as to laugh her sense of the joke in Annie's face.

"No matter; your papa can, and I'm going to keep you."

Idella let her head fall back against Annie's breast, and began to finger the rings on the hand which Annie laid across her lap to keep her.

"For goodness gracious!" said Mrs. Savor, "who you got there, Miss Kilburn?"

"Mr. Peck's little girl."

"Where'd she spring from?"

Mrs. Gerrish leaned forward and spoke across the six legs of

W. D. Howells

her children, who were all three standing up in their chairs: "You don't mean to say that's Idella Peck? Where's her father?"

"Somewhere, she says," said Annie, willing to answer Mrs. Gerrish with the child's nonchalance.

"Well, that's great!" said Mrs. Gerrish. "I should think he better be looking after her—or some one."

The music ceased, and the last act of the play began. Before it ended, Idella had fallen asleep, and Annie sat still with her after the crowd around her began to break up. Mrs. Savor kept her seat beside Annie. She said, "Don't you want I should spell you a little while, Miss Kilburn?" She leaned over the face of the sleeping child. "Why, she ain't much more than a baby! William, you go and see if you can't find Mr. Peck. I'm goin' to stay here with Miss Kilburn." Her husband humoured her whim, and made his way through the knots and clumps of people toward the rope enclosing the tennis-court. "Won't you let me hold her, Miss Kilburn?" she pleaded again.

"No, no; she isn't heavy; I like to hold her," replied Annie. Then something occurred to her, and she started in amazement at herself.

"Or yes, Mrs. Savor, you *may* take her a while;" and she put the child into the arms of the bereaved creature, who had fallen desolately back in her chair. She hugged Idella up to her breast, and hungrily mumbled her with kisses, and moaned out over her, "Oh dear! Oh my! Oh my!"

XVII

The people beyond the rope had nearly all gone away, and Mr. Savor was coming back across the court with Mr. Peck. The players appeared from the grove at the other end of the court in their vivid costumes, chatting and laughing with their friends, who went down from the piazzas and terraces to congratulate them. Mrs. Munger hurried about among them, saying something to each group. She caught sight of Mr. Peck and Mr. Savor, and she ran after them, arriving with them where Annie sat.

"I hope you were not anxious about Idella," Annie said, laughing.

"No; I didn't miss her at once," said the minister simply; "and then I thought she had merely gone off with some of the other children who were playing about."

"You shall talk all that over later," said Mrs. Munger. "Now, Miss Kilburn, I want you and Mr. Peck and Mr. and Mrs. Savor to stay for a cup of coffee that I'm going to give our friends out there. Don't you think they deserve it? Wasn't it a wonderful success? They must be frightfully exhausted. Just go right out to them. I'll be with you in one moment. Oh yes, the child! Well, bring her into the house, Mrs. Savor; I'll find a place for her, and then you can go out with me."

"I guess you won't get Maria away from her very easy," said Mr. Savor, laughing. His wife stood with the child's cheek pressed tight against hers.

"Oh, I'll manage that," said Mrs. Munger. "I'm counting on Mrs. Savor." She added in a hurried undertone to Annie: "I've asked a number of the workpeople to stay—representative workpeople, the foremen in the different shops and their families—and you'll find your friends of all classes together. It's a great day for the Social Union!" she said aloud. "I'm sure *you* must feel that, Mr. Peck. Miss Kilburn and I have to thank you for saving us from a great mistake at the outset, and now your staying," she continued, "will give it just the appearance we want. I'm going to keep your little girl as a hostage, and you shall not go till I let you. Come, Mrs. Savor!" She bustled away with Mrs. Savor, and Mr. Peck reluctantly accompanied Annie down over the lawn.

He was silent, but Mr. Savor was hilarious. "Well, Mr. Putney," he said, when he joined the group of which Putney was the centre, "you done that in apple-pie order. I never see anything much better than the way you carried on with Mrs. Wilmington."

"Thank you, Mr. Savor," said Putney; "I'm glad you liked it. You couldn't say I was trying to flatter her up much, anyway."

"No, no!" Mr. Savor assented, with delight in the joke.

"Well, Annie," said Putney. He shook hands with her, and Mrs. Putney, who was there with Dr. Morrell, asked her where she had sat.

"We kept looking all round for you."

"Yes," said Putney, with his hand on his boy's shoulder, "we wanted to know how you liked the Mercutio."

"Ralph, it was incomparable!"

"Well, that will do for a beginning. It's a little cold, but it's in the right spirit. You mean that the Mercutio wasn't comparable to the Nurse."

"Oh, Lyra was wonderful!" said Annie. "Don't you think so, Ellen?"

"She was Lyra," said Mrs. Putney definitely.

"No; she wasn't Lyra at all!" retorted Annie. "That was the marvel of it. She was Juliet's nurse."

"Perhaps she was a little of both," suggested Putney. "What did you think of the performance, Mr. Peck? I don't want a personal tribute, but if you offer it, I shall not be ungrateful."

"I have been very much interested," said the minister. "It was all very new to me. I realised for the first time in my life the great power that the theatre must be. I felt how much the drama could do—how much good."

"Well, that's what we're after," said Putney. "We had no personal motive; good, right straight along, was our motto. Nobody wanted to outshine anybody else. I kept my Mercutio down all through, so's not to get ahead of Romeo or Tybalt in the public esteem. Did our friends outside the rope catch on to my idea?" Mr. Peck smiled at the banter, but he seemed not to know just what to say, and Putney went on: "That's why I made it so bad. I didn't want anybody to go home feeling sorry that Mercutio was killed. I don't suppose Winthrop could have slept."

"You won't sleep yourself to-night, I'm afraid," said his wife.

"Oh, Mrs. Munger has promised me a particularly weak cup of coffee. She has got us all in, it seems, for a sort of supper, in spite of everything. I understand it includes representatives of all the stations and conditions present except the outcasts beyond the rope. I don't see what you're doing here, Mr. Peck."

"Was Mr. Peck really outside the rope?" Annie asked Dr. Morrell, as they dropped apart from the others a little.

"I believe he gave his chair to one of the women from the outside," said the doctor.

Annie moved with him toward Lyra, who was joking with some of the hands.

With all her good-nature, she had the effect of patronising them, as she stood talking about the play with them in her drawl, which she had got back to again. They were admiring her, in her dress of the querulous old nurse, and told her how they never would have known her. But there was an insincerity in the effusion of some of the more nervous women, and in the reticence of the others, who were holding back out of self-respect.

She met Annie and Morrell with eager relief. "Well, Annie?"

"Perfect!"

"Well, now, that's very nice; you can't go beyond perfect, you know. I *did* do it pretty well, didn't I? Poor Mr. Brandreth! Have you seen him? You must say something comforting to him. He's really been sacrificed in this business. You know he wanted Miss Chapley. She would have made a lovely Juliet. Of course she blames him for it. She thinks he wanted to make up to Miss Northwick, when Miss Northwick was just flinging herself at Jack. Look at her!"

Jack Wilmington and Miss Sue Northwick were standing together near her father and a party of her friends, and she was smiling and talking at him. Eyes, lips, gestures, attitude expressed in the proud girl a fawning eagerness to please the man, who received her homage rather as if it bored him. His indifferent manner may have been one secret of his power over her, and perhaps she was not capable of all the suffering she was capable of inflicting.

Lyra turned to walk toward the house, deflecting a little in the direction of her nephew and Miss Northwick. "Jack!" she drawled over the shoulder next them as she passed, "I wish you'd bring your aunty's wrap to her on the piazza."

"Why, stay here!" Putney called after her. "They're going to fetch the refreshments out here."

"Yes, but I'm tired, Ralph, and I can't sit on the grass, at my age."

She moved on, with her sweeping, lounging pace, and Jack Wilmington, after a moment's hesitation, bowed to Miss Northwick and went after her.

The girl remained apart from her friends, as if expecting his return.

Silhouetted against the bright windows, Lyra waited till Jack Wilmington reappeared with a shawl and laid it on her shoulders. Then she sank into a chair. The young man stood beside her talking down upon her. Something restive and insistent expressed itself in their respective attitudes. He sat down at her side.

Miss Northwick joined her friends carelessly.

"Ah, Miss Kilburn," said Mr. Brandreth's voice at Annie's ear, "I'm glad to find you. I've just run home with mother—she feels the night air—and I was afraid you would slip through our fingers before I got back. This little business of the refreshments was an afterthought of Mrs. Munger's, and we meant it for a surprise—we knew you'd approve of it in the form it took." He looked round at the straggling workpeople, who represented the harmonisation of classes, keeping to themselves as if they had been there alone.

"Yes," Annie was obliged to say; "it's very pleasant." She added: "You must all be rather hungry, Mr. Brandreth. If the

Social Union ever gets on its feet, it will have *you* to thank more than any one."

"Oh, don't speak of me, Miss Kilburn! Do you know, we've netted about two hundred dollars. Isn't that pretty good, doctor?"

"Very," said the doctor. "Hadn't we better follow Mrs. Wilmington's example, and get up under the piazza roof? I'm afraid you'll be the worse for the night air, Miss Kilburn. Putney," he called to his friend, "we're going up to the house."

"All right. I guess that's a good idea."

The doctor called to the different knots and groups, telling them to come up to the house. Some of the workpeople slipped away through the grounds and did not come. The Northwicks and their friends moved toward the house.

Mrs. Munger came down the lawn to meet her guests. "Ah, that's right. It's much better indoors. I was just coming for you." She addressed herself more particularly to the Northwicks. "Coffee will be ready in a few moments. We've met with a little delay."

"I'm afraid we must say good night at once," said Mr. Northwick. "We had arranged to have our friends and some other guests with us at home. And we're quite late now."

Mrs. Munger protested. "Take our Juliet from us! Oh, Miss Northwick, how can I thank you enough? The whole play turned upon you!"

"It's just as well," she said to Annie, as the Northwicks and their friends walked across the lawn to the gate, where they had carriages waiting. 'They'd have been difficult to manage, and everybody else will feel a little more at home without them. Poor Mr. Brandreth, I'm sure *you* will! I did pity you so, with such a Juliet on your hands!"

In-doors the representatives of the lower classes were less at ease than they were without. Some of the ministers mingled with them, and tried to form a bond between them and the other villagers. Mr. Peck took no part in this work; he stood holding his elbows with his hands, and talking with a perfunctory air to an old lady of his congregation.

The young ladies of South Hatboro', as Mrs. Munger's assistants, went about impartially to high and low with trays of refreshments. Annie saw Putney, where he stood with his wife and boy, refuse coffee, and she watched him anxiously when the claret-cup came. He waved his hand over it, and said, "No; I'll take some of the lemonade." As he lifted a glass of it toward his lips he stopped and made as if to put it down again, and his hand shook so that he spilled some of it. Then he dashed it off, and reached for another glass. "I want some more," he said, with a laugh; "I'm thirsty." He drank a second glass, and when he saw a tray coming toward Annie, where Dr. Morrell had joined her, he came over and exchanged his empty glass for a full one.

"Not much to brag of as lemonade," he said, "but first-rate rum punch."

"Look here, Putney," whispered the doctor, laying his hand on his arm, "don't you take any more of that. Give me that glass!"

"Oh, all right!" laughed Putney, dashing it off. "You're welcome to the tumbler, if you want it, Doc."

XVIII

Mrs. Munger's guests kept on talking and laughing. With the coffee and the punch there began to be a little more freedom. Some prohibitionists among the working people went away when they found that the lemonade was punch; but Mrs. Munger did not know it, and she saw the ideal of a Social Union figuratively accomplished in her own house. She stirred about among her guests till she produced a fleeting, empty good-fellowship among them. One of the shoe-shop hands, with an inextinguishable scent of leather and the character of a droll, seconded her efforts with noisy jokes. He proposed games, and would not be snubbed by the refusal of his boss to countenance him, he had the applause of so many others. Mrs. Munger approved of the idea.

"Don't you think it would be great fun, Mrs. Gerrish?" she asked.

"Well, now, if Squire Putney would lead off," said the joker, looking round.

Putney could not be found, nor Dr. Morrell.

"They're off somewhere for a smoke," said Mrs. Munger. "Well, that's right. I want everybody to feel that my house is their own to-night, and to come and go just as they like. Do you suppose Mr. Peck is offended?" she asked, under her breath, as she passed Annie. "He *couldn't* feel that this is the same thing; but I can't see him anywhere. He wouldn't go without taking leave, you don't suppose?"

Annie joined Mrs. Putney. They talked at first with those who came to ask where Putney and the doctor were; but finally they withdrew into a little alcove from the parlour, where Mrs. Munger approved of their being when she discovered them; they must be very tired, and ought to rest on the lounge there. Her theory of the exhaustion of those who had taken part in the play embraced their families.

The time wore on toward midnight, and her guests got themselves away with more or less difficulty as they attempted the formality of leave-taking or not. Some of the hands who thought this necessary found it a serious affair; but most of them slipped off without saying good night to Mrs. Munger or expressing that rapture with the whole evening from beginning to end which the ladies of South Hatboro' professed. The ladies of South Hatboro' and Old Hatboro' had met in a general intimacy not approached before, and they parted with a flow of mutual esteem. The Gerrish children had dropped asleep in nooks and corners, from which Mr. Gerrish hunted them up and put them together for departure, while his wife remained with Mrs. Munger, unable to stop talking, and no longer amenable to the looks with which he governed her in public.

Lyra came downstairs, hooded and wrapped for departure, with Jack Wilmington by her side. "Why, *Ellen*!" she said, looking into the little alcove from the hall. "Are you here yet? And Annie! Where in the world is Ralph?" At the pleading look with which Mrs. Putney replied, she exclaimed: "Oh, it's what I was afraid of! I don't see what the woman could have been about! But of course she didn't think of poor Ralph. Ellen, let me take you and Winthrop home! Dr. Morrell will be sure to bring Ralph."

"Well," said Mrs. Putney passively, but without rising.

"Annie can come too. There's plenty of room. Jack can walk."

Jack Wilmington joined Lyra in urging Annie to take his place. He said to her, apart, "Young Munger has been telling me that Putney got at the sideboard and carried off the rum. I'll stay and help look after him."

A crazy laugh came into the parlour from the piazza outside, and the group in the alcove started forward. Putney stood at a window, resting one arm on the bar of the long lower sash, which was raised to its full height, and looking ironically in upon Mrs. Munger and her remaining guests. He was still in his Mercutio dress, but he had lost his plumed cap, and was bareheaded. A pace or two behind him stood Mr. Peck, regarding the effect of this apparition upon the company with the same dreamy, indrawn presence he had in the pulpit.

"Well, Mrs. Munger, I'm glad I got back in time to tell you how much I've enjoyed it. Brother Peck wanted me to go home, but I told him, Not till I've thanked Mrs. Munger, Brother Peck; not till I've drunk her health in her own old particular Jamaica." He put to his lips the black bottle which he had been holding in his right hand behind him; then he took it away, looked at it, and flung it rolling-along the piazza floor. "Didn't get hold of the inexhaustible bottle that time; never do. But it's a good article; a better article than you used to sell on the sly, Bill Gerrish. You'll excuse my helping myself, Mrs. Munger; I knew you'd want me to. Well, it's been a great occasion, Mrs. Munger." He winked at the hostess. "You've had your little invited supper, after all. You're a manager, Mrs. Munger. You've made even the wrath of Brother Peck to praise you."

The ladies involuntarily shrank backward as Putney suddenly entered through the window and gained the corner of the piano at a dash. He stayed himself against it, slightly swaying, and turned his flaming eyes from one to another, as if questioning whom he should attack next.

Except for the wild look in them, which was not so much wilder than they wore in all times of excitement, and an occasional halt at a difficult word, he gave no sign of being drunk. The liquor had as yet merely intensified him.

Mrs. Munger had the inspiration to treat him as one caresses a dangerous lunatic. "I'm sure you're very kind, Mr. Putney, to come back. Do sit down!"

"Why?" demanded Putney. "Everybody else standing."

"That's true," said Mrs. Munger. "I'm sure I don't know why—"

"Oh yes, you do, Mrs. Munger. It's because they want to have a good view of a man who's made a fool of himself—"

"Oh, now, Mr. *Putney*!" said Mrs. Munger, with hospitable deprecation. "I'm sure no one wants to do anything of the kind." She looked round at the company for corroboration, but no one cared to attract Putney's attention by any sound or sign.

"But I'll tell you what," said Putney, with a savage burst, "that a woman who puts hell-fire before a poor devil who can't keep out of it when he sees it, is better worth looking at."

"Mr. Putney, I assure you," said Mrs. Munger, "that it was the *mildest* punch! And I really didn't think—I didn't remember—"

She turned toward Mrs. Putney with her explanation, but Putney seemed to have forgotten her, and he turned upon Mr. Gerrish, "How's that drunkard's grave getting along that you've dug for your porter?" Gerrish remained prudently silent. "I know you, Billy. You're all right. You've got the pull on your conscience; we all have, one way or another. Here's Annie Kilburn, come back from Rome, where she couldn't seem to fix it up with hers to suit her, and she's trying to get round it in Hatboro' with good works. Why, there isn't any occasion for good works in Hatboro'. I could have told you that before you came," he said, addressing Annie directly. "What we want is faith, and lots of it. The church is going to pieces because we haven't got any faith."

His hand slipped from the piano, and he dropped heavily back upon a chair that stood near. The concussion seemed to complete in his brain the transition from his normal dispositions to their opposite, which had already begun. "Bill Gerrish has done more for Hatboro' than any other man in the place. He's the only man that holds the church together, because he knows the value of *faith*." He said this without a trace of irony, glaring at Annie with fierce defiance. "You come back here, and try to set up for a saint in a town where William B. Gerrish has done—has done more to establish the dry-goods business on a metro-me-tro-politan basis than any other man out of New York or Boston."

He stopped and looked round, mystified, as if this were not the point which he had been aiming at.

Lyra broke into a spluttering laugh, and suddenly checked herself. Putney smiled slightly. "Pretty good, eh? Say, where was I?" he asked slyly. Lyra hid her face behind Annie's shoulder. "What's that dress you got on? What's all this about, anyway? Oh yes, I know. *Romeo and Juliet*—Social Union. Well," he resumed, with a frown, "there's too much *Romeo and Juliet*, too much Social Union, in this town already." He stopped, and seemed preparing to launch some deadly phrase at Mrs. Wilmington, but he only said, "You're all right, Lyra."

"Mrs. Munger," said Mr. Gerrish, "we must be going. Good night, ma'am. Mrs. Gerrish, it's time the children were at home."

"Of course it is," said Putney, watching the Gerrishes getting their children together. He waved his hand after them, and called out, "William Gerrish, you're a man; I honour you."

He laid hold of the piano and pulled himself to his feet, and seemed to become aware, for the first time, of his wife, where she stood with their boy beside her.

"What you doing here with that child at this time of night?" he shouted at her, all that was left of the man in his eyes changing into the glare of a pitiless brute. "Why don't you go home? You want to show people what I did to him? You want to publish my shame, do you? Is that it? Look here!"

He began to work himself along toward her by help of the piano. A step was heard on the piazza without, and Dr. Morrell entered through the open window.

"Come now, Putney," he said gently. The other men closed round them.

Putney stopped. "What's this? Interfering in family matters? You better go home and look after your own wives, if you got any. Get out the way, 'n' you mind your own business, Doc. Morrell. You meddle too much." His speech was thickening and breaking. "You think science going do everything— evolution! Talk me about evolution! What's evolution done for Hatboro'? 'Volved Gerrish's store. One day of Christianity— real Christianity—Where's that boy? If I get hold of him—"

He lunged forward, and Jack Wilmington and young Munger stepped before him.

Mrs. Putney had not moved, nor lost the look of sad, passive vigilance which she had worn since her husband reappeared.

She pushed the men aside.

"Ralph, behave yourself! *Here's* Winthrop, and we want you to take us home. Come now!" She passed her arm through his, and the boy took his other hand. The action, so full of fearless custom and wonted affection from them both, seemed with her words to operate another total change in his mood.

"All right; I'm going, Ellen. Got to say good night Mrs. Munger, that's all." He managed to get to her, with his wife on his arm and his boy at his side. "Want to thank you for a pleasant evening, Mrs. Munger—want to thank you—"

"And *I* want to thank you *too*, Mrs. Munger," said Mrs. Putney, with an intensity of bitterness no repetition of the words could give, "It's been a pleasant evening for *me*!"

Putney wished to stop and explain, but his wife pulled him away.

Dr. Morrell and Annie followed to get them safely into the carriage; he went with them, and when she came back Mrs. Munger was saying: "I will leave it to Mr. Wilmington, or any one, if I'm to blame. It had quite gone out of my head about Mr. Putney. There was plenty of coffee, besides, and if everything that could harm particular persons had to be kept out of the way, society couldn't go on. We ought to consider the greatest good of the greatest number." She looked round from one to another for support. No one said anything, and Mrs. Munger, trembling on the verge of a collapse, made a direct appeal: "Don't you think so, Mr. Peck?"

The minister broke his silence with reluctance. "It's sometimes best to have the effect of error unmistakable. Then we are sure it's error."

Mrs. Munger gave a sob of relief into her handkerchief. "Yes, that's just what I say."

Lyra bent her face on her arm, and Jack Wilmington put his head out of the window where he stood.

Mr. Peck remained staring at Mrs. Munger, as if doubtful what to do. Then he said: "You seem not to have understood me, ma'am. I should be to blame if I left you in doubt. You have been guilty of forgetting your brother's weakness, and if the consequence has promptly followed in his shame, it is for you to realise it. I wish you a good evening."

He went out with a dignity that thrilled Annie. Lyra leaned toward her and said, choking with laughter, "He's left Idella asleep upstairs. We haven't *any* of us got *perfect* memories, have we?"

"Run after him!" Annie said to Jack Wilmington, in undertone, "and get him into my carriage. I'll get the little girl. Lyra, *don't* speak of it."

"Never!" said Mrs. Wilmington, with delight. "I'm solid for Mr. Peck every time."

XIX

Annie made up a bed for Idella on a wide, old-fashioned lounge in her room, and put her away in it, swathed in a night-gown which she found among the survivals of her own childish clothing in that old chest of drawers. When she woke in the morning she looked across at the little creature, with a tender sense of possession and protection suffusing her troubled recollections of the night before. Idella stirred, stretched herself with a long sigh, and then sat up and stared round the strange place as if she were still in a dream.

"Would you like to come in here with me?" Annie suggested from her bed.

The child pushed back her hair with her little hands, and after waiting to realise the situation to the limit of her small experience, she said, with a smile that showed her pretty teeth, "Yes."

"Then come."

Idella tumbled out of bed, pulling up the nightgown, which was too long for her, and softly thumped across the carpet. Annie leaned over and lifted her up, and pressed the little face to her own, and felt the play of the quick, light breath over her cheek.

"Would you like to stay with me—live with me—Idella?" she asked.

The child turned her face away, and hid a roguish smile in the pillow. "I don't know."

"Would you like to be my little girl?"

"No."

"No? Why not?"

"Because—because"—she seemed to search her mind—"because your night-gowns are too long."

"Oh, is that all? That's no reason. Think of something else."

Idella rubbed her face hard on the pillow. "You dress up cats."

She lifted her face, and looked with eyes of laughing malice into Annie's, and Annie pushed her face against Idella's neck and cried, "You're a rogue!"

The little one screamed with laughter and gurgled: "Oh, you tickle! You tickle!"

They had a childish romp, prolonged through the details of Idella's washing and dressing, and Annie tried to lose, in her frolic with the child, the anxieties that had beset her waking; she succeeded in confusing them with one another in one dull, indefinite pain.

She wondered when Mr. Peck would come for Idella, but they were still at their belated breakfast when Mrs. Bolton came in to say that Bolton had met the minister on his way up, and had asked him if Idella might not stay the week out with them.

"I don' know but he done more'n he'd ought.

"But she can be with us the rest part, when you've got done with her."

"I haven't begun to get done with her," said Annie. "I'm glad Mr. Bolton asked."

After breakfast Bolton himself appeared, to ask if Idella might go up to the orchard with him. Idella ran out of the room and came back with her hat on, and tugging to get into her shabby little sack. Annie helped her with it, and Idella tucked her hand into Bolton's loose, hard fist, and gave it a pull toward the door.

"Well, I don't see but what she's goin'," he said.

"Yes; you'd better ask her the next time if *I* can go," said Annie.

"Well, why don't you?" asked Bolton, humouring the joke. "I guess you'd enjoy it about as well as any. We're just goin' for a basket of wind-falls for pies. I guess we ain't a-goin' to be gone a great while."

Annie watched them up the lane from the library window with a queer grudge at heart; Bolton stiffly lumbering forward at an angle of forty-five degrees, the child whirling and dancing at his side, and now before and now after him.

At the sound of wheels on the gravel before the front door, Annie turned away with such an imperative need of its being Dr. Morrell's buggy that it was almost an intolerable disappointment to find it Mrs. Munger's phaeton.

Mrs. Munger burst in upon her in an excitement which somehow had an effect of premeditation.

"Miss Kilburn, I wish to know what you think of Mr. and Mrs. Putney's behaviour to me, and Mr. Peck's, in my own house, last night. They are friends of yours, and I wish to know if you approve of it. I come to you *as* their friend, and I am sure you will feel as I do that my hospitality has been abused. It was an outrage for Mr. Putney to get intoxicated in my house; and for Mr. Peck to attack me as he did before everybody, because Mr. Putney had taken advantage of his privileges, was abominable. I am not a member of his church; and even if I were, he would have had no right to speak so to me."

Annie felt the blood fly to her head, and she waited a moment to regain her coolness. "I wonder you came to ask me, Mrs. Munger, if you were so sure that I agreed with you. I'm certainly Mr. and Mrs. Putney's friend, and so far as admiring Mr. Peck's sincerity and goodness is concerned, I'm *his* friend. But I'm obliged to say that you're mistaken about the rest."

She folded her hands at her waist, and stood up very straight, looking firmly at Mrs. Munger, who made a show of taking a new grip of her senses as she sank unbidden into a chair.

"Why, what do you mean, Miss Kilburn?"

"It seems to me that I needn't say."

"Why, but you must! You *must*, you know. I can't be *left* so! I must know where I *stand*! I must be sure of my *ground*! I can't go on without understanding just how much you mean by my being mistaken."

She looked Annie in the face with eyes superficially expressive of indignant surprise, and Annie perceived that she wished to restore herself in her own esteem by browbeating some one else into the affirmation of her innocence.

"Well, if you must know, Mrs. Munger, I mean that you ought to have remembered Mr. Putney's infirmity, and that it was cruel to put temptation in his way. Everybody knows that he can't resist it, and that he is making such a hard fight to keep out of it. And then, if you press me for an opinion, I must say that you were not justifiable in asking Mr. Peck to take part in a social entertainment when we had explicitly dropped that part of the affair."

Mrs. Munger had not pressed Annie for an opinion on this point at all; but in their interest in it they both ignored the fact. Mrs. Munger tacitly admitted her position in retorting, "He needn't have stayed."

"You made him stay—you remember how—and he couldn't have got away without being rude."

"And you think he wasn't rude to scold me before my guests?"

"He told you the truth. He didn't wish to say anything, but you forced him to speak, just as you have forced me."

"Forced *you*? Miss Kilburn!"

"Yes. I don't at all agree with Mr. Peck in many things, but he is a good man, and last night he spoke the truth. I shouldn't be speaking it if I didn't tell you I thought so."

"Very well, then," said Mrs. Munger, rising.

"After this you can't expect me to have anything to do with the Social Union; you couldn't *wish* me to, if that's your opinion of my character."

"I haven't expressed any opinion of your character, Mrs. Munger, if you'll remember, please; and as for the Social Union, I shall have nothing further to do with it myself."

Annie drew herself up a little higher, and silently waited for her visitor to go.

But Mrs. Munger remained.

"I don't believe Mrs. Putney herself would say what you have said," she remarked, after an embarrassing moment. "If it were really so I should be willing to make any reparation—to acknowledge it. Will you go with me to Mrs. Putney's? I have my phaeton here, and—"

"I shouldn't dream of going to Mrs. Putney's with you."

Mrs. Munger urged, with the effect of invincible argument: "I've been down in the village, and I've talked to a good many about it—some of them hadn't heard of it before—and I must say, Miss Kilburn, that people generally take a very different view of it from what you do. They think that my hospitality has been shamefully abused. Mr. Gates said he should think I would have Mr. Putney arrested. But I don't care for all that. What I wish is to prove to you that I am right; and if I can go with you to call on Mrs. Putney, I shall not care what any one else says. Will you come?"

"Certainly not," cried Annie.

They both stood a moment, and in this moment Dr. Morrell drove up, and dropped his hitching-weight beyond Mrs. Munger's phaeton.

As he entered she said: "We will let Dr. Morrell decide. I've been asking Miss Kilburn to go with me to Mrs. Putney's. I think it would be a graceful and proper thing for me to do, to express my sympathy and interest, and to hear what Mrs. Putney really has to say. Don't *you* think I ought to go to see her, doctor?"

The doctor laughed. "I can't prescribe in matters of social duty. But what do you want to see Mrs. Putney for?"

"What for? Why, doctor, on account of Mr. Putney—what took place last night."

"Yes? What was that?"

"What was *that*? Why, his strange behaviour—his—his intoxication."

"Was he intoxicated? Did you think so?"

"Why, you were there, doctor. Didn't you think so?"

Annie looked at him with as much astonishment as Mrs. Munger.

The doctor laughed again. "You can't always tell when Putney's joking; he's a great joker. Perhaps he was hoaxing."

"Oh doctor, do you think he *could* have been?" said Mrs. Munger, with clasped hands. "It would make me the happiest woman in the world! I'd forgive him all he's made me suffer. But *you're* joking *now*, doctor?"

"You can't tell when people are joking. If I'm not, does it follow that I'm really intoxicated?"

"Oh, but that's nonsense, Dr. Morrell. That's mere—what do you call it?—chop logic. But I don't mind it. I grasp at a straw." Mrs. Munger grasped at a straw of the mind, to show how. "But what *do* you mean?"

"Well, Mrs. Putney wasn't intoxicated last night, but she's not well this morning. I'm afraid she couldn't see you."

"Just as you *say*, doctor," cried Mrs. Munger, with mounting cheerfulness. "I *wish* I knew just how much you meant, and how little." She moved closer to the doctor, and bent a look of candid fondness upon him. "But I know you're trying to mystify me."

She pursued him with questions which he easily parried, smiling and laughing. At the end she left him to Annie, with adieux that were almost radiant. "Anyhow, I shall take the benefit of the doubt, and if Mr. Putney was hoaxing, I shall not give myself away. *Do* find out what he means, Miss Kilburn, won't you?" She took hold of Annie's unoffered hand, and pressed it in a double leathern grasp, and ran out of the room with a lightness of spirit which her physical bulk imperfectly expressed.

XX

"Well?" said Annie, to the change which came over Morrell's face when Mrs. Munger was gone.

"Oh, it's a miserable business! He must go on now to the end of his debauch. He's got past doing any mischief, I'm thankful to say. But I had hoped to tide him over a while longer, and now that fool has spoiled everything. Well!"

Annie's heart warmed to his vexation, and she postponed another emotion. "Yes, she *is* a fool. I wish you had qualified the term, doctor."

They looked at each other solemnly, and then laughed. "It won't do for a physician to swear," said Morrell. "I wish you'd give me a cup of coffee. I've been up all night."

"With Ralph?"

"With Putney."

"You shall have it instantly; that is, as instantly as Mrs. Bolton can kindle up a fire and make it." She went out to the kitchen, and gave the order with an imperiousness which she softened in Dr. Morrell's interest by explaining rather fully to Mrs. Bolton.

When she came back she wanted to talk seriously, tragically, about Putney. But the doctor would not. He said that it paid to sit up with Putney, drunk or sober, and hear him go on. He repeated some things Putney said about Mr. Peck, about Gerrish, about Mrs. Munger.

"But why did you try to put her off in that way—to make her believe he wasn't intoxicated?" asked Annie, venting her postponed emotion, which was of disapproval.

"I don't know. It came into my head. But she knows better."

"It was rather cruel; not that she deserves any mercy. She caught so at the idea."

"Oh yes, I saw that. She'll humbug herself with it, and you'll see that before night there'll be two theories of Putney's escapade. I think the last will be the popular one. It will jump with the general opinion of Putney's ability to carry anything out. And Mrs. Munger will do all she can to support it."

Mrs. Bolton brought in the coffee-pot, and Annie hesitated a moment, with her hand on it, before pouring out a cup.

"I don't like it," she said.

"I know you don't. But you can say that it wasn't Putney who hoaxed Mrs. Munger, but Dr. Morrell."

"Oh, you didn't either of you hoax her."

"Well, then, there's no harm done."

"I'm not so sure."

"And you won't give me any coffee?"

"Oh yes, I'll give you some *coffee*," said Annie, with a sigh of baffled scrupulosity that made them both laugh.

He broke out again after he had begun to drink his coffee.

"Well?" she demanded, from her own lapse into silence.

"Oh, nothing! Only Putney. He wants Brother Peck, as he calls him, to unite all the religious elements of Hatboro' in a church of his own, and send out missionaries to the heathen of South Hatboro' to preach a practical Christianity. He makes South Hatboro' stand for all that's worldly and depraved."

"Poor Ralph! Is that the way he talks?"

"Oh, not all the time. He talks a great many other ways."

"I wonder you can laugh."

"He's been very severe on Brother Peck for neglecting the discipline of his child. He says he ought to remember his duty to others, and save the community from having the child grow up into a capricious, wilful woman. Putney was very hard upon your sex, Miss Kilburn. He attributed nearly all the trouble in the world to women's wilfulness and caprice."

He looked across the table at her with his merry eyes, whose sweetness she felt even in her sudden preoccupation with the notion which she now launched upon him, leaning forward and pushing some books and magazines aside, as if she wished to have nothing between her need and his response.

"Dr. Morrell, what should you think of my asking Mr. Peck to give me his little girl?"

"To give you his—"

"Yes. Let me take Idella—keep her—adopt her! I've nothing to do, as you know very well, and she'd be an occupation; and it would be far better for her. What Ralph says is true. She's growing up without any sort of training; and I think if she keeps on she will be mischievous to herself and every one else."

"Really?" asked the doctor. "Is it so bad as that?"

"Of course not. And of course I don't want Mr. Peck to renounce all claim to his child; but to let me have her for the present, or indefinitely, and get her some decent clothes, and trim her hair properly, and give her some sort of instruction—"

"May I come in?" drawled Mrs. Wilmington's mellow voice, and Annie turned and saw Lyra peering round the edge of the half-opened library door. "I've been discreetly hemming and scraping and hammering on the wood-work so as not to overhear, and I'd have gone away if I hadn't been afraid of being overheard."

"Oh, come in, Lyra," said Annie; and she hoped that she had kept the spirit of resignation with which she spoke out of her voice.

Dr. Morrell jumped up with an apparent desire to escape that wounded and exasperated her. She put out her hand quite haughtily to him and asked, "Oh, must you go?"

"Yes. How do you do, Mrs. Wilmington? You'd better get Miss Kilburn to give you a cup of her coffee."

"Oh, I will," said Lyra. She forbore any reference, even by a look, to the intimate little situation she had disturbed.

Morrell added to Annie: "I like your plan. It 'a the best thing you could do."

She found she had been keeping his hand, and in the revulsion from wrath to joy she violently wrung it.

"I'm *so* glad!" She could not help following him to the door, in the hope that he would say something more, but he did not, and she could only repeat her rapturous gratitude in several forms of incoherency.

She ran back to Mrs. Wilmington. "Lyra, what do you think of my taking Mr. Peck's little girl?"

Mrs. Wilmington never allowed herself to seem surprised at anything; she was, in fact, surprised at very few things. She had got into the easiest chair in the room, and she answered from it, with a luxurious interest in the affair, "Well, you know what people will say, Annie."

"No, I don't. *What* will they say?"

"That you're after Mr. Peck pretty openly."

Annie turned scarlet. "And when they find I'm *not*?" she demanded with severity, that had no effect upon Lyra.

"Then they'll say you couldn't get him."

"They may say what they please. What do you think of the plan?"

"I think it would be the greatest blessing for the poor little thing," said Lyra, with a nearer approach to seriousness than she usually made. "And the greatest care for you," she added, after a moment.

"I shall not care for the care. I shall be glad of it—thankful for it," cried Annie fervidly.

"If you can get it," Lyra suggested.

"I believe I can get it. I believe I can make Mr. Peck see that it's a duty. I shall ask him to regard it as a charity to me—as a mercy."

"Well, that's a good way to work upon Mr. Peck's feelings," said Lyra demurely. "Was that the plan that Dr. Morrell approved of so highly?"

"Yes."

"I didn't know but it was some course of treatment. You pressed his hand so affectionately. I said to myself, Well, Annie's either an enthusiastic patient, or else—"

"What?" demanded Annie, at the little stop Lyra made.

"Well, you know what people do *say*, Annie."

"What?"

"Why, that you're very much out of health, or—" Lyra made another of her tantalising stops.

"Or what?"

"Or Dr. Morrell is very much in love."

"Lyra, I can't allow you to say such things to me."

"No; that's what I've kept saying to myself all the time. But you would have it *out* of me. *I* didn't want to say it."

It was impossible to resist Lyra's pretended deprecation. Annie laughed. "I suppose I can't help people's talking, and I ought to be too old to care."

"You ought, but you're not," said Lyra flatteringly. "Well, Annie, what do you think of our little evening at Mrs. Munger's in the dim retrospect? Poor Ralph! What did the doctor say about him?" She listened with so keen a relish for the report of Putney's sayings that Annie felt as if she had been turning the affair into comedy for Lyra's amusement. "Oh dear, I wish I could hear him! I thought I should have died last night when he came back, and began to scare everybody blue with his highly personal remarks. I wish he'd had time to get round to the Northwicks."

"Lyra," said Annie, nerving herself to the office; "don't you think it was wicked to treat that poor girl as you did?"

"Well, I suppose that's the way some people might look at it," said Lyra dispassionately.

"Then how—*how* could you do it?"

"Oh, it's easy enough to behave wickedly, Annie, when you feel like it," said Lyra, much amused by Annie's fervour, apparently. "Besides, I don't know that it was so *very* wicked. What makes you think it was?"

"Oh, it wasn't that merely. Lyra, may I—*may* I speak to you plainly, frankly—like a sister?" Annie's heart filled with tenderness for Lyra, with the wish to help her, to save a person who charmed her so much.

"Well, like a *step*-sister, you may," said Lyra demurely.

"It wasn't for her sake alone that I hated to see it. It was for your sake—for *his* sake."

"Well, that's very kind of you, Annie," said Lyra, without the least resentment. "And I know what you mean. But it really doesn't hurt either Jack or me. I'm not very goody-goody, Annie; I don't pretend to be; but I'm not very baddy-baddy either. I assure you"—Lyra laughed mischievously—"I'm one of the very few persons in Hatboro' who a re better than they should be."

"I know it, Lyra—I know it. But you have no right to keep him from taking a fancy to some young girl—and marrying her; to keep him to yourself; to make people talk."

"There's something in that," Lyra assented, with impartiality. "But I don't think it would be well for Jack to marry yet; and if I see him taking a fancy to any real nice girl, I sha'n't interfere with him. But I shall be very *particular*, Annie."

She looked at Annie with such a droll mock earnest, and shook her head with such a burlesque of grandmotherly solicitude, that Annie laughed in spite of herself. "Oh, Lyra, Lyra!"

"And as for me," Lyra went on, "I assure you I don't care for the little bit of harm it does me."

"But you ought—you ought!" cried Annie. "You ought to respect yourself enough to care. You ought to respect other women enough."

"Oh, I guess I'd let the balance of the sex slide, Annie," said Lyra.

"No, you mustn't; you can't. We are all bound together; we owe everything to each other."

"Isn't that rather Peckish?" Lyra suggested.

"I don't know. But it's true, Lyra. And I shouldn't be ashamed of getting it from Mr. Peck."

"Oh, I didn't say you would be."

"And I hope you won't be hurt with me. I know that it's a most unwarrantable thing to speak to you about such a matter; but you know why I do it."

"Yes, I suppose it's because you like me; and I appreciate that, I assure you, Annie."

Lyra was soberer than she had yet been, and Annie felt that she was really gaining ground. "And your husband; you ought to respect *him*—"

Lyra laughed out with great relish. "Oh, now, Annie, you *are* joking! Why in the *world* should I respect Mr. Wilmington? An old man like him marrying a young girl like me!" She jumped up and laughed at the look in Annie's face. "Will you go round with me to the Putneys? thought Ellen might like to see us."

"No, no. I can't go," said Annie, finding it impossible to recover at once from the quite unanswerable blow her sense of decorum—she thought it her moral sense—had received.

"Well, you'll be glad to have *me* go, anyway," said Lyra. She saw Annie shrinking from her, and she took hold of her, and pulled her up and kissed her. "You dear old thing! I wouldn't hurt your feelings for the world. And whichever it is, Annie, the parson or the doctor, I wish him joy."

That afternoon, as Annie was walking to the village, the doctor drove up to the sidewalk, and stopped near her. "Miss Kilburn, I've got a letter from home. They write me about my mother in a way that makes me rather anxious, and I shall run down to Chelsea this evening."

"Oh, I'm sorry for your bad news. I hope it's nothing serious."

"She's old; that's the only cause for anxiety. But of course I must go."

"Oh yes, indeed. I do hope you'll find all right with her."

"Thank you very much. I'm sorry that I must leave Putney at such a time. But I leave him with Mr. Peck, who's promised to be with him. I thought you'd like to know."

"Yes, I do; it's very kind of you—very kind indeed."

"Thank you," said the doctor. It was not the phrase exactly, but it served the purpose of the cordial interest in which they parted as well as another.

XXI

During the days that Mr. Peck had consented to leave Idella with her Annie took the whole charge of the child, and grew into an intimacy with her that was very sweet. It was not necessary to this that Idella should be always tractable and docile, which she was not, but only that she should be affectionate and dependent; Annie found that she even liked her to be a little baddish; it gave her something to forgive; and she experienced a perverse pleasure in discovering that the child of a man so self-forgetful as Mr. Peck was rather more covetous than most children. It also amused her that when some of Idella's shabby playmates from Over the Track casually found their way to the woods past Annie's house, and tried to tempt Idella to go with them, the child disowned them, and ran into the house from them; so soon was she alienated from her former life by her present social advantages. She apparently distinguished between Annie and the Boltons, or if not quite this, she showed a distinct preference for her company, and for her part of the house. She hung about Annie with a flattering curiosity and interest in all she did. She lost every trace of shyness with her, but developed an intense admiration for her in every way—for her dresses, her rings, her laces, for the elegancies that marked her a gentlewoman. She pronounced them prettier than Mrs. Warner's things, and the house prettier and larger.

"Should you like to live with me?" Annie asked.

The child seemed to reflect. Then she said, with the

indirection of her age and sex, pushing against Annie's knee, "I don't know what your name is."

"Have you never heard my name? It's Annie. How do you like it?"

"It's—it's too short," said the child, from her readiness always to answer something that charmed Annie.

"Well, then you can make it longer. You can call me Aunt Annie. I think that will be better for a little girl; don't you?"

"Mothers can whip, but aunts can't," said Idella, bringing a practical knowledge, acquired from her observation of life Over the Track, to a consideration of the proposed relation.

"I know *one* aunt who won't," said Annie, touched by the reply.

Saturday evening Idella's father came for her; and with a preamble which seemed to have been unnecessary when he understood it, Annie asked him to let her keep the child, at least till he had settled himself in a house of his own, or, she hinted, in some way more comfortable for Idella than he was now living. In her anxiety to make him believe that she was not taking too great a burden on her hands, she became slowly aware that no fear of this had apparently troubled him, and that he was looking at the whole matter from a point outside of questions of polite ceremonial, even of personal feeling.

She was vexed a little with his insensibility to the favour she meant the child, and she could not help trying to make him realise it. "I don't promise always to be the best guide, philosopher, and friend that Idella could have"—she took this light tone because she found herself afraid of him—"but I think I shall be a little improvement on some of her friends Over the Track. At least, if she wants my cat, she shall have it without fighting for it."

W. D. Howells

Mr. Peck looked up with question, and she went on to tell him of a struggle which she had seen one day between Idella and a small Irish boy for a kitten; it really belonged to the boy, but Idella carried it off.

The minister listened attentively. At the end: "Yes," he said, "that lust of possession is something all but impossible, even with constant care, to root out of children. I have tried to teach Idella that nothing is rightfully hers except while she can use it; but it is hard to make her understand, and when she is with other children she forgets."

Annie could not believe at first that he was serious, and then she was disposed to laugh. "Really, Mr. Peck," she began, "I can't think it's so important that a little thing like Idella should be kept from coveting a kitten as that she should be kept from using naughty words and from scratching and biting."

"I know," Mr. Peck consented. "That is the usual way of looking at such things."

"It seems to me," said Annie, "that it's the common-sense way."

"Perhaps. But upon the whole, I don't agree with you. It is bad for the child to use naughty words and to scratch and bite; that's part of the warfare in which we all live; but it's worse for her to covet, and to wish to keep others from having."

"I don't wonder you find it hard to make her understand that."

"Yes, it's hard with all of us. But if it is ever to be easier we must begin with the children."

He was silent, and Annie did not say anything. She was afraid that she had not helped her cause. "At least," she finally ventured, "you can't object to giving Idella a little rest from the fray. Perhaps if she finds that she can get things without fighting for them, she'll not covet them so much."

"Yes," he said, with a dim smile that left him sad again, "there is some truth in that. But I'm not sure that I have the right to give her advantages of any kind, to lift her above the lot, the chance, of the least fortunate—"

"Surely, we are bound to provide for those of our own household," said Annie.

"Who are those of our own household?" asked the minister. "All mankind are those of our own household. These are my mother and my brother and my sister."

"Yes, I know," said Annie, somewhat eagerly quitting this difficult ground. "But you can leave her with me at least till you get settled," she faltered, "if you don't wish it to be for longer."

"Perhaps it may not be for long," he answered, "if you mean my settlement in Hatboro'. I doubt," he continued, lifting his eyes to the question in hers, "whether I shall remain here."

"Oh, I hope you will," cried Annie. She thought she must make a pretence of misunderstanding him. "I supposed you were very much satisfied with your work here."

"I am not satisfied with myself in my work," replied the minister; "and I know that I am far from acceptable to many others in it."

"You are acceptable to those who are best able to appreciate you, Mr. Peck," she protested, "and to people of every kind. I'm sure it's only a question of time when you will be thoroughly acceptable to all. I want you to understand, Mr. Peck," she added, "that I was shocked and ashamed the other night at your being tricked into countenancing a part of the entertainment you were promised should be dropped. I had nothing to do with it."

W. D. Howells

"It was very unimportant, after all," the minister said, "as far as I was concerned. In fact, I was interested to see the experiment of bringing the different grades of society together."

"It seems to me it was an utter failure," suggested Annie.

"Quite. But it was what I expected."

There appeared an uncandour in this which Annie could not let pass even if it imperilled her present object to bring up the matter of past contention. "But when we first talked of the Social Union you opposed it because it wouldn't bring the different classes together."

"Did you understand that? Then I failed to make myself clear. I wished merely to argue that the well-meaning ladies who suggested it were not intending a social union at all. In fact, such a union in our present condition of things, with its division of classes, is impossible—as Mrs. Munger's experiment showed—with the best will on both sides. But, as I said, the experiment was interesting, though unimportant, except as it resulted in heart-burning and offence."

They were on the same ground, but they had reached it from starting-points so opposite that Annie felt it very unsafe. In her fear of getting into some controversy with Mr. Peck that might interfere with her designs regarding Idella, she had a little insincerity in saying: "Mrs. Munger's bad faith in that was certainly unimportant compared with her part in poor Mr. Putney's misfortune. That was the worst thing; that's what I *can't* forgive."

Mr. Peck said nothing to this, and Annie, somewhat daunted by his silence, proceeded. "I've had the satisfaction of telling her what I thought on both points. But Ralph—Mr. Putney— I hear, has escaped this time with less than his usual—"

She did not know what lady-like word to use for spree, and so she stopped.

Mr. Peck merely said, "He has shown great self-control;" and she perceived that he was not going to say more. He listened patiently to the reasons she gave for not having offered Mrs. Putney anything more than passive sympathy at a time when help could only have cumbered and kindness wounded her, but he made no sign of thinking them either necessary or sufficient. In the meantime he had not formally consented to Idella's remaining with her, and Annie prepared to lead back to that affair as artfully as she could.

"I really want you to believe, Mr. Peck, that I think very differently on *some* points from what I did when we first talked about the Social Union, and I have you to thank for seeing things in a new light. And you needn't," she added lightly, "be afraid of my contaminating Idella's mind with any wicked ideas. I'll do my best to keep her from coveting kittens or property of any kind; though I've always heard my father say that civilisation was founded upon the instinct of ownership, and that it was the only thing that had advanced the world. And if you dread the danger of giving her advantages, as you say, or bettering her worldly lot," she continued, with a smile for his quixotic scruples, "why, I'll do my best to reduce her blessings to a minimum; though I don't see why the poor little thing shouldn't get some good from the inequalities that there always must be in the world."

"I am not sure there always must be inequalities in the world," answered the minister.

"There always have been," cried Annie.

"There always had been slavery, up to a certain time," he replied.

"Oh, but surely you don't compare the two!" Annie pleaded with what she really regarded as a kind of lunacy in the good man. "In the freest society, I've heard my father say, there is naturally an upward and downward tendency; a perfect level is impossible. Some must rise, and some must sink."

"But what do you mean by rising? If you mean in material things, in wealth and the power over others that it gives—"

"I don't mean that altogether. But there are other ways—in cultivation, refinement, higher tastes and aims than the great mass of people can have. You have risen yourself, Mr. Peck."

"I have risen, as you call it," he said, with a meek sufferance of the application of the point to himself. "Those who rise above the necessity of work for daily bread are in great danger of losing their right relation to other men, as I said when we talked of this before."

A point had remained in Annie's mind from her first talk with Dr. Morrell. "Yes; and you said once that there could be no sympathy between the rich and the poor—no real love— because they had not had the same experience of life. But how is it about the poor who become rich? They have had the same experience."

"Too often they make haste to forget that they were poor; they become hard masters to those they have left behind them. They are eager to identify themselves with those who have been rich longer than they. Some working-men who now see this clearly have the courage to refuse to rise. Miss Kilburn, why should I let you take my child out of the conditions of self-denial and self-help to which she was born?"

"I don't know," said Annie rather blankly. Then she added impetuously: "Because I love her and want her. I don't—I won't—pretend that it's for her sake. It's for *my* sake, though I can take better care of her than you can. But I'm all alone in the world; I've neither kith nor kin; nothing but my miserable money. I've set my heart on the child; I must have her. At least let me keep her a while. I will be honest with you, Mr. Peck. If I find I'm doing her harm and not good, I'll give her up. I should wish you to feel that she is yours as much as ever, and if you *will* feel so, and come often to see her—I—I shall—be very glad, and—" she stopped, and Mr. Peck rose.

"Where is the child?" he asked, with a troubled air; and she silently led the way to the kitchen, and left him at the door to Idella and the Boltons. When she ventured back later he was gone, but the child remained.

Half exultant and half ashamed, she promised herself that she really would be true as far as possible to the odd notions of the minister in her treatment of his child. When she undressed Idella for bed she noticed again the shabbiness of her poor little clothes. She went through the bureau that held her own childish things once more, but found them all too large for Idella, and too hopelessly antiquated. She said to herself that on this point at least she must be a law to herself.

She went down to see Mrs. Bolton. "Isn't there some place in the village where they have children's ready-made clothes for sale?" she asked.

"Mr. Gerrish's," said Mrs. Bolton briefly.

Annie shook her head, drawing in her breath. "I shouldn't want to go there. Is there nowhere else?"

"There's a Jew place. They say he cheats."

"I dare say he doesn't cheat more than most Christians," said Annie, jumping from her chair. "I'll try the Jew place. I want you to come with me, Mrs. Bolton."

They went together, and found a dress that they both decided would fit Idella, and a hat that matched it.

"I don't know as he'd like to have anything quite so nice," said Mrs. Bolton coldly.

"I don't know as he has anything to say about it," said Annie, mimicking Mrs. Bolton's accent and syntax.

They both meant Mr. Peck. Mrs. Bolton turned away to hide

W. D. Howells

her pleasure in Annie's audacity and extravagance.

"Want I should carry 'em?" she asked, when they were out of the store.

"No, I can carry them," said Annie.

She put them where Idella must see them as soon as she woke.

It was late before she slept, and Idella's voice broke upon her dreams. The child was sitting up in her bed, gloating upon the dress and hat hung and perched upon the chair-back in the middle of the room. "Oh, whose is it? Whose is it? Whose is it?" she screamed; and as Annie lifted herself on her elbow, and looked over at her: "Is it mine? Is it mine?"

Annie had thought of playing some joke; of pretending not to understand; of delaying the child's pleasure; playing with it; teasing. But in the face of this rapturous longing, she could only answer, "Yes."

"Mine? My very own? To have? To keep always?"

"Yes."

Idella sprang from her bed, and flew upon the things with a primitive, greedy transport in their possession. She could scarcely be held long enough to be washed before the dress could be put on.

"Be careful—be careful not to get it soiled now," said Annie.

"No; I won't spoil it." She went quietly downstairs, and when Annie followed, she found her posing before the long pier-glass in the parlour, and twisting and turning for this effect and that. All the morning she moved about prim and anxious; the wild-wood flower was like a hot-house blossom wired for a bouquet. At the church door she asked Idella, "Would you rather sit with Mrs. Bolton?"

"No, no," gasped the child intensely; "with *you*!" and she pushed her hand into Annie's, and held fast to it.

Annie's question had been suggested by a belated reluctance to appear before so much of Hatboro' in charge of the minister's child. But now she could not retreat, and with Idella's hand in hers she advanced blushing up the aisle to her pew.

W. D. Howells

XXII

The farmers' carry-alls filled the long shed beside the church, and their leathern faces looked up, with their wives' and children's, at Mr. Peck where he sat high behind the pulpit; a patient expectance suggested itself in the men's bald or grizzled crowns, and in the fantastic hats and bonnets of their women folks. The village ladies were all in the perfection of their street costumes, and they compared well with three or four of the ladies from South Hatboro', but the men with them spoiled all by the inadequacy of their fashion. Mrs. Gates, the second of her name, was very stylish, but the provision-man had honestly the effect of having got for the day only into the black coat which he had bought ready-made for his first wife's funeral. Mr. Wilmington, who appeared much shorter than his wife as he sat beside her, was as much inferior to her in dress; he wore, with the carelessness of a rich man who could afford simplicity, a loose alpaca coat and a cambric neckcloth, over which he twisted his shrivelled neck to catch sight of Annie, as she rustled up the aisle. Mrs. Gerrish—so much as could be seen of her—was a mound of bugled velvet, topped by a small bonnet, which seemed to have gone much to a fat black pompon; she sat far within her pew, and their children stretched in a row from her side to that of Mr. Gerrish, next the door. He did not look round at Annie, but kept an attitude of fixed self-concentration, in harmony with the severe old-school respectability of his dress; his wife leaned well forward to see, and let all her censure appear in her eyes.

Colonel Marvin, of the largest shoe-shop, showed the side of his large florid face, with the kindly smile that seemed to hang loosely upon it; and there was a good number of the hat-shop and shoe-shop hands of different ages and sexes scattered about. The gallery, commonly empty or almost so, showed groups and single figures dropped about here and there on its seats.

The Putneys were in their pew, the little lame boy between the father and mother, as their custom was. They each looked up at her as she passed, and smiled in the slight measure of recognition which people permit themselves in church. Putney was sitting with his head hanging forward in pathetic dejection; his face, when he first lifted it to look at Annie in passing, was haggard, but otherwise there was no consciousness in it of what had passed since they had sat there the Sunday before. When his glance took in Idella too, in her sudden finery, a light of friendly mocking came into it, and seemed to comment the relation Annie had assumed to the child.

Annie's pew was just in front of Lyra's, and Lyra pursed her mouth in burlesque surprise as Annie got into it with Idella and turned round to lift the child to the seat. While Mr. Peck was giving out the hymn, Lyra leaned forward and whispered—

"Don't imagine that this turnout is *all* on your account, Annie. He's going to preach against the Social Union and the social glass."

The banter echoed a mechanical expectation in Annie's heart, which was probably present in many others there. It was some time before she could cast it out, even after he had taken his text, "I am the Resurrection and the Life," and she followed him with a mechanical disappointment at his failure to meet it.

He began by saying that he wished to dissociate his text in his hearers' minds from the scent of the upturned earth, and the fall of clods upon the coffin lid, and he asked them to join him in attempting to find in it another meaning beside that which it usually carried. He believed that those words of Christ ought to speak to us of this world as well as the next, and enjoin upon us the example which we might all find in Him, as well as promise us immortality with Him. As the minister went on, Annie followed him with the interest which her belief that she heard between the words inspired, and occasionally in a discontent with what seemed a mystical, almost a fantastical, quality of his thought.

"There is an evolution," he continued, "in the moral as well as in the material world, and good unfolds in greater good; that which was once best ceases to be in that which is better. In the political world we have striven forward to liberty as to the final good, but with this achieved we find that liberty is only a means and not an end, and that we shall abuse it as a means if we do not use it, even sacrifice it, to promote equality; or in other words, equality is the perfect work, the evolution of liberty. Patriotism has been the virtue which has secured an image of brotherhood, rude and imperfect, to large numbers of men within certain limits, but nationality must perish before the universal ideal of fraternity is realised. Charity is the holiest of the agencies which have hitherto wrought to redeem the race from savagery and despair; but there is something holier yet than charity, something higher, something purer and further from selfishness, something into which charity shall willingly grow and cease, and that is *justice*. Not the justice of our Christless codes, with their penalties, but the instinct of righteous shame which, however dumbly, however obscurely, stirs in every honest man's heart when his superfluity is confronted with another's destitution, and which is destined to increase in power till it becomes the social as well as the individual conscience. Then, in the truly Christian state, there shall be no more asking and no more giving, no more gratitude and no more merit, no more charity, but only and evermore justice; all shall share alike, and want and luxury and killing toil and heartless indolence shall all cease together.

"It is in the spirit of this justice that I believe Christ shall come to judge the world; not to condemn and punish so much as to reconcile and to right. We live in an age of seeming preparation for indefinite war. The lines are drawn harder and faster between the rich and the poor, and on either side the forces are embattled. The working-men are combined in vast organisations to withstand the strength of the capitalists, and these are taking the lesson and uniting in trusts. The smaller industries are gone, and the smaller commerce is being devoured by the larger. Where many little shops existed one huge factory assembles manufacture; one large store, in which many different branches of trade are united, swallows up the small dealers. Yet in the labour organisations, which have their bad side, their weak side, through which the forces of hell enter, I see evidence of the fact that the poor have at last had pity on the poor, and will no more betray and underbid and desert one another, but will stand and fall together as brothers; and the monopolies, though they are founded upon ruin, though they know no pity and no relenting, have a final significance which we must not lose sight of. They prophesy the end of competition; *they eliminate* one element of strife, of rivalry, of warfare. But woe to them through whose evil this good comes, to any man who prospers on to ease and fortune, forgetful or ignorant of the ruin on which his success is built. For that death the resurrection and the life seem not to be. Whatever his creed or his religious profession, his state is more pitiable than that of the sceptic, whose words perhaps deny Christ, but whose works affirm Him. There has been much anxiety in the Church for the future of the world abandoned to the godlessness of science, but I cannot share it. If God is, nothing exists but from Him. He directs the very reason that questions Him, and Christ rises anew in the doubt of him that the sins of Christendom inspire. So far from dreading such misgiving as comes from contemplating the disparity between the Church's profession and her performance, I welcome it as another resurrection and a new life."

The minister paused and seemed about to resume, when a scuffling and knocking noise drew all eyes toward the pew of the Gerrish family. Mr. Gerrish had risen and flung open the door so sharply that it struck against the frame-work of the pew, and he stood pulling his children, whom Mrs. Gerrish urged from behind, one after another, into the aisle beside him. One of them had been asleep, and he now gave way to the alarm which seizes a small boy suddenly awakened. His mother tried to still him, stooping over him and twitching him by the hand, with repeated "Sh! 'sh's!" as mothers do, till her husband got her before him, and marched his family down the aisle and out of the door. The noise of their feet over the floor of the vestibule died away upon the stone steps outside. The minister allowed the pause he had made to prolong itself painfully. He wavered, after clearing his throat, as if to go on with his sermon, and then he said sadly, "Let us pray!"

XXIII

Putney stopped with his wife and boy and waited for Annie at the corner of the street where their ways parted. She had eluded Lyra Wilmington in coming down the aisle, and she had hurried to escape the sensation which broke into eager talk among the people before they got out of church, and which began with question whether one of the Gerrish children was sick, and ended in the more satisfactory conviction that Mr. Gerrish was offended at something in the sermon.

"Well, Annie," said Putney, with a satirical smile.

"Oh, Ralph—Ellen—what does it mean?"

"It means that Brother Gerrish thought Mr. Peck was hitting at him in that talk about the large commerce, and it means business," said Putney. "Brother Gerrish has made a beginning, and I guess it's the beginning of the end, unless we're all ready to take hold against him. What are you going to do?"

"Do? Anything! Everything! It was abominable! It was atrocious!" she shuddered out with disgust. "How could he imagine that Mr. Peck would do such a thing?"

"Well, he's imagined it. But he doesn't mean to stay out of church; he means to put Brother Peck out."

"We mustn't let him. That would be outrageous."

W. D. Howells

"That's the way Ellen and I feel about it," said Putney; "but we don't know how much of a party there is with us."

"But everybody—everybody must feel the same way about Mr. Gerrish's behaviour? I don't see how you can be so quiet about it—you and Ellen!"

Annie looked from one to another indignantly, and Putney laughed.

"We're not *feeling* quietly about it," said Mrs. Putney.

Putney took out a piece of tobacco, and bit off a large corner, and began to chew vehemently upon it. "Hello, Idella!" he said to the little girl, holding by Annie's hand and looking up intently at him, with childish interest in what he was eating. "What a pretty dress you've got on!"

"It's mine," said the child. To keep."

"Is that so? Well, it's a beauty."

"I'm going to wear it all the time."

"Is that so? Well, now, you and Winthrop step on ahead a little; I want to see how you look in it. Splendid!" he said, as she took the boy's hand and looked back over her shoulder for Putney's applause. "Lyra tells us you've adopted her for the time being, Annie. I guess you'll have your hands full. But, as I was going to say, about feeling differently, my experience is that there's always a good-sized party for the perverse, simply because it seems to answer a need in human nature. There's a fascination in it; a man feels as if there must be something in it besides the perversity, and because it's so obviously wrong it must be right. Don't you believe but what a good half of the people in church to-day are pretty sure that Gerrish had a good reason for behaving indecently. The very fact that he did so carries conviction to some minds, and those are the minds we have got to deal with. When he gets up in the next Society meeting there's a mighty great danger that he'll have a strong party to back him."

"I can't believe it," Annie broke out, but she was greatly troubled. "What do you think, Ellen; that there's any danger of his carrying the day against Mr. Peck?"

"There's a great deal of dissatisfaction with Mr. Peck already, you know, and I guess Ralph's right about the rest of it."

"Well, I'm glad I've taken a pew. I'm with you for Mr. Peck, Ralph, heart and soul."

"As Brother Brandreth says about the Social Union. Well, that's right. I shall count upon you. And speaking of the Social Union, I haven't seen you, Annie, since that night at Mrs. Munger's. I suppose you don't expect me to say anything in self-defence?"

"No, Ralph, and you needn't; *I've* defended you sufficiently—justified you."

"That won't do," said Putney. "Ellen and I have thought that all out, and we find that I—or something that stood for me—was to blame, whoever else was to blame, too; we won't mention the hospitable Mrs. Munger. When Dr. Morrell had to go away Brother Peck took hold with me, and he suggested good resolutions. I told him I'd tried 'em, and they never did me the least good; but his sort really seemed to work. I don't know whether they would work again; Ellen thinks they would. *I* think we sha'n't ever need anything again; but that's what I always think when I come out of it—like a man with chills and fever."

"It was Dr. Morrell who asked Mr. Peck to come," said Mrs. Putney; "and it turned out for the best. Ralph got well quicker than he ever did before. Of course, Annie," she explained, "it must seem strange to you hearing us talk of it as if it were a disease; but that's just like what it is—a raging disease; and I can't feel differently about anything that happens in it, though I do blame people for it." Annie followed with tender interest the loving pride that exonerated and idealised Putney in the words of the woman who had suffered so much with him, and must suffer. "I couldn't help speaking as I did to Mrs. Munger."

"She deserved it every word," said Annie. "I wonder you didn't say more."

"Oh, hold on!" Putney interposed. "We'll allow that the local influences were malarial, but I guess we can't excuse the invalid altogether. That's Brother Peck's view; and I must say I found it decidedly tonic; it helped to brace me up."

"I think he was too severe with you altogether," said his wife.

Putney laughed. "It was all I could do to keep Ellen from getting up and going out of church too, when Brother Gerrish set the example. She's a Gerrishite at heart."

"Well, remember, Ralph," said Annie, "that I'm with you in whatever you do to defeat that man. It's a good cause—a righteous cause—the cause of justice; and we must do everything for it," she said fervently.

"Yes, any enormity is justifiable against injustice," he suggested, "or the unjust; it's the same thing."

"You know I don't mean that. I can trust you."

"I shall keep within the law, at any rate," said Putney.

"Well, Mrs. Bolton!" Annie called out, when she entered her house, and she pushed on into the kitchen; she had not the patience to wait for her to bring in the dinner before speaking about the exciting event at church. But Mrs. Bolton would not be led up to the subject by a tacit invitation, and after a suspense in which her zeal for Mr. Peck began to take a colour of resentment toward Mrs. Bolton, Annie demanded, "What do you think of Mr. Gerrish's scandalous behaviour?"

Mrs. Bolton gave herself time to put a stick of wood into the stove, and to punch it with the stove-lid handle before answering. "I don't know as it's anything more than I expected."

Annie went on: "It was shameful! Do you suppose he really thought Mr. Peck was referring to him in his sermon?"

"I presume he felt the cap fit. But if it hadn't b'en one thing, 'twould b'en another. Mr. Peck was bound to roil the brook for Mr. Gerrish's drinkin', wherever he stood, up stream or down."

"Yes. He *is* a wolf! A wolf in sheep's clothing," said Annie excitedly.

"I d'know as you can call him a *wolf*, exactly," returned Mrs. Bolton dryly. "He's got his good points, I presume."

Annie was astounded. "Why, Mrs. Bolton, you're surely not going to justify him?"

Mrs. Bolton erected herself from cutting a loaf of her best bread into slices, and stood with the knife in her hand, like a figure of Justice. "Well, I *guess* you no need to ask me a question like that, Miss Kilburn. I hain't obliged to make up to Mr. Peck, though, for what I done in the beginnin' by condemnin' everybuddy else without mercy now." Mrs. Bolton's eyes did not flash fire, but they sent out an icy gleam that went as sharply to Annie's heart.

Bolton came in from feeding the horse and cow in the barn, with a mealy tin pan in his hand, from which came a mild, subdued radiance like that of his countenance. He was not sensible of arriving upon a dramatic moment, and he said, without noticing the attitude of either lady: "I see you walkin' home with Mr. Putney, Miss Kilburn. What'd *he* say?"

W. D. Howells

"You mean about Mr. Gerrish? He thinks as we all do; that it was a challenge to Mr. Peck's friends, and that we must take it up."

A light of melancholy satisfaction shone from Bolton's deeply shaded eyes. "Well, he ain't one to lose time, not a great deal. I presume he's goin' to work?"

"At once," said Annie. "He says Mr. Gerrish will be sure to bring his grievance up at the next Society meeting, and we must be ready to meet him, and out-talk him and out-vote him." She reported these phrases from Putney's lips.

"Well, I guess if it was out-talkin', Mr. Putney wouldn't have much trouble about it. And as far forth as votin' goes, I don't believe but what we can carry the day."

"We couldn't," said Mrs. Bolton from the pantry, where she had gone to put the bread away in its stone jar, "if it was left to the church." She accented the last word with the click of the jar lid, and came out.

"Well, it ain't a church question. It's a Society question."

Mrs. Bolton replied, on her passage to the dining-room with the plate of sliced bread: "I can't make it seem right to have the minister a Society question. Seems to me that the church members'd ought have the say."

"Well, you can't make the discipline over to suit everybody," said Bolton. "I presume it was ordered for a wise purpose."

"Why, land alive, Oliver Bolton," his wife shouted back from the remoteness to which his words had followed her, "the statute provisions and rules of the Society wa'n't ordered by Providence."

"Well, not directly, as you may say," said Bolton, beginning high, and lowering his voice as she rejoined them, "but I presume the hearts of them that made them was moved."

Mrs. Bolton could not combat a position of such unimpregn-able piety in words, but she permitted herself a contemptuous sniff, and went on getting the things into the dining-room.

"And I guess it's all goin' to work together for good. I ain't afraid any but what it's goin' to come out all right. But we got to be up and doin', as they say about 'lection times. The Lord helps them that helps themselves," said Bolton, and then, as if he felt the weakness of this position as compared with that of entire trust in Providence, he winked his mild eyes, and added, "if they're on the right side, and put their faith in His promises."

"Well, your dinner's ready now," Mrs. Bolton said to Annie.

Idella had clung fast to Annie's hand; as Annie started toward the dining-room she got before her, and whispered vehemently.

"What?" asked Annie, bending down; she laughed, in lifting her head, "I promised Idella you'd let us have some preserves to-day, Mrs. Bolton."

Mrs. Bolton smiled with grim pleasure. "I see all the while her mind was set on something. She ain't one to let you forget *your* promises. Well, I guess if Mr. Peck had a little more of *her* disposition there wouldn't be much doubt about the way it would all come out."

"Well, you don't often see pairents take after their children," said Bolton, venturing a small joke.

"No, nor husbands after their wives, either," said Mrs. Bolton sharply. "The more's the pity."

XXIV

Dr. Morrell came to see Annie late the next Wednesday evening.

"I didn't know you'd come back," she said. She returned to the rocking-chair, from which she came forward to greet him, and he dropped into an easy seat near the table piled with books and sewing.

"I didn't know it myself half an hour ago."

"Really? And is this your first visit? I must be a very interesting case."

"You are—always. How have you been?"

"I? I hardly know whether I've been at all," she answered, in mechanical parody of his own reply. "So many other things have been of so much more importance."

She let her eyes rest full upon his, with a sense of returning comfort and safety in his presence, and after a deep breath of satisfaction, she asked, "How did you leave your mother?"

"Very much better—entirely out of danger."

"It's so odd to think of any one's having a family. To me it seems the normal condition not to have any relatives."

"Well, we can't very well dispense with mothers," said the doctor. "We have to begin with them, at any rate."

"Oh, I don't object to them. I only wonder at them."

They fell into a cosy and mutually interesting talk about their separate past, and he gave her glimpses of the life, simple and studious, he had led before he went abroad. She confessed to two mistakes in which she had mechanically persisted concerning him; one that he came from Charlestown instead of Chelsea, and the other that his first name was Joseph instead of James. She did not own that she had always thought it odd he should be willing to remain in a place like Hatboro', and that it must argue a strangely unambitious temperament in a man of his ability. She diverted the impulse to a general satire of village life, and ended by saying that she was getting to be a perfect villager herself.

He laughed, and then, "How has Hatboro' been getting along?" he asked.

"Simply seething with excitement," she answered. "But I should hardly know where to begin if I tried to tell you," she added. "It seems such an age since I saw you."

"Thank you," said the doctor.

"I didn't mean to be *quite* so flattering; but you have certainly marked an epoch. Really, I *don't* know where to begin. I wish you'd seen somebody else first—Ralph and Ellen, or Mrs. Wilmington."

"I might go and see them now."

"No; stay, now you're here, though I know I shall not do justice to the situation." But she was able to possess him of it with impartiality, even with a little humour, all the more because she was at heart intensely partisan and serious. "No one knows what Mr. Gerrish intends to do next. He has kept

W. D. Howells

quietly about his business; and he told some of the ladies who tried to interview him that he was not prepared to talk about the course he had taken. He doesn't seem to be ashamed of his behaviour; and Ralph thinks that he's either satisfied with it, and intends to let it stand as a protest, or else he's going to strike another blow on the next business meeting. But he's even kept Mrs. Gerrish quiet, and all we can do is to unite Mr. Peck's friends provisionally. Ralph's devoted himself to that, and he says he has talked forty-eight hours to the day ever since."

Is he—"

"Yes; perfectly! I could hardly believe it when I saw him at church on Sunday. It was like seeing one risen from the dead. What he must have gone through, and Ellen! She told me how Mr. Peck had helped him in the struggle. She attributes every-thing to him. But of course you think he had nothing to do with it."

"What makes you think that?" he asked.

"Oh, I don't know. Wouldn't that naturally be the attitude of Science?"

"Toward religion? Perhaps. But I'm not Science—with a large S. May be that's the reason why I left the case with Mr. Peck," said the doctor, smiling. "Putney didn't leave off my medicine, did he?"

"He never got well so soon before. They both say that. I didn't think you could be so narrow-minded, Dr. Morrell. But of course your scientific bigotry couldn't admit the effect of the moral influence. It would be too much like a miracle; you would have to allow for a mystery."

"I have to allow for a good many," said the doctor. "The world is full of mysteries for me, if you mean things that science hasn't explored yet. But I hope that they'll all yield to the light, and that somewhere there'll be light enough to clear up even the spiritual mysteries."

"Do you really?" she demanded eagerly. "Then you believe in a life hereafter? You believe in a moral government of the—"

He retreated, laughing, from her ardent pursuit. "Oh, I'm not going to commit myself. But I'll go so far as to say that I like to hear Mr. Peck preach, and that I want him to stay. I don't say he had nothing to do with Putney's straightening up. Putney had a great deal to do with it himself. What does he think Mr. Peck's chances are?"

"If Mr. Gerrish tries to get him dismissed? He doesn't know; he's quite in the dark. He says the party of the perverse—the people who think Mr. Gerrish must have had some good reason for his behaviour, simply because they can't see any—is unexpectedly large; and it doesn't help matters with the more respectable people that the most respectable, like Mr. Wilmington and Colonel Marvin, are Mr. Peck's friends. They think there must be something wrong if such good men are opposed to Mr. Gerrish."

"And I suspect," said Dr. Morrell soberly, "that Putney's championship isn't altogether an advantage. The people all concede his brilliancy, and they are prouder of him on account of his infirmity; but I guess they like to feel their superiority to him in practical matters. They admire him, but they don't want to follow him."

"Oh, I suppose so," said Annie disconsolately. "And I imagine that Mr. Wilmington's course is attributed to Lyra, and that doesn't help Mr. Peck much with the husbands of the ladies who don't approve of her."

The doctor tacitly declined to touch this delicate point. He asked, after a pause, "You'll be at the meeting?"

"I couldn't keep away. But I've no vote, that's the worst. I can only suffer in the cause." The doctor smiled. "You must go, too," she added eagerly.

"Oh, I shall go; I couldn't keep away either. Besides, I can vote. How are you getting on with your little *protegee*?

"Idella? Well, it isn't such a simple matter as I supposed, quite. Did you ever hear anything about her mother?"

"Nothing more than what every one has. Why?" asked the doctor, with scientific curiosity. "Do you find traits that the father doesn't account for?'

"Yes. She is very vain and greedy and quick-tempered."

"Are those traits uncommon in children?"

"In such a degree I should think they were. But she's very affectionate, too, and you can do anything with her through her love of praise. She puzzles me a good deal. I wish I knew something about her mother. But Mr. Peck himself is a puzzle. With all my respect for him and regard and admiration, I can't help seeing that he's a very imperfect character."

Doctor Morrell laughed. "There's a great deal of human nature in man."

"There isn't enough in Mr. Peck," Annie retorted. "From the very first he has said things that have stirred me up and put me in a fever; but he always seems to be cold and passive himself."

"Perhaps he *is* cold," said the doctor.

"But has he any *right* to be so?" retorted Annie, with certainly no coldness of her own.

"Well, I don't know. I never thought of the right or wrong of a man's being what he was born. Perhaps we might justly blame his ancestors."

Annie broke into a laugh at herself: "Of course. But don't you think that a man who is able to put things as he does—who can make you see, for example, the stupidity and cruelty of things that always seemed right and proper before—don't you think that he's guilty of a kind of hypocrisy if he doesn't *feel* as well as see?"

"No, I can't say that I do," said the doctor, with pleasure in the feminine excess of her demand. "And there are so many ways of feeling. We're apt to think that our own way is the only way, of course; but I suppose that most philanthropists—men who have done the most to better conditions—have been people of cold temperaments; and yet you can't say they are unfeeling."

"No, certainly. Do you think Mr. Peck is a real philanthropist?"

"How you do get back to the personal always!" said Dr. Morrell. "What makes you ask?"

"Because I can't understand his indifference to his child. It seems to me that real philanthropy would begin at home. But twice he has distinctly forgotten her existence, and he always seems bored with it. Or not that quite; but she seems no more to him than any other child."

"There's something very curious about all that," said the doctor. "In most things the greater includes the less, but in philanthropy it seems to exclude it. If a man's heart is open to the whole world, to all men, it's shut sometimes against the individual, even the nearest and dearest. You see I'm willing to admit all you can say against a rival practitioner."

"Oh, I understand," said Annie. "But I'm not going to gratify your spite." At the same time she tacitly consented to the slight for Mr. Peck which their joking about him involved. In such cases we excuse our disloyalty as merely temporary, and intend to turn serious again and make full amends for it. "He made very short work," she continued, "of that notion of yours that there could be any good feeling between the poor and the rich who had once been poor themselves."

"Did I have any such notion as that?"

She recalled the time and place of its expression to him, and he said, "Oh yes! Well?"

"He says that rich people like that are apt to be the hardest masters, and are eager to forget they ever were poor, and are only anxious to identify themselves with the rich."

Dr. Morrell seemed to enjoy this immensely. "That does rather settle it," he said recreantly.

She tried to be severe with him, but she only kept on laughing and joking; she was aware that he was luring her away from her seriousness.

Mrs. Bolton brought in the lamp, and set it on the library table, showing her gaunt outline a moment against it before she left it to throw its softened light into the parlour where they sat. The autumn moonshine, almost as mellow, fell in through the open windows, which let in the shrilling of the crickets and grasshoppers, and wafts of the warm night wind.

"Does life," Annie was asking, at the end of half an hour, "seem more simple or more complicated as you live on? That sounds awfully abstruse, doesn't it? And I don't know why I'm always asking you abstruse things, but I am."

"Oh, I don't mind it," said the doctor. "Perhaps I haven't lived on long enough to answer this particular question; I'm only thirty-six, you know."

"*Only*? I'm thirty-one, and I feel a hundred!" she broke in.

"You don't look it. But I believe I rather like abstruse

questions. You know Putney and I have discussed a great many. But just what do you mean by this particular abstraction?"

He took from the table a large ivory paper-knife which he was in the habit of playing with in his visits, and laid first one side and then the other side of its smooth cool blade in the palm of his left hand, as he leaned forward, with his elbows on his knees, and bent his smiling eyes keenly upon her.

She stopped rocking herself, and said imperatively, "Will you please put that back, Dr. Morrell?"

"This paper-knife?"

"Yes. And not look at me just in that way? When you get that knife and that look, I feel a little too much as if you were diagnosing me."

"Diagnosticating," suggested the doctor.

"Is it? I always supposed it was diagnosing. But it doesn't matter. It wasn't the name I was objecting to."

He put the knife back and changed his posture, with a smile that left nothing of professional scrutiny in his look. "Very well, then; you shall diagnose yourself."

"Diagnosticate, please."

"Oh, I thought you preferred the other."

"No, it sounds undignified, now that I know there's a larger word. Where was I?"

"The personal bearing of the question whether life isn't more and more complicated?"

"How did you know it had a personal bearing?"

"I suspected as much."

"Yes, it has. I mean that within the last four or five months—since I've been in Hatboro'—I seem to have lost my old point of view; or, rather, I don't find it satisfactory any more. I'm ashamed to think of the simple plans, or dreams, that I came home with. I hardly remember what they were; but I must have expected to be a sort of Lady Bountiful here; and now I think a Lady Bountiful one of the most mischievous persons that could infest any community."

"You don't mean that charity is played out?" asked the doctor.

"In the old-fashioned way, yes."

"But they say poverty is on the increase. What is to be done?"

"Justice," said Annie. "Those who do most of the work in the world ought to share in its comforts as a right, and not be put off with what we idlers have a mind to give them from our superfluity as a grace."

"Yes, that's all very true. But what till justice *is* done?"

"Oh, we must continue to do charity," cried Annie, with self-contempt that amused him. "But don't you see how much more complicated it is? That's what I meant by life not being simple any more. It was easy enough to do charity when it used to seem the right and proper remedy for suffering; but now, when I can't make it appear a finality, but only something provisional, temporary—Don't you see?"

"Yes, I see. But I don't see how you're going to help it At the same time, I'll allow that it makes life more difficult."

For a moment they were both serious and silent. Then she said: "Sometimes I think the fault is all in myself, and that if I were not so sophisticated and—and—selfish, I should find the old way of doing good just as effective and natural as ever.

Then again, I think the conditions are all wrong, and that we ought to be fairer to people, and then we needn't be so good to them. I should prefer that. I hate being good to people I don't like, and I can't like people who don't interest me. I think I must be very hard-hearted."

The doctor laughed at this.

"Oh, I know," said Annie, "I know the fraudulent reputation I've got for good works."

"Your charity to tramps is the opprobrium of Hatboro'," the doctor consented.

"Oh, I don't mind that. It's easy when people ask you for food or money, but the horrible thing is when they ask you for work. Think of me, who never did anything to earn a cent in my life, being humbly asked by a fellow-creature to let him work for something to eat and drink! It's hideous! It's abominable! At first I used to be flattered by it, and try to conjure up something for them to do, and to believe that I was helping the deserving poor. Now I give all of them money, and tell them that they needn't even pretend to work for it. *I* don't work for my money, and I don't see why they should."

"They'd find that an unanswerable argument if you put it to them," said the doctor. He reached out his hand for the paper-cutter, and then withdrew it in a way that made her laugh.

"But the worst of it is," she resumed, "that I don't love any of the people that I help, or hurt, whichever it is. I did feel remorseful toward Mrs. Savor for a while, but I didn't love her, and I knew that I only pitied myself through her. Don't you see?"

"No, I don't," said the doctor.

"You don't, because you're too polite. The only kind of creature that I can have any sympathy with is some little

W. D. Howells

wretch like Idella, who is perfectly selfish and naughty every way, but seems to want me to like her, and a reprobate like Lyra, or some broken creature like poor Ralph. I think there's something in the air, the atmosphere, that won't allow you to live in the old way if you've got a grain of conscience or humanity. I don't mean that *I* have. But it seems to me as if the world couldn't go on as it has been doing. Even here in America, where I used to think we had the millennium because slavery was abolished, people have more liberty, but they seem just as far off as ever from justice. That is what paralyses me and mocks me and laughs in my face when I remember how I used to dream of doing good after I came home. I had better stayed at Rome."

The doctor said vaguely, "I'm glad you didn't," and he let his eyes dwell on her with a return of the professional interest which she was too lost in her self reproach to be able to resent.

"I blame myself for trying to excuse my own failure on the plea that things generally have gone wrong. At times it seems to me that I'm responsible for having lost my faith in what I used to think was the right thing to do; and then again it seems as if the world were all so bad that no real good could be done in the old way, and that my faith is gone because there's nothing for it to rest on any longer. I feel that something must be done; but I don't know what."

"It would be hard to say," said the doctor.

She perceived that her exaltation amused him, but she was too much in earnest to care. "Then we are guilty—all guilty—till we find out and begin to do it. If the world has come to such a pass that you can t do anything but harm in it—"

"Oh, is it so bad as that?" he protested.

"It's *quite* as bad," she insisted. "Just see what mischief I've done since I came back to Hatboro'. I took hold of that miserable Social Union because I was outside of all the life about me, and it seemed my only chance of getting into it; and I've done more harm by it in one summer than I could undo in a lifetime. Just think of poor Mr. Brandreth's love affair with Miss Chapley broken off, and Lyra's lamentable triumph over Miss Northwick, and Mrs. Munger's duplicity, and Ralph's escapade—all because I wanted to do good!"

A note of exaggeration had begun to prevail in her self-upbraiding, which was real enough, and the time came for him to suggest, "I think you're a little morbid, Miss Kilburn."

"Morbid! Of course I am! But that doesn't alter the fact that everything is wrong, does it?"

"Everything!"

"Why, you don't pretend yourself, do you, that everything is right?"

"A true American ought to do so, oughtn't he?" teased the doctor. "One mustn't be a bad citizen."

"But if you *were* a bad citizen?" she persisted.

"Oh, then I might agree with you on some points. But I shouldn't say such things to my patients, Miss Kilburn."

"It would be a great comfort to them if you did," she sighed.

The doctor broke out in a laugh of delight at her perfervid concentration. "Oh, no, no! They're mostly nervous women, and it would be the death of them—if they understood me. In fact, what's the use of brooding upon such ideas? We can't hurry any change, but we can make ourselves uncomfortable."

"Why should I be comfortable?" she asked, with a solemnity that made him laugh again.

"Why shouldn't you be?"

"Yes, that's what I often ask myself. But I can't be," she said sadly.

They had risen, and he looked at her with his professional interest now openly dominant, as he stood holding her hand. "I'm going to send you a little more of that tonic, Miss Kilburn."

She pulled her hand away. "No, I shall not take any more medicine. You think everything is physical. Why don't you ask at once to see my tongue?"

He went out laughing, and she stood looking wistfully at the door he had passed through.

XXV

The bell on the orthodox church called the members of Mr. Peck's society together for the business meeting with the same plangent, lacerant note that summoned them to worship on Sundays. Among those who crowded the house were many who had not been there before, and seldom in any place of the kind. There were admirers of Putney: workmen of rebellious repute and of advanced opinions on social and religious questions; nonsuited plaintiffs and defendants of shady record, for whom he had at one time or another done what he could. A good number of the summer folk from South Hatboro' were present, with the expectation of something dramatic, which every one felt, and every one hid with the discipline that subdues the outside of life in a New England town to a decorous passivity.

At the appointed time Mr. Peck rose to open the meeting with prayer; then, as if nothing unusual were likely to come before it, he declared it ready to proceed to business. Some people who had been gathering in the vestibule during his prayer came in; and the electric globes, which had been recently hung above the pulpit and on the front of the gallery in substitution of the old gas chandelier, shed their moony glare upon a house in which few places were vacant. Mr. Gerrish, sitting erect and solemn beside his wife in their pew, shared with the minister and Putney the tacit interest of the audience.

He permitted the transaction of several minor affairs, and Mr. Peck, as Moderator, conducted the business with his habitual exactness and effect of far-off impersonality. The people waited with exemplary patience, and Putney, who lounged in one corner of his pew, gave no more sign of excitement, with his chin sunk in his rumpled shirt-front, than his sad-faced wife at the other end of the seat.

Mr. Gerrish rose, with the air of rising in his own good time, and said, with dry pomp, "Mr. Moderator, I have prepared a resolution, which I will ask you to read to this meeting."

He held up a paper as he spoke, and then passed it to the minister, who opened and read it—

"*Whereas*, It is indispensable to the prosperity and well-being of any and every organisation, and especially of a Christian church, that the teachings of its minister be in accord with the convictions of a majority of its members upon vital questions of eternal interest, with the end and aim of securing the greatest efficiency of that body in the community, as an example and a shining light before men to guide their steps in the strait and narrow path; therefore

"*Resolved*, That a committee of this society be appointed to inquire if such is the case in the instance of the Rev. Julius W. Peck, and be instructed to report upon the same."

A satisfied expectation expressed itself in the silence that followed the reading of the paper, whatever pain and shame were mixed with the satisfaction. If the contempt of kindly usage shown in offering such a resolution without warning or private notice to the minister shocked many by its brutality, still it was satisfactory to find that Mr. Gerrish had intended to seize the first chance of airing his grievance, as everybody had said he would do.

Mr. Peck looked up from the paper and across the intervening pews at Mr. Gerrish. "Do I understand that you move the adoption of this resolution?"

"Why, certainly, sir," said Mr. Gerrish, with an accent of supercilious surprise.

"You did not say so," said the minister gently. "Does any one second Brother Gerrish's motion?"

A murmur of amusement followed Mr. Peck's reminder to Mr. Gerrish, and an ironical voice called out—

"Mr. Moderator!"

"Mr. Putney."

"I think it important that the sense of the meeting should be taken on the question the resolution raises. I therefore second the motion for its adoption."

Putney sat down, and the murmur now broadened into something like a general laugh, hushed as with a sudden sense of the impropriety.

Mr. Gerrish had gradually sunk into his seat, but now he rose again, and when the minister formally announced the motion before the meeting, he called, sharply, "Mr. Moderator!"

"Brother Gerrish," responded the minister, in recognition.

"I wish to offer a few remarks in support of the resolution which I have had the honour—the duty, I *would* say—of laying before this meeting." He jerked his head forward at the last word, and slid the fingers of his right hand into the breast of his coat like an orator, and stood very straight. "I have no desire, sir, to make this the occasion of a personal question between myself and my pastor. But, sir, the question has been forced upon me against my will and my—my consent; and I was obliged on the last ensuing Sabbath, when I sat in this place, to enter my public protest against it.

"Sir, I came into this community a poor boy, without a penny in my pocket, and unaided and alone and by my own exertions I have built up one of the business interests of the place. I will not stoop to boast of the part I have taken in the prosperity of this place; but I will say that no public object has been wanting—that my support has not been wanting—from the first proposition to concrete the sidewalks of this village to the introduction of city waterworks and an improved system of drainage, and—er—electric lighting. So much for my standing in a public capacity! As for my business capacity, I would gladly let that speak for itself, if that capacity had not been turned in the sanctuary itself against the personal reputation which every man holds dearer than life itself, and which has had a deadly blow aimed at it through that—that very capacity. Sir, I have established in this town a business which I may humbly say that in no other place of the same numerical size throughout the commonwealth will you find another establishment so nearly corresponding to the wants and the—er—facilities of a great city. In no other establishment in a place of the same importance will you find the interests and the demands and the necessities of the whole community so carefully considered. In no other—"

Putney got upon his feet and called out, "Mr. Moderator, will Brother Gerrish allow me to ask him a single question?"

Mr. Peck put the request, and Mr. Gerrish involuntarily made a pause, in which Putney pursued—

"My question is simply this: doesn't Brother Gerrish think it would help us to get at the business in hand sooner if he would print the rest of his advertisement in the Hatboro' *Register*?"

A laugh broke out all over the house as Putney dropped back into his seat. Mr. Gerrish stood apparently undaunted.

"I will attend to you presently, sir," he said, with a school-masterly authority which made an impression in his favour with some. "And I thank the gentleman," he continued, turning again to address the minister, "for recalling me from a side issue. As he acknowledges in the suggestion which he intended to wound my feelings, but I can assure him that my self-respect is beyond the reach of slurs and innuendoes; I care little for them; I care not what quarter they originate from, or have their—their origin; and still less when they spring from a source notoriously incompetent and unworthy to command the respect of this community, which has abused all its privileges and trampled the forbearance of its fellow-citizens under foot, until it has become a—a byword in this place, sir."

Putney sprang up again with, "Mr. Moderator—" "No, sir! no, sir!" pursued Gerrish; "I will not submit to your interruptions. I have the floor, and I intend to keep it. I intend to challenge a full and fearless scrutiny of my motives in this matter, and I intend to probe those motives in others. Why do we find, sir, on the one side of this question as its most active exponent a man outside of the church in organising a force within this society to antagonise the most cherished convictions of that church? We do not asperse his motives; but we ask if these motives coincide with the relations which a Christian minister should sustain to his flock as expressed in the resolution which I have had the privilege to offer, more in sorrow than in anger."

Putney made some starts to rise, but quelled himself, and finally sank back with an air of ironical patience. Gerrish's personalities had turned public sentiment in his favour. Colonel Marvin came over to Putney's pew and shook hands with him before sitting down by his side. He began to talk with him in whisper while Gerrish went on—

"But on the other hand, sir, what do we see? I will not allude to myself in this connection, but I am well aware, sir, that I represent a large and growing majority of this church in the stand I have taken. We are tired, sir—and I say it to you openly, sir, what has been bruited about in secret long enough—of having what I may call a one-sided gospel preached in this church and from this pulpit. We enter our protest against the neglect of very essential elements of

Christianity—not to say the essential—the representation of Christ as—a—a spirit as well as a life. Understand me, sir, we do not object, neither I nor any of those who agree with me, to the preaching of Christ as a life. That is all very well in its place, and it is the wish of every true Christian to conform and adapt his own life as far as—as circumstances will permit of. But when I come to this sanctuary, and *they* come, Sabbath after Sabbath, and hear nothing said of my Redeemer as a— means of salvation, and nothing of Him crucified; and when I find the precious promises of the gospel ignored and neglected continually and—and all the time, and each discourse from yonder pulpit filled up with generalities—glittering generalities, as has been well said by another—in relation to and connection with mere conduct, I am disappointed, sir, and dissatisfied, and I feel to protest against that line of—of preaching. During the last six months, Sabbath after Sabbath, I have listened in vain for the ministrations of the plain gospel and the tenets under which we have been blessed as a church and as—a—people. Instead of this I have heard, as I have said—and I repeat it without fear of contradiction—nothing but one-idea appeals and mere moralisings upon duty to others, which a child and the veriest tyro could not fail therein; and I have culminated—or rather it has been culminated to me—in a covert attack upon my private affairs and my way of conducting my private business in a manner which I could not overlook. For that reason, and for the reasons which I have recapitulated—and I challenge the closest scrutiny—I felt it my duty to enter my public protest and to leave this sanctuary, where I have worshipped ever since it was erected, with my family. And I now urge the adoption of the foregoing resolution because I believe that your usefulness has come to an end to the vast majority of the constituent members of this church; and—and that is all."

Mr. Gerrish stopped so abruptly that Putney, who was engaged in talk with Colonel Marvin, looked up with a startled air, too late to secure the floor. Mr. Peck recognised Mr. Gates, who stood with his wrists caught in either hand across his middle, and looked round with a quizzical glance before he began to speak. Putney lifted his hand in playful threatening toward Colonel Marvin, who got away from him with a face of noiseless laughter, and went and joined Mr. Wilmington where he sat with his wife, who entered into the talk between the men.

"Mr. Moderator," said Gates, "I don't know as I expected to take part in this debate; but you can't always tell what's going to happen to you, even if you're only a member of the church by marriage, as you might say. I presume, though, that I have a right to speak in a meeting like this, because I *am* a member of the society in my own right, and I've got its interests at heart as much as any one. I don't know but what I got the interests of Hatboro' at heart too, but I can't be certain; sometimes you can't; sometimes you think you've got the common good in view, and you come to look a little closer and you find it's the uncommon good; that is to say, it's not so much the public weal you're after as what it is the private weal. But that's neither here nor there. I haven't got anything to say against identifying yourself with things in general; I don't know but what it's a good way; all is, it's apt to make you think you're personally attacked when nobody is meant in particular. *I* think that's what's partly the matter with Brother Gerrish here. I heard that sermon, and I didn't suppose there was anything in it to hurt any one especially; and I was consid'ably surprised to see that Mr. Gerrish seemed to take it to himself, somehow, and worry over it; but I didn't really know just what the trouble was till he explained here tonight. All I was thinking was when it come to that about large commerce devouring the small—sort of lean and fat kine—I wished Jordan and Marsh could hear that, or Stewart's in New York, or Wanamaker's in Philadelphia. I never *thought* of Brother Gerrish once; and I don't presume one out of a hundred did either. I—" The electric light immediately over Gates's head began to hiss and sputter, and to suffer the sort of syncope which overtakes electric lights at such times, and to leave the house in darkness. Gates waited, standing, till it revived, and then added: "I guess I hain't got anything more to say, Mr. Moderator. If I had it's gone from me now. I'm more used to speaking by kerosene, and I always lose my breath when an electric light begins that way."

Putney was on his legs in good time now, and secured
recognition before Mr. Wilmington, who made an effort to
catch the moderator s eye. Gates had put the meeting in good-
humoured expectation of what they might now have from
Putney. They liked Gates's points very well, but they hoped
from Putney something more cruel and unsparing, and the
greater part of those present must have shared his impatience
with Mr. Wilmington's request that he would give way to him
for a moment. Yet they all probably felt the same curiosity
about what was going forward, for it was plain that Mr.
Wilmington and Colonel Marvin were conniving at the same
point. Marvin had now gone to Mr. Gerrish, and had slipped
into the pew beside him with the same sort of hand-shake he
had given Putney.

"Will my friend Mr. Putney give way to me for a moment?"
asked Mr. Wilmington.

"I don't see why I should do that," said Putney.

"I assure him that I will not abuse his courtesy, and that I will
yield the floor to him at any moment."

Putney hesitated a moment, and then, with the contented
laugh of one who securely bides his time, said, "Go ahead."

"It is simply this," said Mr. Wilmington, with a certain formal
neatness of speech: "The point has been touched by the last
speaker, which I think suggested itself to all who heard the
remarks of Brother Gerrish in support of his resolution, and
the point is simply this—whether he has not misapplied the
words of the discourse by which he felt himself aggrieved, and
whether he has not given them a particular bearing foreign to
the intention of their author. If, as I believe, this is the case,
the whole matter can be easily settled by a private conference
between the parties, and we can be saved the public appearance
of disagreement in our society. And I would now ask Brother

Gerrish, in behalf of many who take this view with me, whether he will not consent to reconsider the matter, and whether, in order to arrive at the end proposed, he will not, for the present at least, withdraw the resolution he has offered?"

Mr. Wilmington sat down amidst a general sensation, which was heightened by Putney's failure to anticipate any action on Gerrish's part. Gerrish rapidly finished something he was saying to Colonel Marvin, and then half rose, and said, "Mr. Moderator, I withdraw my resolution—for the time being, and—for the present, sir," and sat down again.

"Mr. Moderator," Putney called sharply, from his place, "this is altogether unparliamentary. That resolution is properly before the meeting. Its adoption has been moved and seconded, and it cannot be withdrawn without leave granted by a vote of the meeting. I wish to discuss the resolution in all its bearings, and I think there are a great many present who share with me a desire to know how far it represents the sense of this society. I don't mean as to the supposed personal reflections which it was intended to punish; that is a very small matter, and as compared with the other questions involved, of no consequence whatever." Putney tossed his head with insolent pleasure in his contempt of Gerrish. His nostrils swelled, and he closed his little jaws with a firmness that made his heavy black moustache hang down below the corners of his chin. He went on with a wicked twinkle in his eye, and a look all round to see that people were waiting to take his next point. "I judge my old friend Brother Gerrish by myself. My old friend Gerrish cares no more really about personal allusions than I do. What he really had at heart in offering his resolution was not any supposed attack upon himself or his shop from the pulpit of this church. He cared no more for that than I should care for a reference to my notorious habits. These are things that we feel may be safely left to the judgment, the charitable judgment, of the community, which will be equally merciful to the man who devours widows' houses and to the man who 'puts an enemy in his mouth to steal away his brains.'"

"Mr. Moderator," said Colonel Marvin, getting upon his feet.

"No, sir!" shouted Putney fiercely; "I can't allow you to speak. Wait till I get done!" He stopped, and then said gently "Excuse me, Colonel; I really must go on. I'm speaking now in behalf of Brother Gerrish, and he doesn't like to have the speaking on his side interrupted. '

"Oh, all right," said Colonel Marvin amiably; "go on."

"What my old friend William Gerrish really designed in offering that resolution was to bring into question the kind of Christianity which has been preached in this place by our pastor—the one-sided gospel, as he aptly called it—and what he and I want to get at is the opinion of the society on that question. Has the gospel preached to us here been one-sided or hasn't it? Brother Gerrish says it has, and Brother Gerrish, as I understand, doesn't change his mind on that point, if he does on any, in asking to withdraw his resolution. He doesn't expect Mr. Peck to convince him in a private conference that he has been preaching an all-round gospel. I don't contend that he has; but I suppose I'm not a very competent judge. I don't propose to give you the opinion of one very fallible and erring man, and I don't set myself up in judgment of others; but I think it's important for all parties concerned to know what the majority of this society think on a question involving its future. That importance must excuse—if anything can excuse—the apparent want of taste, of humanity, of decency, in proposing the inquiry at a meeting over which the person chiefly concerned would naturally preside, unless he were warned to absent himself. Nobody cares for the contemptible point, the wholly insignificant question, whether allusion to Mr. Gerrish's variety store was intended or not. What we are all anxious to know is whether he represents any considerable portion of this society in his general attack upon its pastor. I want a vote on that, and I move the previous question."

No one stopped to inquire whether this was parliamentary or not. Putney sat down, and Colonel Marvin rose to say that if a vote was to be taken, it was only right and just that Mr. Peck should somehow be heard in his own behalf, and half a dozen voices from all parts of the church supported him Mr. Peck, after a moment, said, "I think I have nothing to say;" and he added, "Shall I put the question?"

"Question!" "Question!" came from different quarters.

"It is moved and seconded that the resolution before the meeting be adopted," said the minister formally. "All those in favour will say ay." He waited for a distinct space, but there was no response; Mr. Gerrish himself did not vote. The minister proceeded, "Those opposed will say no."

The word burst forth everywhere, and it was followed by laughter and inarticulate expressions of triumph and mocking. "Order! order!" called the minister gravely, and he announced, "The noes have it."

The electric light began to suffer another syncope. When it recovered, with the usual fizzing and sputtering, Mr. Peck was on his feet, asking to be relieved from his duties as moderator, so that he might make a statement to the meeting. Colonel Marvin was voted into the chair, but refused formally to take possession of it. He stood up and said, "There is no place where we would rather hear you than in that pulpit, Mr. Peck."

"I thank you," said the minister, making himself heard through the approving murmur; "but I stand in this place only to ask to be allowed to leave it. The friendly feeling which has been expressed toward me in the vote upon the resolution you have just rejected is all that reconciles me to its defeat. Its adoption might have spared me a duty which I find painful. But perhaps it is best that I should discharge it. As to the sermon which called forth that resolution it is only just to say that I intended no personalities in it, and I humbly entreat any one who felt himself aggrieved to believe me." Every one looked at Gerrish to see how he took this; he must have felt it the part of self-respect not to change countenance. "My desire in that discourse was, as always, to present the truth as I had seen it, and try to make it a help to all. But I am by no means sure that the author of the resolution was wrong in arraigning me before you for neglecting a very vital part of Christianity in my ministrations here. I think with him, that those who have made an open profession of Christ have a claim to the consolation of His promises, and to the support which good men have found in the mysteries of faith; and I ask his patience and that of others who feel that I have not laid sufficient stress upon these. My shortcoming is something that I would not have you overlook in any survey of my ministry among you; and I am not here now to defend that ministry in any point of view. As I look back over it, by the light of the one ineffable ideal, it seems only a record of failure and defeat." He stopped, and a sympathetic dissent ran through the meeting. "There have been times when I was ready to think that the fault was not in me, but in my office, in the church, in religion. We all have these moments of clouded vision, in which we ourselves loom up in illusory grandeur above the work we have failed to do. But it is in no such error that I stand before you now. Day after day it has been borne in upon me that I had mistaken my work here, and that I ought, if there was any truth in me, to turn from it for reasons which I will give at length should I be spared to preach in this place next Sabbath. I should have willingly acquiesced if our parting had come in the form of my dismissal at your hands. Yet I cannot wholly regret that it has not taken that form, and that in offering my resignation, as I shall formally do to those empowered by the rules of our society to receive it, I can make it a means of restoring concord among you. It would be affectation in me to pretend that I did not know of the dissension which has had my ministry for its object if not its cause; and I earnestly hope that with my withdrawal that dissension may cease, and that this church may become a symbol before the world of the peace of Christ. I conjure such of my friends as have been active in my behalf to unite with their brethren in a cause which can alone merit their devotion. Above all things I beseech you to be at peace one with another. Forbear, forgive, submit, remembering that strife for the better part can only make it the worse, and that for Christians there can be no rivalry but in concession and self-sacrifice."

Colonel Marvin forgot his office and all parliamentary proprieties in the tide of emotion that swept over the meeting when the minister sat down. "I am glad," he said, "that no sort of action need be taken now upon Mr. Peck's proposed resignation, which I for one cannot believe this society will ever agree to accept."

Others echoed his sentiment; they spoke out, sitting and standing, and addressed themselves to no one, till Putney moved an adjournment, which Colonel Marvin sufficiently recollected himself to put to a vote, and declare carried.

Annie walked home with the Putneys and Dr. Morrell. She was aware of something unwholesome in the excitement which ran so wholly in Mr. Peck's favour, but abandoned herself to it with feverish helplessness.

"Ah-h-h!" cried Putney, when they were free of the crowd which pressed upon him with questions and conjectures and comments. "What a slump!—what a slump! That blessed, short-legged little seraph has spoilt the best sport that ever was. Why, he's sent that fool of a Gerrish home with the conviction that he was right in the part of his attack that was the most vilely hypocritical, and he's given that heartless scoundrel the pleasure of feeling like an honest man. I should like to rap Mr. Peck's head up against the back of his pulpit, and I should like to knock the skulls of Colonel Marvin and Mr. Wilmington together and see which was the thickest. Why, I had Gerrish fairly by the throat at last, and I was just reaching for the balm of Gilead with my other hand to give him a dose that would have done him for one while! Ah, it's too bad, too bad! Well! well! But—haw! haw! haw!—didn't Gerrish tangle himself up beautifully in his rhetoric? I guess we shall fix Brother Gerrish yet, and I don't think we shall let Brother Peck off without a tussle. I'm going to try print on Brother Gerrish. I'm going to ask him in the Hatboro' *Register*—he doesn't advertise, and the editor's as independent as a lion where a man don't advertise—"

"Indeed he's not going to do anything of the kind, Annie," said Mrs. Putney. "I shall not let him. I shall make him drop the whole affair now, and let it die out, and let us be at peace again, as Mr. Peck says."

"There seemed to be a good deal of sense in that part of it," said Dr. Morrell. "I don't know but he was right to propose himself as a peace-offering; perhaps there's no other way out."

"Well," said Mrs. Putney, "whether he goes or stays, I think we owe him that much. Don't you, Annie?"

"Oh yes!" sighed Annie, from the exaltation to which the events of the evening had borne her. "And we mustn't let him go. It would be a loss that every one would feel; that—"

"I'm tired of this fighting." Mrs. Putney broke in, "and I think it's ruining Ralph every way. He hasn't slept the last two nights, and he's been all in a quiver for the last fortnight. For my part I don't care what happens now, I'm not going to have Ralph mixed up in it any more. I think we ought all to forgive and forget. I'm willing to overlook everything, and I believe others are the same."

"You'd better ask Mrs. Gerrish the next time she calls," Putney interposed.

Mrs. Putney stopped, and took her hand from her husband's arm. "Well, after what Mr. Gerrish said to-night about you, I *don't* think Emmeline had better call *very* soon!"

"Ha, ha, ha! Ha, ha, ha!" shrieked Putney, and his laugh flapped back at them in derisive echo from the house-front they were passing. "I guess Brother Peck had better stay and

help fight it out. It won't be *all* brotherly love after he goes—
or sisterly either."

XXVI

Annie knew from the light in the kitchen window that Mrs. Bolton, who had not gone to the meeting, was there, and she inferred from the silence of the house that Bolton had not yet come home. She went up to her room, and after a glance at Idella asleep in her crib, she began to lay off her things. Then she sat down provisionally by the open window, and looked out into the still autumnal night. The air was soft and humid, with a scent of smoke in it from remote forest fires. The village lights showed themselves dimmed by the haze that thickened the moonless dark.

She heard steps on the gravel of the lane, and then two men talking, one of whom she knew to be Bolton. In a little while the back entry door was opened and shut, and after a brief murmur of voices in the library Mrs. Bolton knocked on the door-jamb of the room where Annie sat.

"What is it, Mrs. Bolton?"

"You in bed yet?"

"No; I'm here by the window. What is it?"

"Well, I don't know but what you'll think it's pretty late for callers, but Mr. Peck is down in the library. I guess he wants to speak with you about Idella. I told him he better see *you*."

"I will come right down."

She followed Mrs. Bolton to the foot of the stairs, where she kept on to the kitchen, while Annie turned into the library. Mr. Peck stood beside her father's desk, resting one hand on it and holding his hat in the other.

"Won't you be seated, Mr. Peck?"

"I thank you. It's only for a moment. I am going away to-morrow, and I wish to speak with you about Idella."

"Yes, certainly. But surely you are not going to leave Hatboro', Mr. Peck! I hoped—we all did—that after what you had seen of the strong feeling in your favour to-night you would reconsider your determination and stay with us!" She went on impetuously. "You must know—you must understand now—how much good you can do here—more than any one else—more than you could do anywhere else. I don't believe that you realise how much depends upon your staying here. You can't stop the dissensions by going away; it will only make them worse. You saw how Colonel Marvin and Mr. Wilmington were with you; and Mr. Gates—all classes. I oughtn't to speak—to attempt to teach you your duty; I'm not of your church; and I can only tell you how it seems to me: that you never can find another place where your principles—your views—"

He waited for her to go on; but she really had nothing more to say, and he began: "I am not hoping for another charge elsewhere, at least not for the present; but I am satisfied that my usefulness here is at an end, and I do not think that my going away will make matters worse. Whether I go or stay, the dissensions will continue. At any rate, I believe that there are those who need help more, and whom I can help more, in another field—"

"Yes," she broke in, with a woman's relevancy to the immediate point, "there is nothing to do here."

He went on as if she had not spoken: "I am going to Fall River to-morrow, where I have heard that there is work for me—"

"In the mills!" she exclaimed, recurring in thought to what he had once said of his work in them. "Surely you don't mean that!" The sight, the smell, the tumult of the work she had seen that day in the mill with Lyra came upon her with all their offence. "To throw away all that you have learnt, all that you have become to others!"

"I am less and less confident that I have become anything useful to others in turning aside from the life of toil and presuming to attempt the guidance of those who remained in it. But I don't mean work in the mills," he continued, "or not at first, or not unless it seems necessary to my work with those who work in them. I have a plan—or if it hardly deserves that name, a design—of being useful to them in such ways as my own experience of their life in the past shall show me in the light of what I shall see among them now. I needn't trouble you with it."

"Oh yes!" she interposed.

"I do not expect to preach at once, but only to teach in one of the public schools, where I have heard of a vacancy, and—and—perhaps otherwise. With those whose lives are made up of hard work there must be room for willing and peaceful service. And if it should be necessary that I should work in the mills in order to render this, then I will do so; but at present I have another way in view—a social way that shall bring me into immediate relations with the people." She still tried to argue with him, to prove him wrong in going away, but they both ended where they began. He would not or could not explain himself further. At last he said: "But I did not come to urge this matter. I have no wish to impose my will, my theory, upon any one, even my own child."

"Oh yes—Idella!" Annie broke in anxiously. "You will leave her with me, Mr. Peck, won't you? You don't know how much I'm attached to her. I see her faults, and I shall not spoil her.

Leave her with me at least till you see your way clear to having her with you, and then I will send her to you."

A trouble showed itself in his face, ordinarily so impassive, and he seemed at a loss how to answer her; but he said: "I—appreciate your kindness to her, but I shall not ask you to be at the inconvenience longer than till to-morrow. I have arranged with another to take her until I am settled, and then bring her to me."

Annie sat intensely searching his face, with her lips parted to speak. "*Another!*" she said, and the wounded feeling, the resentment of his insensibility to her good-will, that mingled in her heart, must have made itself felt in her voice, for he went on reluctantly—

"It is a family in which she will be brought up to work and to be helpful to herself. They will join me with her. You know the mother—she has lost her own child—Mrs. Savor."

At the name, Annie's spirit fell; the tears started from her eyes. "Yes, she must have her. It is just—it is the only expiation. Don't you remember that it was I who sent Mrs. Savor's baby to the sea-shore, where it died?"

"No; I had forgotten," said the minister, aghast. "I am sorry—"

"It doesn't matter," said Annie lifelessly; "it had to be." After a pause, she asked quietly, "If Mrs. Savor is going to work in the mills, how can she make a home for the child?"

"She is not going into the mills," he answered. "She will keep house for us all, and we hope to have others who are without homes of their own join us in paying the expenses and doing the work, so that all may share its comfort without gain to any one upon their necessity of food and shelter."

She did not heed his explanation, but suddenly entreated: "Let me go with you. I will not be a trouble to you, and I will help as well as I can. I can't give the child up! Why—why"—the thought, crazy as it would have once seemed, was now such a happy solution of the trouble that she smiled hopefully—"why shouldn't I go with Mr. and Mrs. Savor, and help to make a home for Idella there? You will need money to begin your work; I will give you mine. I will give it up—I will give it all up. I will give it to any good object that you approve; or you may have it, to do what you think best with; and I will go with Idella and I will work in the mills there—or anything."

He shook his head, and for the first time in their acquaintance he seemed to feel compassion for her. "It isn't possible. I couldn't take your money; I shouldn't know what to do with it."

"You know what to do with your own," she broke in. "You do good with that!"

"I'm afraid I do harm with it too," he returned. "It's only a little, but little as it has been, I can no longer meet the responsibility it brings."

"But if you took my money," she urged, "you could devote your life to preaching the truth, to writing and publishing books, and all that; and so could others: don't you see?"

He shook his head. "Perhaps others; but I have done with preaching for the present. Later I may have something to say. Now I feel sure of nothing, not even of what I've been saying here."

"Will you send for Idella? When she goes with the Savors I will come too!"

He looked at her sorrowfully. "I think you are a good woman, and you mean what you say. But I am sorry you say it, if any words of mine have caused you to say it, for I know you cannot do it. Even for me it is hard to go back to those associations, and for you they would be impossible."

"You will see," she returned, with exaltation. "I will take Idella to the Savors' to-morrow—or no; I'll have them come here!"

He stood looking at her in perplexity. At last he asked, "Could I see the child?"

"Certainly!" said Annie, with the lofty passion that possessed her, and she led him up into the chamber where Idella lay sleeping in Annie's own crib.

He stood beside it, gazing long at the little one, from whose eyes he shaded the lamp. Then he said, "I thank you," and turned away.

She followed him down-stairs, and at the door she said: "You think I will not come; but I will come. Don't you believe that?"

He turned sadly from her. "You might come, but you couldn't stay. You don't know what it is; you can't imagine it, and you couldn't bear it."

"I will come, and I will stay," she answered; and when he was gone she fell into one of those intense reveries of hers—a rapture in which she prefigured what should happen in that new life before her. At its end Mr. Peck stood beside her grave, reading the lesson of her work to the multitude of grateful and loving poor who thronged to pay the last tribute to her memory. Putney was there with his wife, and Lyra regretful of her lightness, and Mrs. Munger repentant of her mendacities. They talked together in awe-stricken murmurs of the noble career just ended. She heard their voices, and then she began to ask herself what they would really say of her proposing to go to Fall River with the Savors and be a mill-hand.

XXVII

Annie did not sleep. After lying a long time awake she took some of the tonic that Dr. Morrell had left her, upon the chance that it might quiet her; but it did no good. She dressed herself, and sat by the window till morning.

The breaking day showed her purposes grotesque and monstrous. The revulsion that must come, came with a tide that swept before it all prepossessions, all affections. It seemed as if the child, still asleep in her crib, had heard what she said, and would help to hold her to her word.

She choked down a crust of bread with the coffee she drank at breakfast, and instead of romping with Idella at her bath, she dressed the little one silently, and sent her out to Mrs. Bolton. Then she sat down again in the sort of daze in which she had spent the night, and as the day passed, her revolt from what she had pledged herself to do mounted and mounted. It was like the sort of woman she was, not to think of any withdrawal from her pledges; they were all the more sacred with her because they had been purely voluntary, insistent; the fact that they had been refused made them the more obligatory.

She thought some one would come to break in upon the heavy monotony of the time; she expected Ralph or Ellen, or at least Lyra; but she only saw Mrs. Bolton, and heard her about her work. Sometimes the child stole back from the kitchen or the barn, and peeped in upon her with a roguish expectance which her gloomy stare defeated, and then it ran off again.

She lay down in the afternoon and tried to sleep; but her brain was inexorably alert, and she lay making inventory of all the pleasant things she was to leave for that ugly fate she had insisted on. A swarm of fancies gave every detail of the parting dramatic intensity. Amidst the poignancy of her regrets, her shame for her recreancy was sharper still.

By night she could bear it no longer. It was Dr. Morrell's custom to come nearly every night; but she was afraid, because he had walked home with her from the meeting the night before, he might not come now, and she sent for him. It was in quality of medicine-man, as well as physician, that she wished to see him; she meant to tell him all that had passed with Mr. Peck; and this was perfectly easy in the interview she forecast; but at the sound of his buggy wheels in the lane a thought came that seemed to forbid her even to speak of Mr. Peck to him. For the first time it occurred to her that the minister might have inferred a meaning from her eagerness and persistence infinitely more preposterous than even the preposterous letter of her words. A number of little proofs of the conjecture flashed upon her: his anxiety to get away from her, his refusal to let her believe in her own constancy of purpose, his moments of bewilderment and dismay. It needed nothing but this to add the touch of intolerable absurdity to the horror of the whole affair, and to snatch the last hope of help from her.

She let Mrs. Bolton go to the door, and she did not rise to meet the doctor; she saw from his smile that he knew he had a moral rather than a physical trouble to deal with, but she did not relax the severity of her glare in sympathy, as she was tempted from some infinite remoteness to do.

When he said, "You're not well," she whispered solemnly back, "Not at all."

He did not pursue his inquiry into her condition, but said, with an irrelevant cheerfulness that piqued her, "I was coming here this evening at any rate, and I got your message on the way up from my office."

"You are very kind," she said, a little more audibly.

"I wanted to tell you," he went on, "of what a time Putney and I have had to-day working up public sentiment for Mr. Peck, so as to keep him here."

Annie did not change her position, but the expression of her glance changed.

"We've been round in the enemy's camp, everywhere; and I've committed Gerrish himself to an armed neutrality. That wasn't difficult. The difficulty was in another quarter—with Mr. Peck himself. He's more opposed than any one else to his stay in Hatboro'. You know he intended going away this morning?"

"Did he?" Annie asked dishonestly. The question obliged her to say something.

"Yes. He came to Putney before breakfast to thank him and take leave of him, and to tell him of the plan he had for— Imagine what!"

"I don't know," said Annie, hoarsely, after an effort, as if the untruth would not come easily. "I am worse than Mrs. Munger," she thought.

"For going to Fall River to teach school among the mill-hands' children! And to open a night-school for the hands themselves."

The doctor waited for her sensation, and in its absence he looked so disappointed that she was forced to say, "To teach school?"

Then he went on briskly again. "Yes. Putney laboured with him on his knees, so to speak, and got him to postpone his going till to-morrow morning; and then he came to me for help. We enlisted Mrs. Wilmington in the cause, and we've spent the day working up the Peck sentiment to a fever-heat. It's been a very queer campaign; three Gentiles toiling for a saint against the elect, and bringing them all over at last. We've got a paper, signed by a large majority of the members of the church—the church, not the society—asking Mr. Peck to remain; and Putney's gone to him with the paper, and he's coming round here to report Mr. Peck's decision. We all agreed that it wouldn't do to say anything about his plan for the future, and I fancy some of his people signed our petition under the impression that they were keeping a valuable man out of another pulpit."

Annie accompanied the doctor's words, which she took in to the last syllable, with a symphony of conjecture as to how the change in Mr. Peck's plans, if they prevailed with him, would affect her, and the doctor had not ceased to speak before she perceived that it would be deliverance perfect and complete, however inglorious. But the tacit drama so vividly preoccupied her with its minor questions of how to descend to this escape with dignity that still she did not speak, and he took up the word again.

"I confess I've had my misgivings about Mr. Peck, and about his final usefulness in a community like this. In spite of all that Putney can say of his hard-headedness, I'm afraid that he's a good deal of a dreamer. But I gave way to Putney, and I hope you'll appreciate what I've done for your favourite."

"You are very good," she said, in mechanical acknowledgment: her mind was set so strenuously to break from her dishonest reticence that she did not know really what she was saying. "Why—why do you call him a dreamer?" She cast about in that direction at random.

"Why? Well, for one thing, the reason he gave Putney for giving up his luxuries here: that as long as there was hardship and overwork for underpay in the world, he must share them. It seems to me that I might as well say that as long as there were dyspepsia and rheumatism in the world, I must share them. Then he has a queer notion that he can go back and find instruction in the working-men—that they alone have the light and the truth, and know the meaning of life. I don't say anything against them. My observation and my experience is that if others were as good as they are in the ratio of their advantages, Mr. Peck needn't go to them for his ideal. But their conditions warp and dull them; they see things askew, and they don't see them clearly. I might as well expose myself to the small-pox in hopes of treating my fellow-sufferers more intelligently."

She could not perceive where his analogies rang false; they only overwhelmed her with a deeper sense of her own folly.

"But I don't know," he went on, "that a dreamer is such a desperate character, if you can only keep him from trying to realise his dreams; and if Mr. Peck consents to stay in Hatboro', perhaps we can manage it." He drew his chair a little toward the lounge where she reclined, and asked, with the kindliness that was both personal and professional, "What seems to be the matter?"

She started up. "There is nothing—nothing that medicine can help. Why do you call him my favourite?" she demanded violently. "But you have wasted your time. If he had made up his mind to what you say, he would never give it up—never in the world!" she added hysterically. "If you've interfered between any one and his duty in this world, where it seems as if hardly any one had any duty, you've done a very unwarrantable thing." She was aware from his stare that her words were incoherent, if not from the words themselves, but she hurried on: "I am going with him. He was here last night, and I told him I would. I will go with the Savors, and we will keep the child together; and if they will take me, I shall go to work in the mills; and I shall not care what people think, if it's right—"

She stopped and weakly dropped back on the lounge, and hid

her face in the pillow.

"I really don't understand." The doctor began, with a physician's carefulness, to unwind the coil she had flung down to him. "Are the Savors going, and the child?"

"He will give her the child for the one they lost—you know how! And they will take it with them."

"But you—what have you—"

"I must have the child too! I can't give it up, and I shall go with them. There's no other way. You don't know. I've given him my word, and there is no hope!"

"He asked you," said the doctor, to make sure he had heard aright—"he asked you—advised you—to go to work in a cotton-mill?"

"No;" she lifted her face to confront him. "He told me *not* to go; but I said I would."

They sat staring at each other in a silence which neither of them broke, and which promised to last indefinitely. They were still in their daze when Putney's voice came through the open hall door.

"Hello! hello! hello! Hello, Central! *Can't* I make you hear, any one?" His steps advanced into the hall, and he put his head in at the library doorway. "Thought you'd be here," he said, nodding at the doctor. "Well, doctor, Brother Peck's beaten us again. He's going."

"Going?" the doctor echoed.

"Yes. It's no use. I put the whole case before him, and I argued it with a force of logic that would have fetched the twelfth man with eleven stubborn fellows against him on a jury; but it didn't fetch Brother Peck. He was very appreciative and grateful, but he believes he's got a call to give up the ministry, for the present at least. Well, there's some consolation in supposing he may know best, after all. It seemed to us that he had a great opportunity in Hatboro', but if he turns his back on it, perhaps it's a sign he wasn't equal to it. The doctor told you what we've been up to, Annie?"

"Yes," she answered faintly, from the depths of the labyrinth in which she was plunged again.

"I'm sorry for your news about him," said the doctor. "I hoped he was going to stay. It's always a pity when such a man lets his sympathies use him instead of using them. But we must always judge that kind of crank leniently, if he doesn't involve other people in his erase."

She knew that he was shielding and trying to spare her, and she felt inexpressibly degraded by the terms of his forbearance. She could not accept, and she had not the strength to refuse it; and Putney said: "I've not seen anything to make me doubt his sanity; but I must say the present racket shakes my faith in his common-sense, and I rather held by that, you know. But I suppose no man, except the kind of a man that a woman would be if she were a man—excuse me, Annie—is ever absolutely right. I suppose the truth is a constitutional thing, and you can't separate it from the personal consciousness, and so you get it coloured and heated by personality when you get it fresh. That is, we can see what the absolute truth was, but never what it is."

Putney amused himself in speculating on these lines with more or less reference to Mr. Peck, and did not notice that the doctor and Annie gave him only a silent assent. "As to misleading any one else, Mr. Peck's following in his new religion seems to be confined to the Savors, as I understand. They are going with him to help him set up a sort of cooperative boarding-house. Well, I don't know where we shall get a hotter gospeller than Brother Peck. Poor old fellow! I hope he'll get along better in Fall River. It is something to be out of reach of Gerrish."

The doctor asked, "When is he going?"

"Why, he's gone by this time, I suppose," said Putney. "I tried to get him to think about it overnight, but he wouldn't. He's anxious to go and get back, so as to preach his last sermon here Sunday, and he's taken the 9.10, if he hasn't changed his mind." Putney looked at his watch.

"Let's hope he hasn't," said Dr. Morrell.

"Which?" asked Putney.

"Changed his mind. I'm sorry he's coming back."

Annie knew that he was talking at her, though he spoke to Putney; but she was powerless to protest.

XXVIII

They went away together, leaving her to her despair, which had passed into a sort of torpor by the following night, when Dr. Morrell came again, out of what she knew must be mere humanity; he could not respect her any longer. He told her, as if for her comfort, that Putney had gone to the depot to meet Mr. Peck, who was expected back in the eight-o'clock train, and was to labour with him all night long if necessary to get him to change, or at least postpone, his purpose. The feeling in his favour was growing. Putney hoped to put it so strongly to him as a proof of duty that he could not resist it.

Annie listened comfortlessly. Whatever happened, nothing could take away the shame of her weakness now. She even wished, feebly, vaguely, that she might be forced to keep her word.

A sound of running on the gravel-walk outside and a sharp pull at the door-bell seemed to jerk them both to their feet.

Some one stepped into the hall panting, and the face of William Savor showed itself at the door of the room where they stood. "Doc—Doctor Morrell, come—come quick! There's been an accident—at—the depot. Mr.—Peck—" He panted out the story, and Annie saw rather than heard how the minister tried to cross the track from his train, where it had halted short of the station, and the flying express from the other quarter caught him from his feet, and dropped the bleeding fragment that still held his life beside the rail a hundred yards away, and then kept on in brute ignorance into the night.

"Where is he? Where have you got him?" the doctor demanded of Savor.

"At my house."

The doctor ran out of the house, and she heard his buggy whirl away, followed by the fainter sound of Savor's feet as he followed running, after he had stopped to repeat his story to the Boltons. Annie turned to the farmer. "Mr. Bolton, get the carry-all. I must go."

"And me too," said his wife.

"Why, no, Pauliny; I guess you better stay. I guess it'll come out all right in the end," Bolton began. "*I* guess William has exaggerated some may be. Anyrate, who's goin' to look after the little girl if you come?"

"*I* am," Mrs. Bolton snapped back. "She's goin' with me."

"Of course she is. Be quick, Mr. Bolton!" Annie called from the stairs, which she had already mounted half-way.

She caught up the child, limp with sleep, from its crib, and began to dress it. Idella cried, and fought away the hands that tormented her, and made herself now very stiff and now very lax; but Annie and Mrs. Bolton together prevailed against her, and she was dressed, and had fallen asleep again in her clothes while the women were putting on their hats and sacks, and Bolton was driving up to the door with the carry-all.

"Why, I can see," he said, when he got out to help them in, "just how William's got his idee about it. His wife's an excitable kind of a woman, and she's sent him off lickety-split after the doctor without looking to see what the matter was. There hain't never been anybody hurt at our depot, and it

W. D. Howells

don't stand to reason—"

"Oliver Bolton, *will* you hush that noise?" shrieked his wife. "If the world was burnin' up you'd say it was nothing but a chimbley on fire som'er's."

"Well, well, Pauliny, have it your own way, have it your own way," said Bolton. "I ain't sayin' but what there's *some*thin' in William's story; but you'll see't he's exaggerated. Git up!"

"Well, do hurry, and *do* be still!" said his wife.

"Yes, yes. It's all right, Pauliny; all right. Soon's I'm out the lane, you'll see't I'll drive *fast* enough."

Mrs. Bolton kept a grim silence, against which her husband's babble of optimism played like heat-lightning on a night sky.

Idella woke with the rush of cold air, and in the dark and strangeness began to cry, and wailed heart-breakingly between her fits of louder sobbing, and then fell asleep again before they reached the house where her father lay dying.

They had put him in the best bed in Mrs. Savor's little guest-room, and when Annie entered, the minister was apologising to her for spoiling it.

"Now don't you say one word, Mr. Peck," she answered him. "It's all right. I ruthah see you layin' there just's you be than plenty of folks that—" She stopped for want of an apt comparison, and at sight of Annie she said, as if he were a child whose mind was wandering: "Well, I declare, if here ain't Miss Kilburn come to see you, Mr. Peck! And Mis' Bolton! Well, the land!"

Mrs. Savor came and shook hands with them, and in her character of hostess urged them forward from the door, where they had halted. "Want to see Mr. Peck? Well, he's real comf'table now; ain't he, Dr. Morrell? We got him all fixed up nicely, and he ain't in a bit o' pain. It's his spine that's hurt, so't he don't feel nothin'; but he's just as clear in his mind as what you or I be. *Ain't* he, doctor?"

"He's not suffering," said Dr. Morrell, to whom Annie's eye wandered from Mrs. Savor, and there was something in his manner that made her think the minister was not badly hurt. She went forward with Mr. and Mrs. Bolton, and after they had both taken the limp hand that lay outside the covering, she touched it too. It returned no pressure, but his large, wan eyes looked at her with such gentle dignity and intelligence that she began to frame in her mind an excuse for what seemed almost an intrusion.

"We were afraid you were hurt badly, and we thought—we thought you might like to see Idella—and so—we came. She is in the next room."

"Thank you," said the minister. "I presume that I am dying; the doctor tells me that I have but a few hours to live."

Mrs. Savor protested, "Oh, I guess you ain't a-goin' to die *this* time, Mr. Peck." Annie looked from Dr. Morrell to Putney, who stood with him on the other side of the bed, and experienced a shock from their gravity without yet being able to accept the fact it implied. "There's plenty of folks," continued Mrs. Savor, "hurt worse'n what you be that's alive to-day and as well as ever they was."

Bolton seized his chance. "It's just what I said to Pauliny, comin' along. 'You'll see,' said I, 'Mr. Peck'll be out as spry as any of us before a great while.' That's the way I felt about it from the start."

"All you got to do is to keep up courage," said Mrs. Savor.

"That's so; that's half the battle," said Bolton.

There were numbers of people in the room and at the door of

the next. Annie saw Colonel Marvin and Jack Wilmington. She heard afterward that he was going to take the same train to Boston with Mr. Peck, and had helped to bring him to the Savors' house. The stationmaster was there, and some other railroad employes.

The doctor leaned across the bed and lifted slightly the arm that lay there, taking the wrist between his thumb and finger. "I think we had better let Mr. Peck rest a while," he said to the company generally, "We're doing him no good."

The people began to go; some of them said, "Well, good night!" as if they would meet again in the morning. They all made the pretence that it was a slight matter, and treated the wounded man as if he were a child. He did not humour the pretence, but said "Good-bye" in return for their "Good night" with a quiet patience.

Mrs. Savor hastened after her retreating guests. "I ain't a-goin' to let you go without a sup of coffee," she said. "I want you should all stay and git some, and I don't believe but what a little of it would do Mr. Peck good."

The surface of her lugubrious nature was broken up, and whatever was kindly and cheerful in its depths floated to the top; she was almost gay in the demand which the calamity made upon her. Annie knew that she must have seen and helped to soothe the horror of mutilation which she could not even let her fancy figure, and she followed her foolish bustle and chatter with respectful awe.

"Rebecca'll have it right off the stove in half a minute now," Mrs. Savor concluded; and from a further room came the cheerful click of cups, and then a wandering whiff of the coffee; life in its vulgar kindliness touched and made friends with death, claiming it a part of nature too.

The night at Mrs. Munger's came back to Annie from the immeasurable remoteness into which all the past had lapsed.

She looked up at Dr. Morrell across the bed.

"Would you like to speak with Mr. Peck?" he asked officially. "Better do it now," he said, with one of his short nods.

Putney came and set her a chair. She would have liked to fall on her knees beside the bed; but she took the chair, and drew the minister's hand into hers, stretching her arm above his head on the pillow. He lay like some poor little wounded boy, like Putney's Winthrop; the mother that is in every woman's heart gushed out of hers in pity upon him, mixed with filial reverence. She had thought that she should confess her baseness to him, and ask his forgiveness, and offer to fulfil with the people he had chosen for the guardians of his child that interrupted purpose of his. But in the presence of death, so august, so simple, all the concerns of life seemed trivial, and she found herself without words. She sobbed over the poor hand she held. He turned his eyes upon her and tried to speak, but his lips only let out a moaning, shuddering sound, inarticulate of all that she hoped or feared he might prophesy to shape her future.

Life alone has any message for life, but from the beginning of time it has put its ear to the cold lips that must for ever remain dumb.

XXIX

The evening after the funeral Annie took Idella, with the child's clothes and toys in a bundle, and Bolton drove them down Over the Track to the Savors'. She had thought it all out, and she perceived that whatever the minister's final intention might have been, she was bound by the purpose he had expressed to her, and must give up the child. For fear she might be acting from the false conscientiousness of which she was beginning to have some notion in herself, she put the case to Mrs. Bolton. She knew what she must do in any event, but it was a comfort to be stayed so firmly in her duty by Mrs. Bolton, who did not spare some doubts of Mrs. Savor's fitness for the charge, and reflected a subdued censure even upon the judgment of Mr. Peck himself, as she bustled about and helped Annie get Idella and her belongings ready. The child watched the preparations with suspicion. At the end, when she was dressed, and Annie tried to lift her into the carriage, she broke out in sudden rebellion; she cried, she shrieked, she fought; the two good women who were obeying the dead minister's behest were obliged to descend to the foolish lies of the nursery; they told her she was going on a visit to the Savors, who would take her on the cars with them, and then bring her back to Aunt Annie's house. Before they could reconcile her to this fabled prospect they had to give it verisimilitude by taking off her everyday clothes and putting on her best dress.

She did not like Mrs. Savor's house when she came to it, nor Mrs. Savor, who stopped, all blowzed and work-deranged from trying to put it in order after the death in it, and gave Idella a motherly welcome. Annie fancied a certain surprise in her manner, and her own ideal of duty was put to proof by Mrs. Savor's owning that she had not expected Annie to bring Idella to her right away.

"If I had not done it at once, I never could have done it," Annie explained.

"Well, I presume it's a cross," said Mrs. Savor, "and I don't feel right to take her. If it wa'n't for what her father—"

"'Sh!" Annie said, with a significant glance.

"It's an ugly house!" screamed the child. "I want to go back to my Aunt Annie's house. I want to go on the cars."

"Yes, yes," answered Mrs. Savor, blindly groping to share in whatever cheat had been practised on the child, "just as soon as the cars starts. Here, William, you take her out and show her the pretty coop you be'n makin' the pigeons, to keep the cats out."

They got rid of her with Savor's connivance for the moment, and Annie hastened to escape.

"We had to tell her she was going a journey, or we never could have got her into the carriage," she explained, feeling like a thief.

"Yes, yes. It's all right," said Mrs. Savor. "I see you'd be'n putting up some kind of job on her the minute she mentioned the cars. Don't you fret any, Miss Kilburn. Rebecca and me'll get along with her, you needn't be afraid."

Annie could not look at the empty crib where it stood in its alcove when she went to bed; and she cried upon her own pillow with heart-sickness for the child, and with a humiliating doubt of her own part in hurrying to give it up without thought of Mrs. Savor's convenience. What had seemed so noble, so exemplary, began to wear another colour; and she drowsed, worn out at last by the swarming fears, shames, and despairs, which resolved themselves into a fantastic medley of dream images. There was a cat trying to get at the pigeons in the coop which Mr. Savor had carried Idella to see. It clawed and miauled at the lattice-work of lath, and its caterwauling became like the cry of a child, so like that it woke Annie from her sleep, and still kept on. She lay shuddering a moment; it seemed as if the dead minister's ghost flitted from the room, while the crying defined and located itself more and more, till she knew it a child's wail at the door of her house. Then she heard, "Aunt Annie! Aunt Annie!" and soft, faint thumps as of a little fist upon the door panels.

She had no experience of more than one motion from her bed to the door, which the same impulse flung open and let her crush to her breast the little tumult of sobs and moans from the threshold.

"Oh, wicked, selfish, heartless wretch!" she stormed out over the child. "But now I will never, never, never give you up! Oh, my poor little baby! my darling! God has sent you back to me, and I will keep you. I don't care what happens! What a cruel wretch I have been—oh, what a cruel wretch, my pretty!—to tear you from your home! But now you shall never leave it; no one shall take you away." She gripped it in a succession of fierce hugs, and mumbled it—face and neck, and little cold wet hands and feet—with her kisses; and all the time she did not know the child was in its night-dress like herself, or that her own feet were bare, and her drapery as scanty as Idella's.

A sense of the fact evanescently gleamed upon her with the appearance of Mrs. Bolton, lamp in hand, and the instantaneous appearance and disappearance of her husband at the back door through which she emerged. The two women spent the first moments of the lamp-light in making certain that Idella was sound and whole in every part, and then in making uncertain for ever how she came to be there. Whether she had wandered out in her sleep, and found her way home with dream-led feet, or whether she had watched till the house was quiet, and then stolen away, was what she could not tell them, and must always remain a mystery.

"I don't believe but what Mr. Bolton had better go and wake up the Savors. You got to keep her for the night, I presume, but they'd ought to know where she is, and you can take her over there agin, come daylight."

"*Mrs.* Bolton!" shouted Annie, in a voice so deep and hoarse that it shook the heart of a woman who had never known fear of man. "If you say such a thing to me—if you ever say such a thing again—I—I—I will *hit* you! Send Mr. Bolton for Idella's things—right away!"

*   *   *   *   *

"Land!" said Mrs. Savor, when Bolton, after a long conciliatory preamble, explained that he did not believe Miss Kilburn felt a great deal like giving the child up again. "*I* don't want it without it's satisfied to stay. I see last night it was just breakin' its heart for her, and I told William when we first missed her this mornin', and he was in such a pucker about her, I bet anything he was a mind to that the child had gone back to Miss Kilburn's. That's just the words I used; didn't I, Rebecca? I couldn't stand it to have no child *grievin'* around."

Beyond this sentimental reluctance, Mrs. Savor later confessed to Annie herself that she was really accepting the charge of Idella in the same spirit of self-sacrifice as that in which Annie was surrendering it, and that she felt, when Mr. Peck first suggested it, that the child was better off with Miss Kilburn; only she hated to say so. Her husband seemed to think it would make up to her for the one they lost, but nothing could really do that.

XXX

In a reverie of rare vividness following her recovery of the minister's child, Annie Kilburn dramatised an escape from all the failures and humiliations of her life in Hatboro'. She took Idella with her and went back to Rome, accomplishing the whole affair so smoothly and rapidly that she wondered at herself for not having thought of such a simple solution of her difficulties before. She even began to put some little things together for her flight, while she explained to old friends in the American colony that Idella was the orphan child of a country minister, which she had adopted. That old lady who had found her motives in returning to Hatboro' insufficient questioned her sharply *why* she had adopted the minister's child, and did not find her answers satisfactory. They were such as also failed to pacify inquiry in Hatboro', where Annie remained, in spite of her reverie; but people accepted the fact, and accounted for it in their own way, and approved it, even though they could not quite approve her.

The dramatic impressiveness of the minister's death won him undisputed favour, yet it failed to establish unity in his society. Supply after supply filled his pulpit, but the people found them all unsatisfactory when they remembered his preaching, and could not make up their minds to any one of them. They were more divided than ever, except upon the point of regretting Mr. Peck. But they distinguished, in honouring his memory. They revered his goodness and his wisdom, but they regarded his conduct of life as unpractical. They said there never was a more inspired teacher, but it was impossible to follow him, and he could not himself have kept the course he had marked out. They said, now that he was beyond recall, no one else could have built up the church in Hatboro' as he could, if he could only have let impracticable theories alone. Mr. Gerrish called many people to witness that this was what he had always said. He contended that it was the spirit of the gospel which you were to follow. He said that if Mr. Peck had gone to teaching among the mill hands, he would have been sick of it inside of six weeks; but he was a good Christian man, and no one wished less than Mr. Gerrish to reproach him for what was, after all, more an error of the head than the heart. His critics had it their own way in this, for he had not lived to offer that full exposition of his theory and justification of his purpose which he had been expected to give on the Sunday after he was killed; and his death was in no wise exegetic. It said no more to his people than it had said to Annie; it was a mere casualty; and his past life, broken and unfulfilled, with only its intimations and intentions of performance, alone remained.

When people learned, as they could hardly help doing from Mrs. Savor's volubility, what his plan with regard to Idella had been, they instanced that in proof of the injuriousness of his idealism as applied to real life; and they held that she had been remanded in that strange way to Miss Kilburn's charge for some purpose which she must not attempt to cross. As the minister had been thwarted in another intent by death, it was a sign that he was wrong in this too, and that she could do better by the child than he had proposed.

This was the sum of popular opinion; and it was further the opinion of Mrs. Gerrish, who gave more attention to the case than many others, that Annie had first taken the child because she hoped to get Mr. Peck, when she found she could not get Dr. Morrell; and that she would have been very glad to be rid of it if she had known how, but that she would have to keep it now for shame's sake.

For shame's sake certainly, Annie would have done several

other things, and chief of these would have been never to see Dr. Morrell again. She believed that he not only knew the folly she had confessed to him, but that he had divined the cowardice and meanness in which she had repented it, and she felt intolerably disgraced before the thought of him. She had imagined mainly because of him that escape to Rome which never has yet been effected, though it might have been attempted if Idella had not wakened ill from the sleep she sobbed herself into when she found herself safe in Annie's crib again.

She had taken a heavy cold, and she moped lifelessly about during the day, and drowsed early again in the troubled cough-broken slumber.

"That child ought to have the doctor," said Mrs. Bolton, with the grim impartiality in which she masked her interference.

"Well," said Annie helplessly.

At the end of the lung fever which followed, "It was a narrow chance," said the doctor one morning; "but now I needn't come any more unless you send for me."

Annie stood at the door, where he spoke with his hand on the dash-board of his buggy before getting into it.

She answered with one of those impulses that come from something deeper than intention. "I will send for you, then— to tell you how generous you are," and in the look with which she spoke she uttered the full meaning that her words withheld.

He flushed for pleasure of conscious desert, but he had to laugh and turn it off lightly. "I don't think I could come for that. But I'll look in to see Idella unprofessionally."

He drove away, and she remained at her door looking up at the summer blue sky that held a few soft white clouds, such as might have overhung the same place at the same hour thousands of years before, and such as would lazily drift over it in a thousand years to come. The morning had an immeasurable vastness, through which some crows flying across the pasture above the house sent their voices on the spacious stillness. A perception of the unity of all things under the sun flashed and faded upon her, as such glimpses do. Of her high intentions, nothing had resulted. An inexorable centrifugality had thrown her off at every point where she tried to cling. Nothing of what was established and regulated had desired her intervention; a few accidents and irregularities had alone accepted it. But now she felt that nothing withal had been lost; a magnitude, a serenity, a tolerance, intimated itself in the universal frame of things, where her failure, her recreancy, her folly, seemed for the moment to come into true perspective, and to show venial and unimportant, to be limited to itself, and to be even good in its effect of humbling her to patience with all imperfection and shortcoming, even her own. She was aware of the cessation of a struggle that has never since renewed itself with the old intensity; her wishes, her propensities, ceased in that degree to represent evil in conflict with the portion of good in her; they seemed so mixed and interwoven with the good that they could no longer be antagonised; for the moment they seemed in their way even wiser and better, and ever after to be the nature out of which good as well as evil might come.

As she remained standing there, Mr. Brandreth came round the corner of the house, looking very bright and happy.

"Miss Kilburn," he said abruptly, "I want you to congratulate me. I'm engaged to Miss Chapley."

"Are you indeed, Mr. Brandreth? I do congratulate you with all my heart. She is a lovely girl."

"Yes, it's all right now," said Mr. Brandreth. "I've come to tell you the first one, because you seemed to take an interest in it when I told you of the trouble about the Juliet. We hadn't come to any understanding before that, but that seemed to bring us both to the point, and—and we're engaged. Mother and I are going to New York for the winter; we think she can risk it; and at any rate she won't be separated from me; and we shall be back in our little home next May. You know that I'm to be with Mr. Chapley in his business?"

"Why, no! This is *great* news, Mr. Brandreth! I don't know what to say."

"You're very kind," said the young man, and for the third or fourth time he wrung her hand. "It isn't a partnership, of course; but he thinks I can be of use to him."

"I know you can!" Annie adventured.

"We are very busy getting ready—nearly everybody else is gone—and mother sent her kindest regards—you know she don't make calls—and I just ran up to tell you. Well, *good-*bye!"

"*Good-*bye! Give my love to your mother, and to your-to Miss Chapley."

"I will." He hurried off, and then came running back. "Oh, I forgot! About the Social Union fund. You know we've got about two hundred dollars from the theatricals, but the matter seems to have stopped there, and some of us think there'd better be some other disposition of the money. Have you any suggestion to make?"

"No, none."

"Then I'll tell you. It's proposed to devote the money to beautifying the grounds around the soldiers' monument. They ought to be fenced and planted with flowers—turned into a little public garden. Everybody appreciates the interest you took in the Union, and we hoped you'd be pleased with that disposition of the money."

"It is very kind," said Annie, with a meek submission that must have made him believe she was deeply touched.

"As I'm not to be here this winter," he continued, "we thought we had better leave the whole matter in your hands, and the money has been deposited in the bank subject to your order. It was Mrs. Munger's idea. I don't think she's ever felt just right about that evening of the dramatics, don't you know. *Good-bye!*"

He ran off to escape her thanks for this proof of confidence in her taste and judgment, and he was gone beyond her protest before she emerged from her daze into a full sense of the absurdity of the situation.

"Well, it's a very simple matter to let the money lie in the bank," said Dr. Morrell, who came that evening to make his first unprofessional visit, and received with pure amusement the account of the affair, which she gave him with a strong infusion of vexation.

"The way I was involved in this odious Social Union business from the first, and now have it left on my hands in the end, is maddening. Why, I can't get rid of it!" she replied.

"Then, perhaps," he comfortably suggested, "it's a sign you're not intended to get rid of it."

"What *do* you mean?"

"Why don't you go on," he irresponsibly adventured further, "and establish a Social Union?"

"Do you *mean* it?"

"What was that notion of his"—they usually spoke of the minister pronominally—"about getting the Savors going in a co-operative boarding-house at Fall River? Putney said something about it."

Annie explained, as she had heard it from him, and from the Savors since his death, the minister's scheme for a club, in which the members should contribute the labour and the provisions, and should live cheaply and wholesomely under the management of the Savors at first, and afterward should continue them in charge, or not, as they chose. "He seemed to have thought it out very carefully. But I supposed, of course, it was unpractical."

"Was that why you were going in for it?" asked the doctor; and then he spared her confusion in adding: "I don't see why it was unpractical. It seems to me a very good notion for a Social Union. Why not try it here? There isn't the same pressing necessity that there is in a big factory town; but you have the money, and you have the Savors to make a beginning."

His tone was still half bantering; but it had become more and more serious, so that she could say in earnest: "But the money is one of the drawbacks. It was Mr. Peck's idea that the working people ought to do it all themselves."

"Well, I should say that two-thirds of that money in the bank had come from them. They turned out in great force to Mr. Brandreth's theatricals. And wouldn't it be rather high-handed to use their money for anything but the Union?"

"You don't suppose," said Annie hotly, "that I would spend a cent of it on the grounds of that idiotic monument? I would pay for having it blown up with dynamite! No, I can't have anything more to do with the wretched affair. My touch is fatal." The doctor laughed, and she added: "Besides, I believe most heartily with Mr. Peck that no person of means and leisure can meet working people except in the odious character of a patron, and if I didn't respect them, I respect myself too much for that. If I were ready to go in with them and start the Social Union on his basis, by helping do house-work—*scullion*-work—for it, and eating and living with them, I might try; but I know from experience I'm not. I haven't the need, and to pretend that I have, to forego my comforts and luxuries in a make-believe that I haven't them, would be too ghastly a farce, and I won't."

"Well, then, don't," said the doctor, bent more perhaps on carrying his point in argument than on promoting the actual establishment of the Social Union. "But my idea is this: Take two-thirds or one-half of that money, and go to Savor, and say: 'Here! This is what Mr. Brandreth's theatricals swindled the shop-hands out of. It's honestly theirs, at least to control; and if you want to try that experiment of Mr. Peck's here in Hatboro', it's yours. We people of leisure, or comparative leisure, have really nothing in common with you people who work with your hands for a living; and as we really can't be friends with you, we won't patronise you. We won't advise you, and we won't help you; but here's the money. If you fail, you fail; and if you succeed, you won't succeed by our aid and comfort.'"

The plan that Annie and Doctor Morrell talked over half in joke took a more and more serious character in her sense of duty to the minister's memory and the wish to be of use, which was not extinct in her, however she mocked and defied it. It was part of the irony of her fate that the people who were best able to counsel with her in regard to it were Lyra, whom she could not approve, and Jack Wilmington, whom she had always disliked. He was able to contribute some facts about the working of the Thayer Club at the Harvard Memorial Hall in Cambridge, and Lyra because she had been herself a hand, and would not forget it, was of use in bringing the scheme into favour with the hands. They felt easy with her, as they did with Putney, and for much the same reason: it is one of the pleasing facts of our conditions that people who are socially inferior like best those above them who are morally anomalous. It was really through Lyra that Annie got at the working people, and when it came to a formal conference, there was no one who could command their confidence like Putney, whom they saw mad-drunk two or three times a year, but always pulling up and fighting back to sanity against the enemy whose power some of them had felt too.

No theory is so perfect as not to be subject to exceptions in the experiment, and in spite of her conviction of the truth of Mr. Peck's social philosophy, Annie is aware, through her simple and frank relations with the hands in a business matter, of mutual kindness which it does not account for. But perhaps the philosophy and the experiment were not contradictory; perhaps it was intended to cover only the cases in which they had no common interest. At anyrate, when the Peck Social Union, as its members voted to call it, at the suggestion of one of their own number, got in working order, she was as cordially welcomed to the charge of its funds and accounts as if she had been a hat-shop hand or a shoe-binder. She is really of use, for its working is by no means ideal, and with her wider knowledge she has suggested improvements and expedients for making both ends meet which were sometimes so reluctant to meet. She has kept a conscience against subsidising the Union from her own means; and she even accepts for her services a small salary, which its members think they ought to pay her. She owns this ridiculous, like all the make-believe work of rich people; a travesty which has no reality except the little sum it added to the greater sum of her superabundance. She is aware that she is a pensioner upon the real members of the Social Union for a chance to be useful, and that the work they let her do is the right of some one who needs it. She has thought of doing the work and giving the pay to another; but she sees that this would be pauperising and degrading another. So she dwells in a vicious circle, and waits, and mostly forgets, and is mostly happy.

The Social Union itself, though not a brilliant success in all points, is still not a failure; and the promise of its future is in the fact that it continues to have a present. The people of Hatboro' are rather proud of it, and strangers visit it as one of the possible solutions of one of the social problems. It is predicted that it cannot go on; that it must either do better or do worse; but it goes on the same.

Putney studies its existence in the light of his own infirmity, to which he still yields from time to time, as he has always done.

He professes to find there a law which would account for a great many facts of human experience otherwise inexplicable. He does not attempt to define this occult preservative principle, but he offers himself and the Social Union as proofs of its existence; and he argues that if they can only last long enough they will finally be established in a virtue and prosperity as great as those of Mr. Gerrish and his store.

Annie sometimes feels that nothing else can explain the maintenance of Lyra Wilmington's peculiar domestic relations at the point which perpetually invites comment and never justifies scandal. The situation seems to her as lamentable as ever. She grieves over Lyra, and likes her, and laughs with her; she no longer detests Jack Wilmington so much since he showed himself so willing and helpful about the Social Union; she thinks there must be a great deal of good in him, and sometimes she is sorry for him, and longs to speak again to Lyra about the wrong she is doing him. One of the dangers of having a very definite point of view is the temptation of abusing it to read the whole riddle of the painful earth. Annie has permitted herself to think of Lyra's position as one which would be impossible in a state of things where there was neither poverty nor riches, and there was neither luxury on one hand to allure, nor the fear of want to constrain on the other.

When her recoil from the fulfilment of her volunteer pledge to Mr. Peck brought her face to face with her own weakness, there were two ways back to self-respect, either of which she might take. She might revert to her first opinion of him, and fortify herself in that contempt and rejection of his ideas, or she might abandon herself to them, with a vague intention of reparation to him, and accept them to the last insinuation of their logic. This was what she did, and while her life remained the same outwardly, it was inwardly all changed. She never could tell by what steps she reached her agreement with the minister's philosophy; perhaps, as a woman, it was not possible she should; but she had a faith concerning it to which she bore unswerving allegiance, and it was Putney's delight to witness its revolutionary effect on an old Hatboro' Kilburn, the

W. D. Howells

daughter of a shrewd lawyer and canny politician like her father, and the heir of an aristocratic tradition, a gentlewoman born and bred. He declared himself a reactionary in comparison with her, and had the habit of taking the conservative side against her. She was in the joke of this; but it was a real trouble to her for a time that Dr. Morrell, after admitting the force of her reasons, should be content to rest in a comfortable inconclusion as to his conduct, till one day she reflected that this was what she was herself doing, and that she differed from him only in the openness with which she proclaimed her opinions. Being a woman, her opinions were treated by the magnates of Hatboro' as a good joke, the harmless fantasies of an old maid, which she would get rid of if she could get anybody to marry her; being a lady, and very well off, they were received with deference, and she was left to their uninterrupted enjoyment. Putney amused himself by saying that she was the fiercest apostle of labour that never did a stroke of work; but no one cared half so much for all that as for the question whether her affair with Dr. Morrell was a friendship or a courtship. They saw an activity of attention on his part which would justify the most devout belief in the latter, and yet they were confronted with the fact that it so long remained eventless. The two theories, one that she was amusing herself with him, and the other that he was just playing with her, divided public opinion, but they did not molest either of the parties to the mystery; and the village, after a season of acute conjecture, quiesced into that sarcastic sufferance of the anomaly into which it may have been noticed that small communities are apt to subside from such occasions. Except for some such irreconcilable as Mrs. Gerrish, it was a good joke that if you could not find Dr. Morrell in his office after tea, you could always find him at Miss Kilburn's. Perhaps it might have helped solve the mystery if it had been known that she could not accept the situation, whatever it really was, without satisfying herself upon two points, which resolved themselves into one in the process of the inquiry.

She asked, apparently as preliminary to answering a question of his, "Have you heard that gossip about my—being in—caring for the poor man?"

"Yes."

"And did you—what did you think?"

"That it wasn't true. I knew if there were anything in it, you couldn't have talked him over with me."

She was silent. Then she said, in a low voice: "No, there couldn't have been. But not for that reason alone, though it's very delicate and generous of you to think of it, very large-minded; but because it *couldn't* have been. I could have worshipped him, but I couldn't have loved him—any more," she added, with an implication that entirely satisfied him, "than I could have worshipped *you*."

ABOUT THE AUTHOR

 **William Dean Howells** (March 1, 1837 – May 11, 1920) was an American realist author and literary critic.

Born in Martins Ferry, Ohio, originally Martinsville, to William Cooper and Mary Dean Howells, Howells was the second of eight children. His father was a newspaper editor and printer, and the father moved frequently around Ohio. Howells began to help his father with typesetting and printing work at an early age. In 1852, his father arranged to have one of Howells' poems published in the Ohio State Journal without telling him.

He wrote his first novel, The Wedding Journey, in 1872, but his literary reputation took off with the realist novel, A Modern Instance, published in 1882, which described the decay of a marriage. His 1885 novel The Rise of Silas Lapham is perhaps his best known, describing the rise and fall of an American entrepreneur in the paint business. His social views were also strongly reflected in the novels Annie Kilburn (1888) and A Hazard of New Fortunes (1890). He was particularly outraged by the trials resulting from the Haymarket Riot.

In 1904, he was one of the first seven chosen for membership in the American Academy of Arts and Letters, of which he became president.

Choose from Thousands of 1stWorldLibrary Classics By

A. M. Barnard
Ada Leverson
Adolphus William Ward
Aesop
Agatha Christie
Alexander Aaronsohn
Alexander Kielland
Alexandre Dumas
Alfred Gatty
Alfred Ollivant
Alice Duer Miller
Alice Turner Curtis
Alice Dunbar
Allen Chapman
Alleyne Ireland
Ambrose Bierce
Amelia E. Barr
Amory H. Bradford
Andrew Lang
Andrew McFarland Davis
Andy Adams
Angela Brazil
Anna Alice Chapin
Anna Sewell
Annie Besant
Annie Hamilton Donnell
Annie Payson Call
Annie Roe Carr
Annonaymous
Anton Chekhov
Archibald Lee Fletcher
Arnold Bennett
Arthur C. Benson
Arthur Conan Doyle
Arthur M. Winfield
Arthur Ransome
Arthur Schnitzler
Arthur Train
Atticus
B.H. Baden-Powell
B. M. Bower
B. C. Chatterjee
Baroness Emmuska Orczy
Baroness Orczy
Basil King
Bayard Taylor
Ben Macomber
Bertha Muzzy Bower
Bjornstjerne Bjornson

Booth Tarkington
Boyd Cable
Bram Stoker
C. Collodi
C. E. Orr
C. M. Ingleby
Carolyn Wells
Catherine Parr Traill
Charles A. Eastman
Charles Amory Beach
Charles Dickens
Charles Dudley Warner
Charles Farrar Browne
Charles Ives
Charles Kingsley
Charles Klein
Charles Hanson Towne
Charles Lathrop Pack
Charles Romyn Dake
Charles Whibley
Charles Willing Beale
Charlotte M. Braeme
Charlotte M. Yonge
Charlotte Perkins Stetson
Clair W. Hayes
Clarence Day Jr.
Clarence E. Mulford
Clemence Housman
Confucius
Coningsby Dawson
Cornelis DeWitt Wilcox
Cyril Burleigh
D. H. Lawrence
Daniel Defoe
David Garnett
Dinah Craik
Don Carlos Janes
Donald Keyhoe
Dorothy Kilner
Dougan Clark
Douglas Fairbanks
E. Nesbit
E. P. Roe
E. Phillips Oppenheim
E. S. Brooks
Earl Barnes
Edgar Rice Burroughs
Edith Van Dyne
Edith Wharton

Edward Everett Hale
Edward J. O'Biren
Edward S. Ellis
Edwin L. Arnold
Eleanor Atkins
Eleanor Hallowell Abbott
Eliot Gregory
Elizabeth Gaskell
Elizabeth McCracken
Elizabeth Von Arnim
Ellem Key
Emerson Hough
Emilie F. Carlen
Emily Bronte
Emily Dickinson
Enid Bagnold
Enilor Macartney Lane
Erasmus W. Jones
Ernie Howard Pie
Ethel May Dell
Ethel Turner
Ethel Watts Mumford
Eugene Sue
Eugenie Foa
Eugene Wood
Eustace Hale Ball
Evelyn Everett-green
Everard Cotes
F. H. Cheley
F. J. Cross
F. Marion Crawford
Fannie E. Newberry
Federick Austin Ogg
Ferdinand Ossendowski
Fergus Hume
Florence A. Kilpatrick
Fremont B. Deering
Francis Bacon
Francis Darwin
Frances Hodgson Burnett
Frances Parkinson Keyes
Frank Gee Patchin
Frank Harris
Frank Jewett Mather
Frank L. Packard
Frank V. Webster
Frederic Stewart Isham
Frederick Trevor Hill
Frederick Winslow Taylor

Friedrich Kerst
Friedrich Nietzsche
Fyodor Dostoyevsky
G.A. Henty
G.K. Chesterton
Gabrielle E. Jackson
Garrett P. Serviss
Gaston Leroux
George A. Warren
George Ade
Geroge Bernard Shaw
George Cary Eggleston
George Durston
George Ebers
George Eliot
George Gissing
George MacDonald
George Meredith
George Orwell
George Sylvester Viereck
George Tucker
George W. Cable
George Wharton James
Gertrude Atherton
Gordon Casserly
Grace E. King
Grace Gallatin
Grace Greenwood
Grant Allen
Guillermo A. Sherwell
Gulielma Zollinger
Gustav Flaubert
H. A. Cody
H. B. Irving
H.C. Bailey
H. G. Wells
H. H. Munro
H. Irving Hancock
H. R. Naylor
H. Rider Haggard
H. W. C. Davis
Haldeman Julius
Hall Caine
Hamilton Wright Mabie
Hans Christian Andersen
Harold Avery
Harold McGrath
Harriet Beecher Stowe
Harry Castlemon
Harry Coghill
Harry Houidini

Hayden Carruth
Helen Hunt Jackson
Helen Nicolay
Hendrik Conscience
Hendy David Thoreau
Henri Barbusse
Henrik Ibsen
Henry Adams
Henry Ford
Henry Frost
Henry James
Henry Jones Ford
Henry Seton Merriman
Henry W Longfellow
Herbert A. Giles
Herbert Carter
Herbert N. Casson
Herman Hesse
Hildegard G. Frey
Homer
Honore De Balzac
Horace B. Day
Horace Walpole
Horatio Alger Jr.
Howard Pyle
Howard R. Garis
Hugh Lofting
Hugh Walpole
Humphry Ward
Ian Maclaren
Inez Haynes Gillmore
Irving Bacheller
Isabel Cecilia Williams
Isabel Hornibrook
Israel Abrahams
Ivan Turgenev
J.G.Austin
J. Henri Fabre
J. M. Barrie
J. M. Walsh
J. Macdonald Oxley
J. R. Miller
J. S. Fletcher
J. S. Knowles
J. Storer Clouston
J. W. Duffield
Jack London
Jacob Abbott
James Allen
James Andrews
James Baldwin

James Branch Cabell
James DeMille
James Joyce
James Lane Allen
James Lane Allen
James Oliver Curwood
James Oppenheim
James Otis
James R. Driscoll
Jane Abbott
Jane Austen
Jane L. Stewart
Janet Aldridge
Jens Peter Jacobsen
Jerome K. Jerome
Jessie Graham Flower
John Buchan
John Burroughs
John Cournos
John F. Kennedy
John Gay
John Glasworthy
John Habberton
John Joy Bell
John Kendrick Bangs
John Milton
John Philip Sousa
John Taintor Foote
Jonas Lauritz Idemil Lie
Jonathan Swift
Joseph A. Altsheler
Joseph Carey
Joseph Conrad
Joseph E. Badger Jr
Joseph Hergesheimer
Joseph Jacobs
Jules Vernes
Julian Hawthrone
Julie A Lippmann
Justin Huntly McCarthy
Kakuzo Okakura
Karle Wilson Baker
Kate Chopin
Kenneth Grahame
Kenneth McGaffey
Kate Langley Bosher
Kate Langley Bosher
Katherine Cecil Thurston
Katherine Stokes
L. A. Abbot
L. T. Meade

L. Frank Baum
Latta Griswold
Laura Dent Crane
Laura Lee Hope
Laurence Housman
Lawrence Beasley
Leo Tolstoy
Leonid Andreyev
Lewis Carroll
Lewis Sperry Chafer
Lilian Bell
Lloyd Osbourne
Louis Hughes
Louis Joseph Vance
Louis Tracy
Louisa May Alcott
Lucy Fitch Perkins
Lucy Maud Montgomery
Luther Benson
Lydia Miller Middleton
Lyndon Orr
M. Corvus
M. H. Adams
Margaret E. Sangster
Margret Howth
Margaret Vandercook
Margaret W. Hungerford
Margret Penrose
Maria Edgeworth
Maria Thompson Daviess
Mariano Azuela
Marion Polk Angellotti
Mark Overton
Mark Twain
Mary Austin
Mary Catherine Crowley
Mary Cole
Mary Hastings Bradley
Mary Roberts Rinehart
Mary Rowlandson
M. Wollstonecraft Shelley
Maud Lindsay
Max Beerbohm
Myra Kelly
Nathaniel Hawthrone
Nicolo Machiavelli
O. F. Walton
Oscar Wilde

Owen Johnson
P.G. Wodehouse
Paul and Mabel Thorne
Paul G. Tomlinson
Paul Severing
Percy Brebner
Percy Keese Fitzhugh
Peter B. Kyne
Plato
Quincy Allen
R. Derby Holmes
R. L. Stevenson
R. S. Ball
Rabindranath Tagore
Rahul Alvares
Ralph Bonehill
Ralph Henry Barbour
Ralph Victor
Ralph Waldo Emmerson
Rene Descartes
Ray Cummings
Rex Beach
Rex E. Beach
Richard Harding Davis
Richard Jefferies
Richard Le Gallienne
Robert Barr
Robert Frost
Robert Gordon Anderson
Robert L. Drake
Robert Lansing
Robert Lynd
Robert Michael Ballantyne
Robert W. Chambers
Rosa Nouchette Carey
Rudyard Kipling
Saint Augustine
Samuel B. Allison
Samuel Hopkins Adams
Sarah Bernhardt
Sarah C. Hallowell
Selma Lagerlof
Sherwood Anderson
Sigmund Freud
Standish O'Grady
Stanley Weyman
Stella Benson
Stella M. Francis

Stephen Crane
Stewart Edward White
Stijn Streuvels
Swami Abhedananda
Swami Parmananda
T. S. Ackland
T. S. Arthur
The Princess Der Ling
Thomas A. Janvier
Thomas A Kempis
Thomas Anderton
Thomas Bailey Aldrich
Thomas Bulfinch
Thomas De Quincey
Thomas Dixon
Thomas H. Huxley
Thomas Hardy
Thomas More
Thornton W. Burgess
U. S. Grant
Upton Sinclair
Valentine Williams
Various Authors
Vaughan Kester
Victor Appleton
Victor G. Durham
Victoria Cross
Virginia Woolf
Wadsworth Camp
Walter Camp
Walter Scott
Washington Irving
Wilbur Lawton
Wilkie Collins
Willa Cather
Willard F. Baker
William Dean Howells
William le Queux
W. Makepeace Thackeray
William W. Walter
William Shakespeare
Winston Churchill
Yei Theodora Ozaki
Yogi Ramacharaka
Young E. Allison
Zane Grey